THE DEMON PRINCE

ALSO BY AMANDA AGGIE

HELLS BELLS & DEMON DEALS
The Demon Prince (Book One)
Crown of Ashes
(Book Two – Coming Summer of 2022)
The Crimson Queen
(Book Three – Coming Fall of 2022)

THE HELLS BELLS & DEMON DEALS WORLD CROSS OVER STANDALONES
Must Love Humans
Must Love Hunters
Bloody Hell
Christmas Curses
Wolfsbane
Monster Roommate
Obsidian Wings (Prequel to The Demon Prince)

SERIAL KILLERS NEED LOVE TOO
Beyond the Palms
Killer Sensations
The Hollow 47

THE DEMON PRINCE

BY AMANDA AGGIE

THE DEMON PRINCE
AMANDA AGGIE

This book is a work of fiction. All names, places, characters, and events are products of the author's imagination or are fictitious.

THE DEMON PRINCE. Copyright © 2022 by Amanda Aggie. All rights reserved. Printed in the United States of America. For more information, please visit www.AmandaAggie.com.

Designations used by companies to distinguish their products are often claimed as trademarks. All brand names and product names used in this book and on its cover are trade names, service marks, logos, and registered trademarks of their respective owners. The publishers and the book are not associated with any product or vendor mentioned in this book. None of the companies referenced within the text have endorsed this book.

Library of Congress Cataloging-in-Publication Data
Names: Aggie, Amanda, author.
Title: The Demon Prince / Amanda Aggie
Description: First Edition. | Book Dragon Publishing, 2022.

Printed by Kindle Direct Publishing 2022
Cover Design Copyright © May 2022 by Amanda Aggie
Proofread by Pankow Editorial Services
Developmental & Line Edited by Book Dragon Publishing
ISBN: 9798816550949 (hardcover)
ISBN: 9798816550536 (paperback)
ASIN: B09LBSSF8M (ebook)

To those who aren't afraid to call someone an asshole to their face. To those that are snarky and just trying to thrive in a world full of sharks. To those who feel like a hot mess and run off caffeine most days. I fucking see you and you're not alone. <3

ACKNOWLEDGEMENT

I would first like to thank you for picking up this book! Without readers like you, I wouldn't be able to do the job I love.

To my besties, J.M. Elliott and Michele Lenard. Without you guys, this book would not be. Y'all lit a fire under my ass to get it done and I appreciate your support and input so much!

To my amazing Beta, ARC, and Street Team. You guys are so supportive and without you, people wouldn't know about my books! You're the bread and butter to this operation and I thoroughly enjoy getting to know you all and some of the lovely conversations we have. Thank you so much for being there and encouraging me to buy way too many fucking books lol.

To my family, for being supportive and to my husband. Thank you for putting up with my shit…and for ordering pizza for the kids while I was in my writing hole for four days straight. I love you and thank you for being the inspiration for my book boyfriends!

To my editors at Book Dragon Publishing & Pankow Editorial Services for helping me give my readers the best reading experience possible!

Lastly, to my parents, and their support! They've always pushed me to reach for the stars.

TRIGGER WARNING

** STOP & READ BEFORE PURCHASING **

This book contains triggers! My heroine is snarky and uses adult language—no, she won't apologize for it. My hero is sexy, manly, and might possibly put a damper on your marital sex life. My stories involve magic and paranormal aspects that take you to another world.

If you're someone who thinks 'Harry Potter' is the Devil's work, this book isn't for you. LGBTQ+ aspects will come up later in the series. I am a firm believer in the idea that everyone deserves love, regardless of race, gender, dress size, or wealth status.

Lastly, I'm a sucker for a spicy romance book, but I prefer those with plot lines. I have an open-door policy and my steamy scenes range from jalapeno to ghost pepper in heat and *the series gets spicier as it goes*, so enter at your own risk.**As for major content or trigger warnings, I'll list them below.**

Gore, violence, death, murder, blood, bones, snakes, monsters, spiders, skeletons, and other disturbing images that might not be suitable for all audiences (graphic). There are moments you might cry, but all of my books have a HEA, or in my series, like this one, they at least end with a HFN without a cliffhanger.

There is fantasy drug use, meaning there isn't meth or cocaine, etc. BUT there are mention of Viagra, and stronger, completely made-up forms thereof. There are scenes that have assault, kidnapping, attempt of rape, and graphic animal attacks.

As for sexual aspects, there are explicit sex scenes that are intended for audiences of 18+ years of age. And since the ZON gets fickle if I don't mention this, there are sexual relations with religious figures, such as demons, angels, the Devil, etc. There are various kinks, such as primal kinks, praise kinks, degradation kinks, age gape (sort of, he doesn't grow old…), choking, biting, animalistic behavior (purring), light masochism, orgasm control/denial, sex toys, and edging.

This book takes what we know about Christianity and turns it upside down. It is not meant to be taken as a biblical text, or to be used for religious purposes.

With that said, if you're family — *talking to you, Mom* — and you have to sit around the dinner table with me at Thanksgiving, you've been warned. If you can't handle the heat, then stay out of the kitchen because what you're about to read might make you look at me awkwardly from here on out.

If anything above offended you, leave now or forever hold your peace. None of my books are for you.

If not, read on fellow humans!

SPOTIFY PLAYLIST

Listen to a themed playlist while you read!

THE DEMON PRINCE

BY AMANDA AGGIE

CHAPTER ONE

Alice

An erratic gasp escapes my lips as my eyes slingshot open. Covers jolt in every which way and my leg shoots straight for the heavens, giving me the momentum I need to hurl myself from the bed.

It was him again.

I rub my eyes trying to rid them of the recurring nonsense of a dream I've been having since… well, as long as I can remember. My aunt claims they're nightmares, but they're far from scary. Just awkward and unnerving, but the moment I wake up, it always feels like someone's snapped my soul back into my body. What I wouldn't give to just open my eyes to the sun beaming through the window like a normal person. *Wouldn't that be nice…*

Cautiously, I rise to my feet and stumble toward the bathroom, gathering the nerve to look at my reflection in the mirror. My shirt is drenched in cold sweat and clings to every curve of my torso, and my rogue red curls are tangled in knots, making me appear homeless. Dark circles make my blue eyes look hollow, empty, like something has sucked every drop of energy from my being.

I strip and climb into the shower, letting the hot water wash away the evidence that I slept like shit, but my mind goes back to the dream. It's always the same, yet last night was different... *altered.*

Night after night, a man and I stand on a patio to some old cabin in the woods. My spine tingles with the suspicion that more eyes are watching me, peeling back the layers of my courage, but I only ever see his. The sky's moonless, lit by nothing but a single yellow bulb by the back door, and I can never make out much beyond there being a wall of trees in the distance, surrounding us.

He always wears some sort of formal attire. Most of the time it's a suit. Others, he's business casual; dress shirts and perfectly pressed slacks, but he stands in the same place, leaning against the wooden railing. I've never seen a man that perfect. Not a hair on his head out of place, complete with a devilishly handsome smile that would make any woman's knees weak. It's like he's sin incarnate, clad in the finest linens. And without fail, he always introduces himself as Lucifer, claiming he's come to check on me, and the same three questions roll off his tongue.

Are you okay?
Do you feel like you're being watched?
Can you show me a magic trick?

Like most witches, it wasn't until my fourteenth birthday, when my weak as shit powers came in, that I could fulfill the last request. Even in my dreams, I'm a pathetic excuse for a witch. It is what it is. I've come to accept that magic isn't my strong suit, but science…That is.

My aunt sent me away to the Belphegor Academy in hopes that I'd learn how to use my magic, but every single person there was vastly more capable than me. So, we made a deal. If I could learn how to hide my *gift* from prying eyes, then I could go to human school. I did, and I fucking love it.

Here, I'm normal. I fit in. Hell, I'm even a third-year biochemistry major at our state university, on a full-ride scholarship, and joined a sorority. I'm not at the bottom of the barrel, like I was at the academy. I scrounged to hold my head above water there, and barely had time to breathe, let alone make friends. Here, I have an entire sisterhood.

Still, even though I found my place in the world, the dreams continue every night, like clockwork. I've tried changing my answers to the mystery man's redundant questions, just to spice shit up. It doesn't work. I can think one thing, but what comes out of my mouth is *always* the truth. Like I've been spelled to do so.

My therapist says it's because of stress. It's a comfort dream loop. Where everything about my life has been complete chaos, it stays consistent to give me something *'normal'* to focus on. As if dreaming of the Devil could ever be considered normal.

I'm not sure how much weight I can put into his diagnosis though. He doesn't know about magic and thinks I'm the very definition of a hot mess. I'd love to say that was a joke, but I watched him scribble it down in my chart during our last session. If it was a joke, it wasn't funny.

Last night's dream was different though. There was a fourth question that jarred me. I even got defensive over it, as if he asked it just to spite my shitty love life.

Are you romantically involved with someone?

And of course, my treacherous tongue told him the truth. *No.* I might never be able to forget the way his lips tipped up into a smirk. Almost like my answer pleased him, and now that single word is going to ruin my entire day.

Checking my phone, I roll out of bed to a text that says, **'Call me when you're up,'** from a contact labeled 'Mom,' who's really my aunt, Elise. I tried calling her Mom to her face once, and it bothered her on a molecular level. So, now I just keep her number in my phone as that, in silent protest. She might not want to be called that, but she's the only one I've ever had–at least that I remember. My biological mother, her sister, died twenty years ago today, so I get how calling her that might rub her the wrong way. My uncle, Noah, on the other hand, damn near coached me to call him Dad, but Pops stuck.

I give her a call, and she answers on the first ring.

"Morning, angel! How are you doing today?" her voice chimes through the speaker without a care in the world.

"Good, but I should be asking you that."

"I'm...*okay*."

Pops yells in the background, "Hell no, she isn't. She's baked enough blueberry muffins for the entire fucking town. Don't let her lie to you."

"Ignore him. What time did you want to go?" she asks, and there's no doubt in my mind that she's referring to our tradition.

Every year, we visit my biological parents' graves at the faction cemetery, all the way in New Orleans. We leave flowers, even though the entire cemetery is a massive garden that my mother used to tend to. And lastly, we pray and talk about the things they've missed.

The Belphegor Academy, the place Auntie sent me to learn how to be a witch, is part of the faction and in the same massive-ass building. When I was a student there, I would visit their graves, hoping to learn something about the people they used to be. Sometimes, I just cursed at them for keeping so many secrets, including how and why they died.

Sometimes, I'd vent about how I was different–weaker than the other witches. My biological mother was the faction's head mistress, meaning, in lack of better words, she was the queen of the paranormal creatures in our country and an incredibly powerful witch, yet I can't do a freaking second level spell. For that to happen, all of the magic genes would've had to skip me. Either that, or it has to do with whatever my father was. Elise still won't tell me his species beyond the fact that he wasn't human and at this rate, I'm going to sprout a tail or worse before I find out. I've already purred like a feral cat once and it's not a memory I like to reminisce about. Let's just say, the guy I was on a date with didn't find it kinky; he ran for the hills.

"I can be ready in five," I tell my aunt, rubbing the sleep from my eyes.

"Is your roomie there?"

"No, she has morning classes."

The wind picks up in the room and I already know that her impatient ass is on her way here. I hang up the phone and flop back onto the bed just in time to see my aunt pop into my bedroom. She's a time spinner, so she can just teleport in and out of nowhere, or even cooler, she can astral project through time. It makes these yearly trips from Missouri to New Orleans a breeze.

"You're still in PJs," she says with a huff.

"I said five minutes… You gave me all of five seconds."

Her mouth forms a hard line and the white roses in her hand begin to wilt and die.

"Auntie. You're killing the flowers."

She lets them go and they float as empty, brittle stems and wrinkled petals to the floor.

"Ah shit. It's okay. We can get more there." Elise collects them and tosses them into the trash can as I go get ready. I slip on a black pleated skirt, and tights, along with a band t-shirt that I cut into a crop top, then yank on my combat boots. They were my mother's and have seen better days. Finally, I yank the hair band out of my hair and let my long crimson curls loose.

"It still amazes me how much you look like her," she says, taking a seat on my bed.

"You say that every year."

"I mean it… but you're seriously going to wear that?"

"What? I thought black was for mourning."

It earns me a scowl, but she doesn't fight the subject. Instead, she rolls her eyes and holds out a hand when I finish. I take it and the room fills with light and swirls until it's replaced by the garden cemetery in New Orleans. Birds singing hits my ears before the light fades and two nearly identical headstones come into view. One reads, *Celeste Whittaker*, and the other is only inscribed with my father's first name, *Azazel*.

What kind of man has such a dark, twisted past that even in death, his last name must stay a secret?

"You know, you never told me why there's no last name on my father's stone," I say, reaching out to trace over the A in Azazel. Elise breathes out hard, stopping her pacing only to pinch off a hydrangea bloom from the bush behind us.

I never understood why we give cut flowers as gifts, like *'Here, take this flower I killed and watch it slowly shrivel up as a token of my love.'* It doesn't sit right with me. It's morbid.

"Your parents had secrets, Alice. So many, in fact, that I was left an entire binder of instructions to follow in their passing, up to and including wiping the memory of anyone who knew about their deaths. Ultimately, it has all been to keep you safe from the people who killed them. So, please. Stop pushing."

"I get that, but how am I supposed to hide from them when I don't know who I'm hiding from?" Ignorance isn't bliss. It's a death sentence and right now it has my name all over it.

She's silent for a moment and the hydrangea she just picked begins to die.

"Auntie! Come on." Elise slumps and lifts them to give what's left of the white bloom a once over.

Honestly, I'm sick of hearing that she can't tell me anything. I've heard it for as long as I can remember. Beyond me looking like Celeste, that she ran the faction counsel, and that they died, I don't know anything about them.

They didn't pass down a shoe box with pictures or mementos. There was no letter explaining why they got into whatever they did that put them in wooden boxes six feet below me. Hell, I didn't even have a birth certificate. Elise had to pay a criminal to make me one. The EMTs that found my mother just dropped me off on Elise and Pop's doorstep, with nothing.

Why didn't they kill me too? What kind of murderer spares children? The way I see it, if it were me, and I was going to be a monster, I'll be a fucking monster and finish the job. I wouldn't develop some sick, grey moral code and let a kid grow up an orphan.

"I'm tired of praying to what could possibly be empty caskets," I finally say in a hushed tone. The flower in her hand crumbles into dust.

My aunt's eye twitches, her red curls start sparking, and I can feel the anger rolling off her in heat waves as she speaks through gritted teeth.

"They're down there. *Trust me.* I watched them both be buried."

From what I understand, all of us Whittaker witches inherit anger problems. And my aunt? She's usually the queen of controlling it, but if you set her off, you might as well detonate an atomic bomb. I can't blow shit up, but for what I lack in power, I make up for with snark. The academy taught me that, and while other witches cut people down with magic, I learned words can be just as damaging.

"Great. Another piece of the puzzle that I'll never solve. You know exactly what happened. You just don't want to tell me. Got it," I say, rolling my eyes.

"For your safety!" She bites the inside of her cheek–aka, her tell-tale sign that she's passed the point of being pissed. I want answers, answers she's purposely kept from me, but if I keep pressing…tick, tick, *boom*. It's a risk I'm finally willing to take. I open my mouth to speak but her words make me snap it back shut. "Enough! Can we please just be civil and get through today?"

"No. I don't know these people. I'm taking my life back and moving on." Elise goes still and I know I've struck her fuse, but I won't apologize. It's been twenty years of the same lies and I can't do it anymore. "Beam me home...*please.*"

She stares at me dumbfounded, then slowly takes a step forward, not daring to meet my eyes. "Fine. I'll see you at dinner tonight." Her jaw flexes...She's doing everything she can to keep her shit together and as much as I admire her willpower, I wish that she'd use the energy she's expended trying to keep me in the dark all of these years, to help me.

"I won't be there, not unless you want to tell me something...*Anything*," I say, resisting the urge to look away from her.

"Blackmail, really?" Her eyes close and her teeth grind together hard enough for me to hear it. "You have to be home tonight. This year is more important than ever."

"Why?" I ask, but she shakes her head, refusing to answer me.

"It just is."

"That's not good enough," I snap and hold out my hand, ready to go back to my stuffy dorm room.

She looks at me with tears brimming her eyes and closes the distance between us. I didn't mean to hurt her, but I need this. This is my life and I'm tired of living it in the dark. If she won't tell me, I'll find someone who can.

"I'm sorry about your sister," I say, "but I need answers."

She tucks a chunk of my hair behind my ear. "I'm sorry about your parents, and I hope you get them one day."

Before I can say anything more, she plants a kiss on my forehead and light blinds me, spinning the colors of the world around my body until I'm back into my room, staring at a wide-eyed Charlie. My roommate.

CHAPTER TWO
Alice

Charlie flings her feet over the edge of the bed. "That shit never gets old."

I hold up a finger to shush her until the light fades and the portal closes. "Girl! She doesn't know that you know and believe me, she can hear through the portal. I'm pretty sure she's part bat."

"When you levitate shit in your sleep, it's kind of hard *not* to," she says, crossing her arms in front of her chest. "I mean, come on. You really think that she doesn't know? You're literally the worst at keeping secrets."

"Does it matter? Elise would snatch me back home if she found out and any hope of graduating next year goes out the window. I trust you, but she'd go off the rails, spewing about the Salem Witch Trials. Our relations with humans haven't exactly been sunshine and rainbows."

"I get it." Charlie plants her palms on the mattress and leans her weight back into them. "So, how did the... *tradition* go?" My face scrunches into a grimace. "That bad?"

"You could say that. My aunt won't budge so I kind of told her I was done, that I didn't want to go anymore if she wasn't going to tell me anything."

Her eyes shoot wide. "Jesus. Really?" My head bobs, confirming it. "Shit, Alice. You can't just shut them out entirely."

I flop down onto my bed and say, "I don't plan to, but I won't be going tonight. Maybe then she'll realize that I'm serious." Huffing out the air in my lungs, I look at her. My stomach turns, knowing I've pissed off the only person who volunteered to take me in, to love me.

Gathering my voice, I continue, "I know I'm part witch, but I have no idea what the hell my father was and why it's had such an impact on my magic. Witches get stronger from generation to generation and my mother was one of the strongest there's ever been. I'm a dud and as much as I want to say screw magic and live a normal, human life, I need to know.

I need closure. Elise refuses to answer any of my questions for *my own protection*." I mock her voice and Charlie snorts.

She twists her lips, pushing up from the bed to weave her fingers together in her lap. "What are you going to do tonight then? I'm not leaving you here to sulk at home."

"I haven't gotten that far."

Her head snaps up and a wicked, lopsided grin stretches across her face. "Well, then...buckle up, sweetie. We're going out."

I've been roommates with Charlie for two years and not once have I allowed her to drag me down the strip to go to some party. Honestly, the only ones I've attended are the ones I've been forced to by our sorority–usually because they're downstairs.

"Oh no," I protest, grabbing the pillow to slam it over my face.

"Ohhh, yes baby! We're going to a party! And guess what..." I lift the pillow just enough to look her in the eye. "Cameron Till will be there." My heart flutters in my chest at the mention of his name. I've been imagining the man naked all year. "Maybe since you're turning over a new leaf you can actually go up and talk to him like an adult. Huh? Wouldn't that be a new and improved Alice Whittaker."

"Why would it matter if he's there?" I ask, knowing damn well why. I've never confirmed her suspicions, but it doesn't take a genius to spot me drooling over him in Organic Chemistry.

"Don't be coy. I've gotta go, but I'll meet you back here tonight so we can get ready."

I have a really bad feeling about this, but what else am I going to do? That and the memory of my dream, how I told the Devil I was *unattached,* pushes me over the edge. Fuck it. Why not?

"Fine," I groan, and she blows me a kiss on her way out the door.

Thirty minutes tick by before I move. I've been lost in thought about how I could possibly screw things up more right now, but also satisfied that I finally got the nerve to say something to Elise and stuck to it. I've never made it this far in the conversation and yet, it feels so… *wrong.*

I grab my book and head downstairs to sit in the hammock on the patio. Maybe getting lost in a fantasy world where everything turns out okay will help me stay the course. Even though every atom of my being wants to call her and apologize.

However, I only get three chapters in before someone cracks open the back door and calls my name. Turning around, rather awkwardly, to glimpse through the holes in the net that suspends me, I find one of my sorority sisters peeping out the patio door.

"Your dad is here," she says.

Shit. By now, Elise has likely already returned home and told Pops all about our argument. He's never come to visit me here, it's always been Elise, and that brings all sorts of bad omens. Has she sent him to scold me? To demand I come home?

I hop to my feet and walk inside, where I find him waiting in the corridor wearing leather boots, a plaid shirt, a dusty hat, and his infamous faded jeans. Growing up, all my friends thought he was hot. He was even voted father of the year at our high school assembly, no doubt because of it. But here, in the sorority, I feel like the women are thirstier. A crowd of them ogle from all corners of the room as he checks out the alumni photos on the wall, oblivious. Either that, or he genuinely doesn't care. I shoo them off with a glare that could kill, right as he turns around.

"Love bug!" he says, arms outstretched and ready to wrap me up.

"Hey, Pops... Before you get mad —"

"Relax. I didn't come here for that. I talked to her, but I understand why you're upset. I would be too."

He gets it. My uncle will never tell me that in front of Elise, not that I blame him since she has a wrath that can make gods shrink, but he almost always takes my side and has made it clear that he's got my back. Dragging me against his chest for a hug, he squeezes until the air leaves my lungs.

"I love you, kiddo. So much. Your M-aunt does, too." His hand scoops under my chin when he releases me, tipping my head up so he can kiss my forehead.

"I love you, too," I say, feeling the tears rising but I shove them down deep.

"Here," he says, reaching into his pocket to pull something out. "I wanted to give you something, just in case you really aren't coming home tonight." A necklace dangles from his hand–a blue crystal pendant. Angelite. It has a septagram carved into the smoothed surface and a silver inlay.

"Oh my god… it's beautiful," I say, reaching out to hold it in my hand.

"Your aunt says angelite is supposed to help you communicate between realms. I thought… it might make you feel closure to those you can't simply call or talk to… You know, those *empty caskets*," he says, mocking my insult. His hand taps my shoulder, signaling me to turn around and I do. My uncle brushes my hair away so he can clasp it around my neck.

As soon as the cool stone hits my chest, I shiver but instantly feel the hum of the crystal against my skin and when he's finished, I turn back around to face him with a massive grin, pulling at my cheeks.

I expect to see a happy smile on his face, instead, it almost looks… *sad.* Flicking my gaze down, I grab the pendant and feel something else engraved on the backside. It reads, ***'To my Love Bug-Pops,'*** and it causes tears to brim my eyes, breaking down every barrier I've put up and reinforced.

He steps forward, grabbing the pendant from me to lift it to his lips and kiss it before standing again. "Promise me you'll wear it. That you'll keep it safe."

"Promise."

He nods and dips his hands into the pockets of his jeans. "Well, I gotta get back to the farm, but I love you and hope to see you soon." Without another word, he spins on his heels and is gone.

Why is everyone acting like they're saying goodbye? If I didn't know any better, I'd think I was about to pass into the veil. I mean I said no to dinner and board games. It's not like I'm eloping to Switzerland. Shrugging it off, I head back to the patio.

CHAPTER THREE

Alice

Six o'clock rolls around and Charlie is snapping orders at me in her tight red dress. She has sleek, black, bone-straight hair with ruby-red devil horns and heels sharp enough to stab someone with. In her hand is a tiny miniature pitchfork to complete her outfit.

"I swear I told you it was an early Halloween party."

I study her for a moment, before answering, "I'm pretty sure that never came up."

"It's the first weekend in October. It really should've been assumed. The entire month is nothing but costume parties down the strip. You'd know that if you ever left the house."

Feeling the nerves flush through me, making my ears hot, I pick through the pile of clothes she's set on my bed. "I go places…"

"Like where?"

We lock eyes for a moment. "Um, the coffee shop. The library. Class."

Charlie rolls her eyes and starts digging through her closet for something decent enough for her to be seen with me in. "Those aren't social events, Alice."

Maybe not to you.

I flip open my book while she holds up a bottle of fake blood like a trophy. "Here we go! What about a murder victim?" Climbing to her feet, she unscrews the cap and grimaces. "Oh Lord...maybe not. That smells awful." I watch her dive back into the bottom of her closet and seconds later, she's holding up a white corset dress. "Angel!"

"It's a bit hard to be an angel without wings," I say, flipping the page of my book. When she doesn't answer, I look up to find her holding a miniature pair of cherub wings. *Dammit.*

Reluctantly, I take them and head off to the bathroom and after thirty minutes of her lacing the back, it's finally on. The dress flares at the bottom of the corset and lands a little above the knee, but besides having to breathe weird, the satin fabric is soft against my skin. Charlie helps me slip on the wings before taking a step back to admire her handy work.

"Girl. You need to go outside more."

Letting my head fall back, I groan. "I've told you before. My skin doesn't tan. I just get more freckles."

"Well, either way, white is not your color. You might as well not dress up and tell people you're a ghost. Maybe I have a different dress…"

I think back to my original idea, which was to throw a sheet over my head and do just that. Only now that I'm in this thing, I don't want to spend another half an hour trying to get out of it. So, I snap my fingers and instantly, the dress and wings turn black.

"Ey? I've fallen." *Victim to whatever the fuck you have planned.* I hold my hands out and spin to give her the whole picture. She finally nods her approval and after I quickly fix my hair and makeup, we're off, walking down the sidewalk past all of the Greek houses.

Music booms and parties line the block. Most of the people outside are dressed up as sexy nurses, cops, cats, and all of the other non-traditional Halloween horseshit. What happened to witch hats and brooms or the old faithful–vampires? *Beats me.* Now a days, it seems Halloween is more about getting laid than going out and having fun. I don't quite understand the need to spend hours dressing up just to let some half-baked chucky doll rip it off, but to each their own.

We find the house Charlie wants to go to and head inside. Music rattles my eyeballs as it blares through the speakers and within seconds, my partner in crime ditches me to go talk to other 'friends' she's spotted. I'm almost jealous at how easy it is for her to just walk in and stretch her social butterfly wings.

Shaking my head, I look around, taking in the black gauze covering *everything* and the purple and green lights. Walking through the doorway into the common area, a plastic skeleton jumps off the wall and I resist the urge to punch it in the throat.

I make it into the room without getting an assault charge and make eye contact with my date for the night–the keg on the far side of the room. The man guarding it hands me a red solo cup and stares at my tits–which admittedly look nice in the corset–but instead of talking to me, he talks straight to the girls.

"Come to daddy," he utters, licking his lips.

"No way in hell." I take the solo cup and roll my eyes as I walk toward the empty couch pushed against the far wall.

"If you change your mind, you know where to find me," the dude yells in a singsong voice, but I don't give him the satisfaction of looking back. He'll get to look at the girls again when I need a refill, not a moment sooner.

The weight shifts on the couch as someone joins me and I turn to find a dark-haired man, maybe a year or two older, leaned back against the cushions, legs spread like it's his damn throne. His jaw is chiseled, like it was carved from stone, and massive, drop-dead-gorgeous wings cling to his back. They're pinned between his body and the couch, and my mouth falls open.

Holy shit, those look amazing!

"Nice costume," he says in a low baritone that makes my mouth water. My stomach storms with butterflies as his ember eyes rake over me until they reach my combat boots, and a smirk crosses his angular face.

"Have you seen yours?" I ask, gawking as they move with every simple shift his body makes. What is he? A robotics major? He has to be for them to move like that. It's too lifelike.

The man chuckles under his breath before turning to shoot me a smile that makes my heart stop. "Yeah, I have." His honey-colored eyes return to the crowd, and I can't help but wish they were still looking at me. The way the heat of his gaze warms my skin... the feeling could be bottled and sold as a drug. "What's your name, princess?"

"Alice," I say dryly. "And obviously *not* a princess."

He side-eyes me and I watch his eyebrow bounce once. "Could've fooled me."

The sound of men howling, and yelling draws my attention and I see Cameron walk into the room. People cling to him like a magnet, patting him on the back and parading around like he's a god. That's not what bothers me though. On his arm are two ridiculously hot women and that DNRs any idea I had to talk to him tonight.

So much for being brave.

The man beside me snorts. "Who's that?"

"No one," I say, hearing the irritation evident in my voice. I hoped to hide that better, but I'm not about to entertain the idea of talking about Cam with some random stranger. I have yet to admit to Charlie that I'm interested in him, and I've lived with her for years. I'm sure as hell not going to pull out the Kleenexes with this fool…even if he is hot as shit.

With a flick of my wrist, I chug the rest of my drink, filling up my cheeks like a squirrel stashing nuts for winter and slowly, gulp it down. He observes me but doesn't say anything until I've finished.

"Sweetheart, I just watched you scowl at the man then chug three-fourths of a solo cup of crappy beer. I don't know who he is, but he's definitely not *no one.*"

I fidget with my cup until Charlie bumps my arm, holding out two shot glasses. I take them and pop one back, then immediately bring the second to my lips and she freezes in place.

"One of those was for your friend, *jeesh*."

Turning to the man I say, "Sorry," then shoot it.

"No worries. I think you need it more than me, anyway." I can feel his smile gleaming as his eyes take in every curve of my exposed skin and goosebumps raise in their wake. My magic claws at me, demanding to be let out. It's like having a wildebeest living within you and beckoning you to do things-like move closer to him, to touch him. I shiver and it calms a bit.

Why is it pulling so much at him? It's never done so with a human, unless... he has magic, or is something else. I look him over, not caring that I'm making it blatantly obvious I'm checking him out. I note every nook and cranny of his hard body that's all man-mouthwatering, swoony, man. Nothing in particular stands out. He's definitely not a wolf or vampire, though.

My investigation is cut short by my roommate reaching over to shake his hand. "I'm Charlie! I don't think we've met."

"Kai," he replies, barely entertaining her. He's too busy undressing me–which I guess is fitting, seeing as I just did the same to him.

"Your costume is incredible!" she says before leaning down to whisper in my ear, "You better fuck that man or I will. He looks like a Greek god." She stands back up, shooting him a quick smile and then points to where she'll be before taking off.

"So, she does have friends," he says with a smirk, and I stare daggers into him, but he almost finds it amusing and slides closer to me.

"What the fuck does that mean?"

"It means you're at a party, sitting alone on a couch, staring at your… boyfriend? No… *Crush*?" My lips part at the word. How did he know that? The man sucks in his bottom lip and nods triumphantly. "That's what it is. Well, sweetheart, you can do a hell of a lot better, but I'd be happy to help you stick it to him."

I cross my arms in front of my chest and his eyes flick down, drawn to the motion, but his tongue slides effortlessly between his lips and I remember that I'm in Charlie's dress. Honestly, I'm afraid to look. I'm hoping I just pressed the girls together, but I'm slightly worried that I've slipped a nip. It's cold in places that should *not* be cold. Instead, my gaze stays fixed on his face.

"And by better, you mean *you*?"

His head tips back as his arm circles around my shoulders. "I can't say that's wrong."

I slide to the right, moving farther away from him. "Thanks for the offer but hard pass. I don't do random guys."

He fights the smile that pulls at the corner of his lips, revealing a dimple in his cheek. And in one fluid motion, he slides back to my side, grazing his hip against mine.

"Did you not hear me, asshole?" I snap. "Keep it up. I bite."

He laughs at my threat and the sound is enchanting and causes my thighs to press together as lust pools between them.

"Trust me, princess, that's never deterred me before. But fear not. I only intend to help make him notice you, nothing more." His eyes dip down to my chest again for a split second. "Though that dress… that alone should be enough. Especially for a mouth breather like him."

I squint at him, resisting the urge to smirk at his attempt to insult someone like Cam. Instead, I watch the crooked grin break out across his. He knows that he's already convinced me before he stands and holds his hand out, offering a dance. The song changes, *Hypnotic* by Zella Day starts playing over the speakers as he waits for my reply, calling my bluff.

"No thanks," I say, looking over him toward the people dancing to the music and giggling into drunken oblivion.

"I'm not asking and trust me, you'll enjoy it. When you see the jealousy on his face, it will be worth it."

With a sigh and an eye roll, I take his hand and he pulls me up and spins me at the exact same time, stealing the air out of my lungs. My back collides with his chest with an *umph*.

"Good girl," he says, skimming his fingers over my bare shoulders and sliding the straps to my wings down my arms. I feel the elastic tug tight around my elbows, holding me there. My eyes shoot wide, both oddly curious about what he's planning to do next and terrified by the realization that I couldn't pull away from him if I wanted to.

His lips trail over my shoulder, feather-light, and his warm breath wraps me up. Inadvertently, my body leans against him, craving more like an addict needing a fix. He chuckles deeply in his throat, knowing that my bluff is just that, and places a soft kiss where his mouth has hovered, taunting me. Without missing a beat, he takes the wings off and throws them to the side where they land on the couch in a heap.

"Can't have these getting in the way, can we?" he whispers. My heart rampages in my chest. *What did I just subject myself to and why do I like it so much?*

CHAPTER FOUR

Alice

The music picks up and he tugs me toward the open area that's been turned into a make-shift dance floor, complete with a crappy superstore disco ball. Kai twirls me out until his grip jolts me to a stop, then spins me back in until my back is pressed firmly against him again.

I feel his breath on my ear. "Close your eyes."

"Excuse me?"

"You're nervous, love." I open my mouth to protest but his hand cuts off the words, clamping gently over my lips. "Don't fight me, sweetheart," he says, dropping his hand and nuzzling his nose against my neck. "Close those baby blues for me and let me show you what you do best."

I do as he says, even though I have no intention of keeping my mouth closed too. "And what is that?

Trusting weird men? If so, I deserve an award for allowing you to drag me out here."

His laugh is even sexier when I can feel the reverberations from his throat against my head. "No. It's bringing men to their knees."

"Hah! Yeah. *Okay*." I turn around in his arms, blindly linking my hands behind his neck. "I'm not sure who you think I am, but you've got the wrong girl, bro."

"Are you not, Alice Whittaker? The daughter of the late Headmistress of the faction counsel? You Whittaker witches are the same. All fiery, red hair and sass, with a habit of ignoring everything good for you." His voice hikes up when he says *sass*, like he'd love to devour it. *So, he knows about the faction... .and witches...and my mother...What else does he know?* I can tell he wasn't human; my magic has never called to someone who was, but what is he?

"I'm not sure I agree with the last bit, but yes. Who are you?" I ask, and a ping of fear shoots through me. Could he know about my parent's death? Could he be who Elise has been protecting me from?

If so, dear lord. She should've let him take me. I'm not sure what Heaven looks like, but I'm fairly certain it comes in the form of a six-foot-two, dark-haired man, with eyes so entrancing that I can get lost in them... I mean, that is if I could get over the fact that would mean he killed my parents.

No... There are thousands of paranormal creatures in this world, most of which could sense my magic and know I'm not human either. The odds of him being involved with my parent's death, isn't likely and though he's been forward, he hasn't been malicious in any way.

"I told you. My name is Kai."

I huff out the air in my lungs. "I meant, what–" His weight shifts and he leans in close.

"Do you always fight people trying to help you this much?"

His hand trails around the middle of my torso as he circles around me, and butterflies erupt in my stomach, trailing south until I have to resist the urge to bite my lip. "When they're strangers, yes."

"We could change that," he whispers, not helping my sky-rocketing libido's case. I scoff, knowing I would never let someone so cocky near my lady bits with a ten-foot pole, but right now, it sounds fucking fantastic.

His vibrato is so deep, so mischievous, that my body has arched toward him just to be closer, begging him to fulfill his promise. "Pass," I say, trying to control my breath. I have no intentions of letting on to what his gentle touches do to me, nor how his words make my heart flutter in my chest like a teenage girl getting a love note from her crush.

The song changes to *Horns* by Bryce Fox and his fingers lace with mine, pulling my hand up until our palms are pressed together. I slowly turn in circles as he rotates, pressing my palm in the direction he wants me to go, then reaching for the other to turn me the other way. It's like some sort of sexually charged dosey doe that makes me realize how much the alcohol has hit me. My head threatens to loll from the dance and the shots have stripped me of my equilibrium.

I gear up for him to switch my direction again, but he doesn't, instead, his fingers trail over me as I turn in place, from my stomach, across my arm, my shoulder, until they brush my hair behind my back. Then, his hand laces with mine again and he swings me out and whips me back into his chest. My hands plant hard against his pecs, that are…notably squeezable, and I suck in a breath.

"I got you. I promise," he hums. I can practically feel the smirk stretch across his face, even though my eyes are still closed, impairing me from seeing it. His hand pushes against my lower back, drawing me closer to him until I feel how much he's enjoying this pressed against my stomach. Holy shit. It's *huge*. "He's watching, little witch."

"Who is?" I ask, then remember why this charade began in the first place. Cameron Till. He chuckles in my ear and my eyelids flutter at the noise he makes when he exhales. Could this man be any sexier? No. Let's not find out.

"Forgotten him already?" His nose nuzzles against the crook of my neck, and I feel his chest swell as he drags in a deep breath. My body melts into him, turning me into putty in his hands. "I promise you can do better. The right man for you…

he'll be unforgettable," he whispers, and nips my ear lobe hard enough to make me jump.

Before I can say anything, he spins me out, then back beneath his arm. As I twirl toward him, his other hand connects with my throat and pushes me back into a dip. My hands fly up, collaring around his wrists for dear life, and the feeling of falling overcomes me causing my body to tense as my eyes flare open.

His lips press against mine and all of my fight disappears instantly. My eyes flutter closed, and I sigh against his lips, enjoying the way they consume me. It's deep and sensual, and over all too soon.

Before I've had my fill, he pulls me back to my feet and releases his grip. I pant, my head spinning. My lips part, determined to memorize the taste he's left behind as I wring my fingers. I stare at him, the way he licks his lips, like he wants to do it again… and I'd let him.

Swallowing hard, I try to slow my heart, which is jackhammering away at my rib cage. Just as I'm about to grip his shirt and yank him toward me, to crush my mouth against his, to let him drag me away and do as he wishes, an applause breaks out and I jump. Looking around the room, dozens of eyes are glued on us, the only people on the makeshift dance floor, in awe. Like they've just witnessed a play in a theater, and we're the final act.

My cheeks flare bright pink as heat floods my face and a smile spreads, threatening to split it in two. Then I see Cameron Till, clapping and grinding his teeth together like he's pissed that it wasn't him, twirling me around… Or maybe because for once, he's not the star of the show.

I flick my gaze back to Kai, and he reaches a hand up, tracing his thumb against my bottom lip. "Now, that's the smile you should've worn all night."

He quickly leans in and whispers, just loud enough for me and only me to hear over the music. "I'm sorry for what comes next."

"And why is that?" The heat of his body steps away from mine.

"Because I'm about to wreck your world, princess…I just hope you'll be able to forgive me for it." I cock my head to the side as he lifts our laced hands to his lips and kisses the top of mine, gently. *Fuck yes, wreck my world. Crush it. I don't care. Just please, don't stop.*

Then, the air leaves my lungs as he turns on his heels and starts toward the door. Leaving.

"That's it? You're just going to go?" I ask, when my voice returns to me. He pauses for a second to send me a smirk over his shoulder then carries on his war path without another word.

CHAPTER FIVE

Alice

"Girl!" Charlie runs up to me as soon as he's gone with wide eyes. "What the fuck was that? No. Better question. *Who* the fuck was that?"

"I… I don't know," I say with a stutter, eyes still glued to the front door, like if I stare at it long enough, he'll come back.

Her hands wrap around my shoulders and shake me out of my head. "Why did he just leave?"

"I said, *I don't know*," I snap. *Believe me, I didn't want him to.* My gaze shifts toward her and my face softens. It's not her fault and honestly, I don't know what I feel. Worrying my lips between my teeth, I grab her hand. "I'm sorry. I just… Let's get beer."

She squints at me like Hell just froze over but doesn't protest. Instead, she skips off toward the dude manning the keg. The music picks up, and by the time she gets back with our drinks, I'm on the dance floor, ignoring all of the eyes that watch me in silence. Fuck'em. It's the anniversary of my mother's death. I've had dreams of the fucking Devil. I've pissed off my aunt, the only mother I've ever known, and met a man who left me with more questions than I already had… but damn. I'd do it all again in a heartbeat for another dance with him and that's what scares me the most.

I've lived my life through everyone else; strived to be the perfect human because I never have and never will amount to half the witch my mother was. My aunt has kept me in a shoe box, hidden from anything resembling fun. And yeah, going to college here meant following a list of rules that went beyond the normal things parents tell their daughters like, *don't go out at night* and if you do, *use the buddy system.* No. Elise's rules are much more restricting and take a lot more effort to follow.

-Keep your head down and study.

-No parties or social events unless they directly pertain to your course work or are required by your sorority.

-Never let anyone close enough to figure out what you are. That includes romantic relationships.

-Hide your magic.

-Don't slip up or it's right back to the academy.

She literally printed it out and laminated the list for me to keep it in my purse. Talk about a helicopter aunt.

Well, I've broken them all tonight.

I'm at a party and certainly not keeping to myself, since everyone in this frat house just watched me dance with an enigma of a man. And said guy knows I'm a witch. In fact, he knows about my mother and the faction council. Charlie has known my secret for a minute and there's no doubt in my mind that there will be hell to pay *when* and *if* Elise catches wind of it. So, I might as well enjoy the freedom while it lasts.

***

Three games of beer pong and a couple hours of dancing later, the room spins and tilts like someone has shoved me inside of a marble and rolled it across the floor. It's been a long time since I've been anywhere close to drunk, and I might be able to hold my alcohol well, but it's catching up to me.

After finding Charlie, I yell so she can hear my voice over the music and let her know I'm going home to sleep off the tequila shots. With a wink and flick of her wrist, she sends me on my merry way and continues climbing the stairs with her kryptonite pussy's latest victim.

I'm not sure why, but every single man the woman has slept with, simply never recovers. They fall head over heels, or their life comes crashing down. The last three in a row have dropped out and one of those three unfortunate souls went to jail. I have no idea what she's doing to them, but whatever it is, it should come with a warning label. Regardless, the man follows eagerly in tow, watching her hips sway with every step. It's like watching a siren lead sailors toward the rocky cliff. I shake my head, trying to erase the image from my memory.

Walking over to the couch where Kai threw my cherub wings, I pick them up and trace my fingers over the obsidian feathers. A hand gently touches my arm and I turn to find Cameron Till shooting me a smile that normally would have me pooling into a puddle of liquid lust at his feet. But now, it just seems bland, average, and I don't think I can ever settle for average after knowing what it feels like to have the attention of someone who is more.

"Hey. Alice, right?" he says, his cheeks never faltering from the playboy grin. The man's eyes nearly sparkle as if he knows all he has to do is show a breadcrumb of interest and women just bend over for him. Let's be honest, I probably would be one of those women days ago, but now, it sounds less than appetizing.

"I didn't know you knew my name," I say, picking at the feathers on the wings in my hand, staring anywhere but at his face.

"Well, I didn't until tonight, but you've kind of been the talk of the party. You and… whoever that guy was. No one has seen him before."

My gaze flicks up to meet his and my eyebrows furrow, but everything relaxes into a sweet smile when I see the tick in his jaw. Jealousy is a bad look for him. "His name is Kai."

His eyebrows bounce and his lips mush together, like he could've done without that information. "So, are you two a thing?"

I shake my head no. "I just met him." The spark that lights back up inside him is comical. Like he thinks he has a chance in hell.

"In that case," he says, and without missing a beat, tries to circle his arm around me, "how about we get out of here and–"

Sliding out of the way, I hold up a hand to cut him off, then tuck my wings under my other arm. "What? Two bitches weren't enough for you?" His mouth opens and closes as he scrambles to find something to say. "Sorry, but pass. I'm no one's sloppy seconds, let alone *thirds*." Cameron nods and then makes a quick getaway and I head off through the front door.

The crisp fall air slices against my exposed skin and I rub my arms, cursing at myself for not bringing a jacket. There's hardly anyone outside. Everyone has either paired off for the night, is safely inside one of the Greek houses, or has gone home. Much like I should've hours ago.

This isn't me... or at least it hasn't been. I've never been the girl to go crazy and deal with the repercussions later. Where I started this night, hellbound to have fun, now, my gut twists with regret. My temples have already started to throb with the impending hangover that's waiting for me when I open my eyes tomorrow morning, and ugh! I have a test on Monday that I really needed to study for this weekend and the likelihood of that happening now is null and void. I'll never be able to focus, and I don't think one day with my nose in a book is going to be enough.

My feet ache from standing, my calves and thighs feel like Jell-O from *getting low*. I can guarantee my muscles will be sore as shit in the morning. But was it worth it? I don't know... It was to dance with him, but everything else I could've gone without and never missed.

My breath fogs from the cold, but I'm almost back to my house, walking on the opposite side of the street past the wooded park. It's a beautiful place to trail through and Charlie and I have hundreds of times, but it's much creepier at night. Keeping my pace, I wrap myself up with my arms, feeling the pebbled peeks of goosebumps coating my flesh.

Something crunches in the woods next to me, like a branch under foot, and I nearly jolt out of my skin. My heart hammers hard against my ribs but I stay statue-still, refusing to even breathe as my eyes frantically search the dark for anything that might've made it. I find nothing, and my muscles loosen, chalking it up to a squirrel or some other kind of animal that roams the park reservation at night.

I continue walking but stop dead in my tracks when a snarl tears through the air. My eyes grow wide, and my breath catches in my throat. *What the fuck was that?* I swallow it down, slowly turning to see what made the sound behind me. But there's just an empty sidewalk, and there's nothing around the edge of the tree line either. It's silent except for the crickets and I allow myself to breathe. *Great. Now I'm going crazy.*

When I turn back around, a hand clamps hard over my mouth and an arm circles my waist, clinging me against a tall, muscular body. I scream into his palm until the air can't leave my lungs anymore and my throat is left raw and shredded, but my voice doesn't travel far. The man pulls me with ease into the woods as I flail and buck. My hands reach for his face, desperately trying to gouge out eyes, to scrape against flesh or maim enough for me to run.

I drag in a deep breath and push from within my soul to scream as loud as my lungs will let me, curdling the noise in my throat as it tears through my body. My attacker laughs. *Fucking laughs* at my struggle and my legs thrash out searching for grip, or to kick him, but nothing works. I'm yanked farther and farther into the darkness of the woods, and there wasn't a single witness to my kidnapping.

I'm on my own.

Giving up on the physical escape, I squeeze my eyes shut. I can't see through the tears that stream down my cheeks anyway; I might as well be looking through the curved glass of a fishbowl. My body shakes, as the sobs rip through me at the realization that I might die. The man might kill me, or worse, torture me, and no one will know until Charlie returns home to an empty dorm.

My grip feels weak, and even with the adrenaline rushing through my veins, I can't urge my fingers to squeeze tighter, to hit harder. Instead, I open my palms, allowing him to drag me away faster as I try to summon my magic. Pulling in a deep breath, I try to calm the nerves, focusing on the hum that sings in my blood and lightning crackles around my fingertips before sizzling out. I try again, and again, until his footsteps cease, and we stop.

"You shouldn't walk alone at night, little girl. This was way too easy," a wicked voice says in my ear. I don't recognize it, but something about his tone tells me he knows exactly who I am. This wasn't just a random attack, to yank some girl off the street. This has to be the person who knew and killed my parents, but an odd feeling of relief sweeps through me when the voice isn't Kai's. As if I'll have a chance with him when I'm dead. I scoff at how pathetic that is.

I've been so careful. How could I be so stupid? Whoever this man is, has watched and waited for me to be alone, to be vulnerable. Now, here I am, drunk and alone, and I can't help but kick myself for wanting to go to a human school. Maybe if I had stayed at the Belphegor Academy, I'd be able to use my magic under distress. I'd be able to put up more of a fight.

THE DEMON PRINCE

CHAPTER SIX

Alice

My attacker loosens his grip and I gear up to make a run for it.

"Don't," he threatens. "You run, and this will be worse for you. Trust me, you won't make it out of the trees."

I swallow hard, and the panic sets in. He's right. I can't outrun him, but I have to try, right? If I don't, I might as well stop my heart and hand it to him. At least that way, I'd be dead before the torture starts. The man's hand falls from my mouth and laces around my waist, linking with his other.

"Now. If you would calm down for a moment, princess, I can explain. I'm Alli–" He doesn't get to finish his introduction before my elbow kicks back and slams hard into his ribs, and pain shoots through my arm making my fingers tingle. "Son of a bitch!" he says, doubling over me and coughing hard.

I don't stop. I lurch away from him, falling forward and feeling the splinters of branches and debris bite into the soft skin of my palms and bare knees. Scrambling, I get one foot on the ground and start to push up when his hand clamps on to my boot and yanks me backward. My chin collides with the forest floor and my teeth clash, biting into my tongue and my ears ring from the impact.

Copper floods my mouth and I grind my teeth together to fight off the pain. Reaching forward, I claw my fingertips into the earth and pull as hard as my muscles will allow me to, desperate to get out of his grip. Only for him to pull back again, harder this time as I scream. My voice rips through the night, unfiltered, and for the first time, unmuffled as he flips me on my back in one fluid motion. The remaining air is knocked from my lungs as I hit the ground and my scream cuts off.

"Dammit, Alice. Why did you have to go do that? I'm not trying to h–" Again, he doesn't finish whatever excuse he has for attacking me because my boot collides with his face and he recoils, giving me enough time to flip over and get to my feet.

The darkness is thick around me, and my feet fly across the ground. I make the executive decision to run deeper into the woods, away from the manicured park trails and away from my home. I'd never make it in the open, he was right about that. There's no doubt that he'll prove to be faster than me, but this way, I'm smaller and there has to be places for me to hide.

If I can hide, I can breathe and calm the nerves that spark beneath my skin, and if I can do that, I can do magic. Fear douses me in adrenaline. My body feels weightless as I glide over the leaf covered ground. Brush and thorns catch onto my dress, tearing the fabric and slicing my skin, but I keep pushing, determined to put as much ground between me and that man as possible.

My lungs heave and sting with each gasp, like someone's lit them on fire. The forest is silent, and I pause, daring a glance back in the way I came and seeing no one. My chest pulses and I can hear the blood pumping in my ears as I take a second to look for a place to hide, to escape. There's nothing but trees and bushes, neither of which would hide me for long.

The top layer of my flesh is raw from the cool air and twigs shredding it apart and my face feels like it will crack any moment. Sweat beads and trails down my wind-burnt cheeks, but I wipe it away.

I can hear the sound of the small river that runs by the trails, and I head for it, taking off again, but jogging with haste instead of sprinting to conserve my energy. The sound of rushing water fills my ears as I climb down the eroded bank and snuggle into a dip in the side wall. It resembles a small cave and is just wide enough for me to back into. Clutching my arms under my knees, I collapse into the dirt wall and wait.

Closing my eyes, I try to slow my heart rate and attempt to breathe shallowly, even though my lungs beg me to gasp and gulp in air. I rack my brain for an invisibility spell, and try my best, pushing out the magic, but I won't know if it worked. Not until it's too late. It's a last-ditch effort.

My breath is still fogging in the cold and will give away my hiding spot, but I don't have time to slow it. Crunching sounds above me on the edge of the bank and I clamp a hand over my mouth, realizing it's covered in blood from the cuts and scrapes on my legs.

The foot falls come closer, like he's right outside of the cave I'm hiding in, but when I peek my eyes open, I see nothing. Just the gentle rushing of water a few feet away, but I hear it. The snarl, so deep that the only plausible origin is a monster.

Something snatches onto my boot, and I scream, kicking with my other foot at whatever invisible force has a hold of me. The air shifts, like something is there, just unable to be seen by the human eye and I grab on to the roots that have broken through the muddied clay walls of the cave, clinging to them for dear life.

I'm not strong enough.

Whatever it is, rips me out of the hole and my back drags along the ground and my head dips into the water, shooting it up my nose. I cough and gag and try to push my red curls out of my face. For the first time, I thank God for the corset because it's the only thing protecting the majority of my back from the jagged lime rocks that coat the water's edge.

Then, it starts to pull me up over the bank as I grip my thigh, moving my hands down my leg until I reach the ties of my boot. I yank the string and fight to loosen the laces and just as the thing, creature, whatever it is, reaches the top of the bank, the shoe gives way and I'm falling, slamming into the shallow water.

I sit up, straining to breathe. The cold water soaking my clothes and hair mixes with the wind and my body trembles. Still, I push on and take off running, and climb up the other side of the bank. Once I crest it, I struggle to get to my feet, but before I can, I'm slammed down on to my stomach by something big. Heavy.

Claws nip into my skin, just enough to draw blood on my shoulder blades as it pins me in place. I try to wiggle out of its clutches but teeth snapping by my face cause me to still. I wince. My body shakes beneath its claws, and I feel something wet drip against my back. *Please tell me that's not saliva...*

The man claps slowly, drawing out the space between to taunt me. "I told you not to run. Now. I'm going to have him let you go, but if you run again, I can't promise you they'll be nice." *They?*

"This was nice? What the fuck is that thing?" I seethe. He whistles and the weight pinning me disappears. I flip around, sitting up and come face to face with a wolf-like creature the size of a fucking car. I'm frozen, staring at the fluorescent green eyes watching me, waiting for me to try and test it.

"Yeah, that was nice. Hell hounds. They're feisty creatures, and if you hadn't fucking kicked me, they would still be taking their nap." I turn my gaze to the man, glaring hard and if looks could kill, he'd be six feet deep. Two other beasts circle us, nearly crawling with every step.

"Who are you? What do you want from me? How do you know my name?" I ask, spitting out the blood still pooling in my mouth onto the ground.

"Allister Caine. I'm a crossroads demon and twenty years ago, your mother made me a deal. Now, it's time to pay up."

I scrunch my eyebrows together. *A deal? With a demon? Twenty years ago… today… That means she made it the night she died.*

The man has tattoos covering every square inch of exposed skin, except for his face. Intricate designs and symbols, both foreign and yet, familiar. His blonde hair is short, almost nonexistent by his ears, but long enough to hang mussed at his eyebrows on top. He crouches down next to me, but far enough that I can't kick him again, and I see the shiner forming where my boot connected.

"It wasn't my intention to hurt you, princess, but you didn't leave me much of a choice. Though, I'm pretty sure Kai is going to kill me for delivering you in this condition," he says. *Kai? He's a part of this? God…How naive can I be in one night?*

We sit in a silent stalemate for a moment, and I rub my hands over my legs, attempting to dull the ache. His blue eyes rake over me from head to toe. "Don't fucking kick me again, but I can help. Just hold still, okay?" I watch him as he slowly creeps closer, like he's just as scared of me as I am of him.

His hand hovers over my legs, trailing up one and down the other. Tingling starts where the scrapes on my legs are and slowly, the skin knits itself back together. Then my shoe pops into his hand out of thin air and he slides it over my foot and ties the laces. When he's done, he scoots closer, sitting next to me and his hand reaches to cup my face, but I flinch away. He grabs at it anyway and I feel the wound on my tongue and chin close.

I start to lift my hair to give him access to the claw marks his puppy left on my back, but he taps my wrist. "You don't need to do that. Hell hounds can't actually inflict damage. They just make it feel like they have. The feeling goes away pretty quickly though."

Dropping my locks, I mush my mouth and give a curt nod. I don't look at him when I speak, instead, I stare off into the woods. "What deal did my mother make you?"

He weighs his head from side to side. "Well, not me, directly, but Lucifer." I turn to look at him, searching his face for any hint that he's lying.

"Lucifer," I mutter and his lips tip into a smirk.

"Yeah, and from what I understand, you've met him already." Turning back to the woods, I swallow hard and try to close my trembling hands around my legs to regain some of my dignity. "You have, haven't you?" I nod, yes, remembering the dreams I've had for years, remembering those three, well now *four* questions.

Are you okay?
Do you feel like you're being watched?
Can you show me a magic trick?

Then, the new one from this morning. *Are you romantically involved with someone?*

He lets me connect the pieces for a moment before continuing. "Twenty years ago, your mother made a deal to protect you. Lucifer was to give you twenty years, to live a human, normal life without fear of…" he trails off. "*Enemies.* Then, after that, you were to be brought to Hell."

"Protect me from who?"

Allister pauses, like he's not supposed to tell me anything. "We can't stay long. You screamed and I can't say for certain that no one heard it. So, the questions will have to wait, but I need you to come with me. I promise, you'll get your answers."

He stands up, holding a hand out to me. "Come on, princess. The Devil doesn't wait for anyone."

I scoff but take his hand. "Will you stop calling me princess? I hate it. And I know you said no questions, but answer this one, please. You said Kai would kill you, how does he play into this?" Part of me hopes what Allister is telling me is true, and that the man who danced with me today isn't the person who killed my parents. I can't be certain, but Allister is the only person in my entire life who's promised answers, and even if I wanted to, it's been made abundantly clear that there's no escaping this alive. Not unless I want to become a chew toy.

He chuckles. "Well, Kai is a prince of Hell and seeing as you're about to become his bride, you might want to get used to being called *princess*. A deal is a deal."

My eyes shoot wide, and my body goes still. I flick my gaze up to meet his, not finding a single twitch, or sign that this is a lie. Instead, a crooked grin stretches on his face.

What the hell did my mother get me into?

"So… Without further ado, *mi lady*," he says, rubbing it in. Allister lifts his hand to my face, and I pull away from it. "Trust me. You'll want to be asleep for this. We're about to pop your realm hopping cherry and it's not a pleasant experience the first time."

He reaches for my head again and for the second time, I lean out of reach.

"Can you just let me do my job?" he asks as I scowl at him. He tries again and I tip away for a third time. "Just hold the fuck still! You've already drop kicked me in the face and I'd rather not have you blowing chunks on my new shoes, okay?"

My lips tip into a smirk and he grunts in frustration.

"Jesus, woman. You might not think so, but you and Kai are going to be perfect for each other. You're both assholes."

I lean toward him without a word, and he pokes his finger at my forehead. Everything instantly goes dark. A single thought circulates my mind as I fall into the first dream I've ever had without the Devil in it.

Did Elise and Noah know? Is that why they did all but say goodbye today? My aunt's words ring in my head.... *You have to be home tonight. This year is more important than ever.* She had to know... there's no other explanation.

I'm not sure what hurts worse, that my mother sold me to the Devil, regardless of whatever her reasoning was, or that my aunt knew I'd be kidnapped tonight, and said nothing. She knew my entire life that I was to be dragged to Hell yet said *nothing.*

THE DEMON PRINCE

CHAPTER SEVEN

Alice

Coming to, I peek my eyes open, glimpsing an empty room. A bedroom. And not just any ordinary one either. The room is bright as the sun streams through the *massive* floor to ceiling windows that arch into points at the top. Cathedral style. Sheer black fabric hangs and pools on the floor in heaps next to them. Even if they did draw shut over the glass, it would do little to restrict the light.

The bed I'm lying on is massive. I could starfish in the middle and still have feet to go before my fingers reach the edge. The comforter is black velvet, and the sheets are the same but satin with the gold, royal swirls. It's ridiculously comfy, like laying on a damn cloud. Even the pillow forms perfectly to my head.

I turn onto my back, looking up at the thick wooden canopy that makes an X above me and connects to each of the four carved posts. The same sheer material loops and hangs around the wood and trails to the floor.

Sitting up, I take in the black marble floors that have flecks of gold through the veins. The walls are some sort of mirror like black stone, but the room itself is bigger than Auntie and Pop's farmhouse and at least two stories tall. There's a living room area, complete with two large velvet couches, a coffee table, and an oversized recliner, big enough to seat two. A large fireplace, with the hearth twice as tall as me, sits on the far side of it. Green flames lick at the wood that doesn't seem to be burning.

I roll toward the edge of the bed and slide off until my bare feet hit the cool marble and a shiver rakes through me. My dress is hanging on by a thread, but I'm glad to see that no one has changed me while I was unconscious. Yet, I almost feel guilty for sleeping in the pristine bed and linens.

The massive wooden door jiggles like someone is unlocking it and it slowly swings open. I whip around to face the reality of the situation, remembering being chased through the woods, finding out that my mother made a deal with the Devil. That Allister brought me to Hell. Is this it? *It has to be.*

Looking to the door, I see a familiar face–the man from my dreams. Lucifer.

Power radiates off of him like a furnace, reaching out tendrils of warmth and sliding over everything in the room. His dark brown hair is slicked back, but in the light I can see the salt and pepper and the hint of cherry strands reflecting the light. Stubble lines his jaw, short, but long enough to be noticed, highlighting his angular face.

He's dressed in black slacks and a white button up shirt, though it's not as official as it was in my dreams. Here, his sleeves are rolled to the elbows–*relaxed*. The top buttons are undone, and the collar is left open, revealing a sneak peek of the chiseled planes underneath the thin fabric.

He shoots me a bright, closed lipped, smirk and pauses mid step.

"You're awake, little one."

"Um…" I shuffle and wrap my arms around my body. My dress is torn, dirty, *revealing*, nothing like one should wear in the presence of someone like him. I've never felt more naked in my life. Both mentally and physically. "Yes," I mumble.

"Do you remember me?" he asks. His voice is low but booms through the large room. It's soft but demands the attention worthy of a king.

I nod as he steps closer. Lucifer doesn't appear menacing like I would've expected him to be. Quite the opposite. It's almost like he's… family or a friend that I haven't seen in years. It's awkward, but not odd enough for me to run the other way. Though, I expected horns and a tail. Maybe red skin? He's none of those… I think.

Leaning to the left, I try to see behind him. Maybe the tail is hiding.

He watches me silently, letting me take it all in, and by all, I mean him. Then, his lips tip as if he's fighting the urge to laugh at me. "What are you looking for?"

I jerk to attention, staring straight into his face and clearing my throat. "Nothing." His eyebrows arch up, questioning me, but he doesn't ask, just gives me a curt nod.

"Anyway," he says, snapping his fingers and a *'pop'* rings through the air as folded clothes appear in his waiting hand. "I wanted to personally welcome you, especially after what Allister told me. The hounds were never supposed to get involved, but…" He pauses and his eyes drift down like a memory has surfaced. "From what I understand, you gave it back to him."

My eyes track him as he walks over to the bed and places the outfit down on top of the velvet comforter. "I hope these suit you well. I'll send someone in tonight to fit you for some clothes, since your belongings are still being brought into the realm. I'm sure you have plenty of questions, so once you're… presentable, just come down the hall and you'll see me." His gaze falls back on me, innocent, loving, and I do what I can to push down the nerves and give him a friendly smile.

Lucifer walks toward the door but pauses before leaving and turns back to me. "And Alice…" When my eyes connect with his again, he continues, "It's lovely to see you, even considering the circumstances."

I don't reply, and I don't think he expected me to because he walks through the door and closes it without a word. For a moment, I stand frozen, numb to everything. I'm in Hell. *Literal Hell* and just had a friendly conversation with the Devil. What the heck has my life come to? Yesterday, I was stressing over an Organic Chemistry test and dealing with family drama. Today, I'm waking up to breakfast with Lucifer–assuming that it is still breakfast time.

Who knows how long it's been since Allister poked me.

Then it hits me. As much as I'm dying to get answers about my parents, answers the Devil could give me being that my mother made a deal with him, it might not just be him down the hall, waiting for me. Allister said I was promised to the Prince of Hell… What if Kai is waiting too? Do I want to see him? My vagina does, but seeing him means the possibility of a man I barely know being my fiancé and I don't even want to be in a relationship right now, let alone *married*. I don't even know his last name.

Jesus. This is starting to sound more and more like a bad night in Vegas.

I scrub my hands down my face and walk over to the bed, unfolding the clothes. A midnight blue dress made out of silk and lace hangs from my fingers. Pressing the fabric over the front of my body, it barely reaches mid-thigh. This is a joke, right? There's no chance in hell– *Shit*. I'm going to have to come up with all new phrases now.

If there's one thing that I am not, it's ladylike. I forget to cross my legs when I sit, I grew up on a farm where blue jeans and boots were a requirement. Though I'm not against wearing dresses and looking nice on occasion, I'd prefer to keep my kitty cat for my eyes only, not for the general public to gawk at and with a dress this short, I wouldn't even know how to sit down without flashing everyone in the room.

Just then, there's a knock on the door and a woman's voice lightly carries through the thick wood. "Mi lady, may I come in?" she says sweetly.

THE DEMON PRINCE

"Ye–" I clear my throat, finding it more sore from screaming that I care for. "Yes," I yell and the door creaks open, revealing a short statured, curvy woman with blonde hair and fluorescent red eyes. Jolting back when her gaze meets mine, the smile on her face eases over me and I exhale.

"Sorry to scare you, Miss. I understand it can be a bit *jarring*, coming here for the first time. I'm Clamara and I'm here to help you get cleaned up…" she trails off, taking in my tattered clothes, the leaves in my hair and the dirt caked beneath my nails. "My, my… It looks like we have our work cut out for us." She grins and ushers me toward a door on the other side of the bed.

I follow her, wondering what kind of creature she could be that would make her eyes glow red. As if sensing my question, she says, "I'm an empath. We feel things about people. We can tell when you're happy, sad, and can make you feel calm when you're nervous. It's actually why Lucifer picked me for the job." Unable to speak, I nod, trying not to stare at her eyes, but I step inside a bathroom twice the size of my dorm room. A massive stone shower with a steaming waterfall is on the far side of the room, complete with plush moss-covered stones and a glass wall encasing it.

One could easily fit a speed boat inside of it. The waterfall ends into a dark pool, and small waves waft over the edge of the stone that's level with the floor. I could walk right into it and I immediately wonder how deep it goes. On the right are massive mirrors, a vanity, and dual glass sinks with golden spigots.

"Bathroom is to the right," she says, and I turn to find a normal looking door in the direction her small finger points. "The shower and bath are pretty obvious. Then down the hall is your closet, though your side is pretty empty at the moment. We will be back later to fit you for a wardrobe." Your side… Who's the other? I don't even know why I ask myself that, it's surely my fiancé's…

The bile in my stomach threatens to boil in my throat. Don't get me wrong, the man is fucking HOT but I always thought it would be my decision one day. Certainly not now, but it seems futile to fight the Devil. At this point, I should just be glad that I'm not getting tortured, right? Isn't that what happens in Hell?

I don't know much about my mother, but from what Elise has disclosed, she doesn't seem to be the kind of person that would sell their child to the Devil without a good reason. And I highly doubt any loving mother would do something like this without their best interest in mind. I just wish I knew what my best interest is…

When I look up from where my gaze has been glued to the floor, I find Clamara staring at me with sympathetic eyes. "Do you need help getting undressed, princ–"

I cut her off. "Please don't call me princess," I say, dragging in a shaky breath. "I'm… I don't think I can handle that right now."

She nods. "As you wish." Slowly, she lifts her hand and touches my arm, watching my every reaction as her fingertips collide with my skin. Instantly, my nerves vanish, and a weight is lifted off of my chest. My eyes flutter shut and for the first time since waking up, I *breathe*.

When I open them, the corner of my lips tip up. "Thank you," I say, and she takes a step closer, turning me gently so she can unlace the back of the corset. Her nimble fingers work at the ties, and I watch her fight with them through the mirror. "I'm sorry you have to do this."

"Oh, it's not a problem, mi lady," she says as she yanks the lace through the last hole. "It's my job, and I like my job." Her eyes meet mine for a quick moment in the mirror.

"So, you're not… I–" I say, stuttering to find the right words. I don't want to offend her.

"A slave?" She pauses, staring at me through the reflection in the mirror. "Oh, Heavens, no. I grew up here and it's an honor to work for Lucifer."

My eyes drop and my arms clutch around the thin satin of what's left of my dress. The corset seemed to be the only thing keeping it up after my fight with Allister and his… dog. I shiver, remembering the way his claws nipped into my back, the hot pain that radiated through me, barely numbed by the adrenaline.

Inadvertently, I turn and examine my back in the mirror. He wasn't lying. There isn't a single mark.

Clamara reaches toward the back of my neck to clip my crystal necklace and I jolt away grabbing the pendant in my hand, clinging to the last thing my father gave me before I *descended*. Who knows when I'll see him again. I'll be damned before I let someone take it from me, even if it is to bathe.

She retracts her hand and nods understandingly. "Well, prin–" she pauses, and I turn my attention back to her.

"Alice. You can call me Alice."

"Well, Alice. You should probably get cleaned up. I'll be in the room if you need me and towels are further down, on the counter." She steps to leave, but pauses, letting her fingers touch my arm again, sending another wave of calm rushing through me.

"Thank you," I say, as she closes the bathroom door. I'm not sure she heard me, but I shake it off and head toward the waterfall. I slip off my dress and let it fall to the floor. Stepping toward the stone edge, I dip my toe in and nearly sigh from the warmth that wraps me up and my body itches to be submersed. I sit down on the edge, dangling my feet into the pool and still not finding the bottom. Taking a deep breath, I push off the edge and sink into the heated pool.

The water ripples beneath the obsidian surface and images flash in my head. Noah, holding Elise as she cries. I can hear his voice in my head, telling her *"We always knew this day would come. Lucifer will take care of her. Celeste wouldn't give her to a monster."*

Panicking, my feet hit the bottom of the pool and I kick off, until my head shoots through the surface and I gasp in a breath. What *the fuck* was that? My chest heaves as I swim toward the edge. My arm props onto the rock, holding me up as my other hand fingers the crystal hanging against the hollow of my collarbone.

Noah's words come back to me. *'I thought it might help you stay close to those you can't talk to directly…'*

Dragging in as much air as my lungs can hold, I let go and the water pulls me under until the world goes white. I focus my mind on the moment I saw when I slipped below the water, and it comes into view again.

They're in the living room, sitting on the couch and Elise sobs into my uncle's chest.

"Hey, hey, hey," he says, pulling my aunt off his chest to look her in the eye. *"Alice could be watching. I gave her the crystal so she could scry between realms. So, she could see home when she misses it. We have to be strong for her, okay?"* He lifts her chin and kisses her. *"Alice is going through Hell right now–"*

"This is not the time for your dad jokes, Noah," my aunt snaps and he chuckles, pulling her against his chest again.

"I'm serious. She needs to see you happy, or she'll fight whatever they have planned to keep her safe to get back here." Elise pushes off his chest, and stands up, heading toward the kitchen of their farmhouse.

"Are you okay now?" Noah asks.

Her head snaps at him and I have to resist the urge to laugh, seeing as I'm under water and would drown. *"Does it look like I'm okay? My daughter is in Hell. I'm not okay, you just smell like the cows."*

The laughter that leaves his lips is enough to bring a smile to my face. *"Yeah, okay, maybe I do. I've been working,"* he says, getting up to go stand behind her and wrap his arms around her waist. *"But you know what?"*

She turns in his arms to look at him. *"What?"*

"You called her your daughter." I can't see her face since her back is to me, but I see her go rigid.

"That's because she is… and I never got the chance to tell her that." Elise's voice is quiet, I almost don't hear it over the sound of the muffle of the waterfall hitting the surface of the pool above me.

"You'll get to. She'll come back. She won't be gone forever," Noah says, wrapping her up in his arms.

I push myself up above the water and the sob rips through me. Tears stream from my eyes as I ugly cry against the rock ledge, body heaving as the tremors rake through me.

God, I'm an asshole. How could I be so mean to her? I love the woman more than air and on the last day I had to spend with her, I chose to go to a fucking party instead. I spent it twirling around with the man I'm supposed to spend the rest of my life with instead of the mother I was leaving…

It's not like I moved to another state. I'm in an entirely different realm. There are no plane tickets back home I can save for. Everything from here on out will change and I'd give anything to go back to not knowing. I'd never demand another answer about my parents again if I could.

Letting everything I've locked behind the wall in my mind about being kidnapped, about not being able to see my family, my friends, about my past and my parents, come to a head. I cry until my eyes are swollen, and my fingers and toes prune from the pool.

CHAPTER EIGHT

Alice

Pulling the towel tight around my body, I snuggle into the fluffiness. My towels in my dorm, back home, are the cheapest ones I could find at the store. The broke bitch fund, aka my crying bank account, wouldn't allow for any higher quality. Elise told me as a kid that when I became an adult, I'd appreciate the little things, such as good towels. I laughed. Now, wrapped in the warmth this hotel luxury brand towel provides, I get it.

I bite my lip, trying not to let the idea of who taught me about good towels make me cry again. Instead, I push through the door into the main bedroom area and find Clamara waiting for me, clothes in hand… including the dress that threatens my chastity and that I wouldn't be caught dead in.

"You must feel so much better," she says, flipping through the clothes to hand me the panties before turning around.

"As good as I can be, all things considered."

I finger the lace panties, holding them up to the light. This shit is see-through. Don't get me wrong, I have my own personal share of fancy panties, but these look top shelf. Brand name. Like someone is going to be seeing them somewhere besides the laundry hamper.

Swallowing the lump in my throat, I slip them on while holding up the towel and right as I stand up, Clamara holds up three different bras.

"I didn't know your size, so I guessed. As a big chested woman, I know how important these are. Specifically, how dangerous it can be to run without one. So, if they don't work, I'll make sure we find something for you until your stuff arrives."

I slowly take them from her hand and look at the tags. They all match the same lace style as the panties and as I thumb the tags, I find that one happens to be my size.

"Thank you, I appreciate it," I say.

Next, she hands me the dress and I do all but groan. Clamara looks over her shoulder. "What is it? Does it not fit?"

"No... it's not that. It's just not — it's not something I'd typically wear."

"Hmm," she says, tipping her head. "Well, what is it you'd *typically wear?*"

"Anything that I won't flash people in."

She snorts out a laugh, before turning around, ignoring the fact I'm nearly naked, in just the bra and panties she gave me. "Well, let's go check the closet. Maybe there's something of Prince Malikai's that will fit. Hm?"

I stutter a nod and follow after her like a lost puppy. We trail through the bathroom and into the closet and my jaw hits the floor. Beautifully tailored suits, along with what I assume are his casual clothes line the top rows of one side, then more normal-looking casual clothes — including a collection of gray sweatpants line the bottom. But dear lord, I've never seen so many pairs of leather pants.

On the far end of the closet are two mannequins that hold up two different sets of armor, one gold and one silver each with a raised crest, featuring Hell's best good boy, Cerberus. I slide my fingers over the hangers, finding a simple long sleeve shirt with three buttons by the collar. I pull it off and yank it over my head. It's big but it will work.

I choose to leave the buttons undone then snap my fingers, turning the laced dress into a flowy skirt. There was just barely enough fabric to alter it, but it turned out bomb.

Knotting the shirt around the hemline of the skirt, I twirl and Clamara gives a short applause, pleased with my craftsmanship.

"These are all Kai's?" I ask, resisting the urge to pull the shirt I'm wearing to my face. It smells *divine*, and exactly like I remember him from the other night.

"Yes, ma'am," she says as I follow her out.

"I can't imagine him in leather pants, let alone golden armor," I say, and Clamara shakes her head.

"Believe me, mi lady. Once you do, you'll be dreaming about those leather pants. He's a fine specimen of a man and you're a very lucky woman."

I stop next to the bed. "You know about this?"

"The whole kingdom does. We've been preparing for months," she says, tapping the seat of a chair she's brought out from… somewhere. I sit and she proceeds to try and tame my unruly locks.

"It seems crazy to me," I say softly, remembering Noah's declaration minutes ago, that it truly was in my best interest to be here, to go through with whatever Lucifer has planned. I might not know my biological mother, the woman who cut this deal, but if there was one person I'd trust with my life, it's Pops.

"All will make sense soon. I promise. Lucifer is a good man. He takes care of all of us that live in his kingdom, and he will do so for you as well," she says as she wraps the elastic around my hair, securing it into a braid.

I note how she keeps referring to Hell as a kingdom, not a prison for unfortunate and dangerous souls. My family never coaxed me to believe that Hell was bad, though based on movies and books, and literally every other person on Earth, it's sort of a learned assumption. But one thing I would've never assumed about this place, is it being a kingdom or that I'd otherwise be treated like a person instead of an inmate.

After she finishes getting me ready, she opens the door to the hall and escorts me down it until we reach a massive living room looking area. Fit with two couches and a few beautifully carved accent chairs with blood red velvet seats, the room is equally breathtaking as the one I just left. Exquisite paintings hang in decorative frames and another stone fireplace sits on one wall, lit with the same green flames. A large fur-like rug makes the aseptic marble floor feel homey, but overall, it's exactly what I'd expect a medieval king's sitting room to look like.

Lucifer sits up from where he's lounging on the couch and adjusts his shirt. Was he napping? Not that I blame him. Especially if he waited here this entire time. His fingers thread through his slicked hair and smooth it back to its natural state of perfection and then his other reaches up so he can thumb the corner of his mouth.

The Devil drools in his sleep. Noted.

"Alice," he says, as he slides over to one side of the couch. I opt to take a seat on the one opposite of him, though the gesture is nice. "I take it Clamara helped you find everything."

"Um, yes. Thank you." I turn around to give her a shy smile. "She was very helpful. Thank you." The woman nods at my gratitude before rushing back down the hall.

"Well, I promised some answers. Your aunt tells me you have plenty of questions." *He's talked to Elise? Of course, he has.* A pang of anger tears through me. I can forgive her for everything, not telling me for my safety, even though I don't know from whom. However, she didn't have to go so far as to try and convince me that I was going crazy when I told her about my dreams of the Devil. The woman made me see a shrink... *for twenty years,* for nightmares that didn't even exist.

"My aunt," I say matter of factly, and he scoots toward the edge of his seat, smudging his palms against his slacks like they've grown sweaty. His jaw twitches like he's grinding his teeth.

"I know you're mad, but this truly was the only way. There's so much you don't know and the last thing I want to do is overwhelm you more than you already are." He watches my face, analyzing me as if he's seeking permission to proceed. "Why don't you ask a question? Let's go from there."

I run my tongue over my teeth as my mind flips through a role-a-dex of questions I've asked over and over but never had answers to. Here he is, the answer to all of them and I can't even decide on a single one. Deciding to just come out with it, consequences be damned, I ask, "My mother made you a deal. Why?"

"Well, that's loaded, but in short–" he starts but I interrupt.

"I don't want the short answer. I've waited too long for this. Don't spare me the gory details."

He mushes his lips into a line, nodding slowly and staring at the ground, though he does as I ask and it earns my respect. "Everything you know is about to shatter, but I promise I'll be here to pick up the pieces. Are you ready, little lamb?" Why the little lamb reference? I'm not about to be led to slaughter... at least I don't think. Shoving off the nickname, I nod. "Good. Let me tell you a story first."

CHAPTER NINE

Alice

Lucifer leans forward, resting his elbows on his knees and clasping his hands, only to let them dangle between his legs. "Thousands of years ago, God created a group of angels to watch over his creation, known as The Watcher Brotherhood. They were the second set of archangels, but no one ever hears about them since they walked among the humans, silently for years. Their grace slowly dwindled the longer they were away from Heaven and as such, they began to experience human emotions. Hatred. Happiness. *Love.*"

I watch his lips tip up at the word, recognizing the story that Elise has told me dozens of times. *The story of the Grigori Angels.* "It was forbidden for angels to form relationships with humans, let alone romantic ones. They were simply there to observe, but then Belphegor married a human, claiming it was to blend in and do his job more effectively. God looked the other way after reminding him of the repercussions, should he sin. It wasn't long after that his wife became pregnant. He hid her, scared of what would come, but before the baby was born, one of the other watchers urged Belphegor to tell God of his sin. They assured him that if he told the truth, God would show leniency."

Lucifer stands and grabs a box off the mantle of the fireplace and returns to his seat while he talks. It's wooden, small, and carved in delicate patterns of angels, wings, and swords. "He did and the archangels, led by Michael descended on Earth and killed the infant before it was born, along with its mother out of fear of what it would become. It sparked a revolution and most of the original watchers were sent to the void, a place of endless darkness. God created new watchers and told those who remained of the old that they physically couldn't bear children. That he had officially made them sterile. The risk of creating something more powerful was too high. And had the baby been born, they might not have been able to rid the world of the abomination."

He opens the box, revealing a single black feather, dipped in gold. "I thought you might want this. It was your father's. He was an archangel and one of the few original watchers to survive the execution. Twenty-five years ago, Michael let the horsemen out in an attempt to get God to step in and resume his place on the throne in Heaven. Your father was sent to Earth to investigate as a ruse, where he fell in love…" Lucifer holds the feather out to me, and I hesitate before taking it into my hands. It's massive, easily the size of my forearm, but beautiful. My mouth gapes as I twirl it in my hands… An angel. I'm part angel. *Holy shit.*

"Michael killed him for it. Your mother found out shortly after that she was pregnant with you, and she managed to keep you a secret. Though, once you were born, the grace that runs through your veins was nothing short of a beacon for the angels to track. Your mother tried to evade them, for years in fact, but she knew sooner or later they would catch up, so I offered her a deal."

I watch his face intently, searching for any sign of a lie, but find nothing. Yet, I can't even begin to wrap my mind around the fact that I'm half angel… *archangel* at that. Where are my wings? My halo? Then it clicks… Kai's wings *were real*. They weren't part of a costume. Will my wings look like that?

Lucifer takes the feather back, placing it into the box and setting it on the couch beside me before taking his seat again. "I spellbound you of your magic and grace, essentially making it impossible for the angels to track you. We knew it was a long shot and it obviously didn't completely work, or you wouldn't be able to use magic at all. The binding was barely holding on by a thread when it bound your soul, we had to protect it, and that meant keeping you in the dark. The more you knew, the more you would've torn at that thread. I promised your mother twenty years of a normal life and I'm honestly surprised it held up."

I've heard of spellbinding, but I've only known of it being done twice to witches. It was the most extensive punishment the faction council imposed for the most ruthless of creatures. The last one who was spellbound was the witch responsible for starting the black plague in England. It's hard to believe that my mother would do that, even if it was to hide me and give me a normal life.

Still, Lucifer continues, "Regardless, the older you got, the more you pushed to know about your parents. Elise wanted to tell you, but she also wanted you to have the normal life your mother gave hers for, and for you to be able to enjoy it as long as possible. It's different now. The moment you crossed into Hell, you became safe from the angels and now you don't have to be kept in the dark. They can't sense your grace here. We made sure of that years ago. Though, your magic and grace will return little by little and it's imperative that you learn to control it. We will help you."

I pick at my fingernails–the simple notion gives me enough courage to ask about the red flag, waving at half-mast in my mind. "What do you get out of this? Out of helping me? This can't be charity."

"Your father and mother are-*were* very dear to me. But you're not wrong. I've been planning a war for thousands of years. My brother isn't a good man, and God has left him to run without a leash in Heaven. Michael might be deemed a saint, but he's sinned more than most and doesn't deserve to run The Silver City. Not to mention that he's raked up more enemies than I thought possible, including your parents. Once you've learned how to control your power, I hope that you'll be willing to avenge your family and to fight by my side along with my son."

Son... Kai? I danced with the Devil's *son? Sweet baby Jesus, I think the room is spinning.* "You specifically are a mix of all the realms of magic. You're a human witch that can tap into Mother Nature's power, your father was in the process of falling when you were conceived, making you have both the grace of an archangel and able to tap into the magic of the eternal fires of Hell. It makes you one of a kind and it would be the tipping point of the war. My son is nephilim, both human and demon. Michael doesn't know he exists and the two of you together... well, you'd out match anyone who stepped in your way. Including me."

Huh. Is he sure he's looking at the right person? I seem to remember not even being able to make myself disappear while being hunted by Allister's hellhound, Sven. I'm still feeling phantom pains from where his claws sank into my flesh. Now the Devil is trying to tell me that I might be more powerful than him? That's a tough pill to swallow and that's one ability that I pride myself on being able to do. Swallow tough answers, or the lack thereof.

"I, um..." I pause, trying to stare anywhere other than into his eyes. Though genuine, they make my skin crawl and drag up stories of torture and torment. Even though I now wonder if they were even real or made up to scare children into complying. "I have one more question."

"Yes, one more, but a short one," he says, sending me a wink and my cheeks flush red hot.

"Allister, the demon who brought me here, said I was supposed to marry someone..." It ended up being more a phrase than a question but judging by the lift of his eyebrow and the way he settles back into the couch, I don't think Allister was supposed to open his mouth so soon.

"Uh, yes. Your spellbinding, like I said, will wear off rather quickly now that you're here but it could still take weeks, months or even years. We don't know. Even I have enemies, Alice. This place was created to judge people and house those that God didn't feel were 'good enough' or that were simply too wicked to walk Earth. As such, I need to know that you're protected while your binding wears off. My son is highly respected. Even those who hate me wouldn't risk his wrath to hurt you and he's offered his hand."

I chew my lip, remembering the way his hands felt on me, the way his lips pressed against my skin. Being with him wouldn't be so bad, right? And just because we'd have the title, doesn't mean we'd have to *be* a married couple, right?

"Is that debatable?" I ask and Lucifer's mouth contorts into a wide grin.

"Not even a little," he says and my shoulders slump. *Fuck me.*

CHAPTER TEN

Kai

"I don't know. I respect you and Lucifer, but I'm not sure I'm willing to put my neck on the line to take on Michael. My answer is the same as it was ten years ago when you asked. Count me out," the man across from me says, using the toothpick in his hand to pull at the chicken wedged between his teeth.

Ogres are… disturbing creatures and this man is the ruler of the lot. I try not to grimace when he picks up the chicken leg to gnaw on the bone and the sound of it crushing beneath his teeth hits my ears.

Twenty more minutes.

Don't kill him.

Dad will be pissed.

"We're not forcing anyone. I understand and I won't take up any more of your time," I say, sliding to the edge of the massive chair and hopping down to my feet.

I've never felt small before, but in this part of Hell, I might as well be an ant. Okay, that might be an exaggeration, but the ogres are easily ten times my size. The man sees me out, being careful not to step on me as we journey through the castle to where my men wait for me outside the front gate.

When we reach it, I pause and turn to him, still not quite giving up on my mission. "Always the pleasure, Thornben, but I do hope you change your mind."

He chuckles, low enough that I can feel the vibrations beneath my feet. "The pleasure is mine, my prince. But I don't foresee that happening. Safe travels home."

Mushing my mouth into a line, I nod and turn on my heels, walking straight through the open gate. Finnick holds the reins to my horse up and waves, as if I couldn't find the group of six, standing in the middle of the open.

As soon as I reach him, he says, "So?" I shake my head and he blows a raspberry. "He'll come around. We'll come back in another decade."

As if we have another decade…

Allister brought Alice into Hell yesterday and there's no doubt in my mind that her being here is going to speed up the timeline. My father has already started buckling down on the war preparations and that alone means it's coming sooner rather than later.

"Ready to head back? Lucifer wanted you back before the third moon's out, right?" Finn asks as we start heading toward the woods.

"Yeah. I'm supposed to *'meet'* my soon to be wife."

He gasps and when I turn to him, his face is brighter than a fucking Christmas tree. His eyes are wide, his mouth is stretched open as far as it will go. He doesn't even need to say it, I already know what's about to fly out of his mouth.

"You met her already?! And you didn't tell me?"

I lean my head and look at him over the top of my eyelids. "If I say yes, will you let it go?"

"Not a chance. We'd freeze first. I need details. *Now*."

Cursing under my breath and rolling my eyes, I pull my horse to a stop and wave for the rest of my men to carry on so we can talk without prying ears. "She's nice," I say, shortly.

"Nice? That's all you got?"

Our horses begin walking again and I weigh my head from side to side, deciding what to disclose and what to keep to myself. I'd prefer to keep it all to myself, but I've known Finn since I was a boy. He won't let it go. "Yeah, nice. And she wears biker boots." I smirk knowing that simple detail will be enough to stump him and hopefully get me out of the conversation.

He's quiet for a moment, then asks, "What the fuck are biker boots?"

"You know, like your metal ones," I nod toward his shoe, and he glimpses down. "just instead of metal, leather. *Biker boots.*"

Finn has never been to Earth to have an inkling of a clue about what a biker is. So, he gives me a skeptical look and then huffs. "Fine. Don't tell me. I didn't want to know what a biker was anyway."

"It's not as fancy as it seems. A biker is someone who rides a metal horse."

"A *metal* horse? Huh... I bet they don't have as much of an attitude when you don't bring carrots."

"Nope. They're a machine, nothing more," I say, watching a raven appear out of thin air and glide toward me, landing on the pommel of my saddle. In its mouth is a note. I take it out and the thing squawks at me. My hands fling, shewing it away and I unravel the rolled-up paper.

'She's up early. I need you back now,' the note says, written in my dad's shitty handwriting.

"Bad news."

"Let me guess, you have to pop back to the castle, leaving little ol me to ride back with the men. Again. Only this time, you'll get to eye fuck your soon to be princess." He squints at me. "How close did I get?"

"Close enough," I say with an awkward smile. He holds his hands out and I hand him the reins, then in a flash, I teleport back to the Hell Hold–the main castle in the main kingdom of Hell.

My armor clinks against the marble floor as I make my way toward my bedroom. Well, *room* might be a stretch, since this entire floor of the keep

THE DEMON PRINCE

is mine. But as I walk into the sitting area, I find Alice and my dad staring up at me.

One of the more unfortunate things about my predicament is that I was hoping to have time to change before seeing Alice again. Compared to what she's used to, seeing me dressed like this, might shock her system. Though, she's going to have to get used to it at some point. It's expected of me, and soon, it will be of her too.

Her mouth hangs open and her ocean eyes scan over me from head to toe. And here Finn thought I was going to be the one eye fucking her. She's just as stunning as she was at the party, though she doesn't seem as nervous as she was then. Maybe she's adjusting better than I thought she would.

"Great timing," my father says, waving me in. He turns to Alice and begins to introduce her to me. Little does he know I've already met her, having gone with Allister to Earth. What can I say, curiosity got to me and if I'm going to be married off to a Whittaker witch, the least I could do is taste her first–more like test drive.

I know this marriage is meant to be all business, but in Hell, there are no divorces. Once a demon finds a mate, they mate for life and as a demon, that's a hell of a lot longer than seventy years, like it is for humans. I needed to know that there was chemistry, that there was something that could grow. And what I found was beyond anything I ever expected.

The way her body fit perfectly against mine. The way she trusted me, a complete stranger, to take control. The way she melted into me, silently begging to be touched more, to feel my hands and lips skim over her flushed skin. It was all the assurance I needed but what scared me was how much I felt it. The lust.

I know it's only primal urges and physical attraction, but maybe one day it could become more-or it can stay as is. Nothing at all. But it gave me peace of mind, seeing her and being with her alone and outside the pressure of an arranged engagement, that I didn't sign my hand away for a cause. Though it's a cause I believe in strongly enough to front line and negotiate allies for.

"We've met," she says quietly and my heart sinks.

Well, mental note. She can't keep a secret. Though, I don't think she knew to keep it, so I'll let it pass.

"I went with Allister last night. Briefly. I didn't stay on Earth long." My dad rolls his eyes and then shoots me a look, silently telling me that we're not done talking about this.

I'll accept whatever ass-chewing he has coming my way. He'd be pissed if he knew that for decades I've gone on escapades to Earth often, though I don't stay long. The last thing I need is Michael picking up on someone 'new' being there. It would take all of the plans Dad's developed for the war and shred them to pieces. But what's that saying? Curiosity killed the cat? Meow.

I step into the room, my heart pounding louder the closer I get to them. The closer I get to *her*... wearing my fucking shirt. My dad stands up and walks toward the way I came from.

"In that case, I'll leave you two alone. Kai, you know the-" I stop him with a nod. *She doesn't leave my sight and she doesn't leave this level of the keep unless she's escorted.* He doesn't have to tell me that. I don't want anyone to harm a pretty hair on her head any more than he does. "Fantastic." He taps the wooden archway frame on his way through it.

The air feels stale and for a moment, I'm scared to breathe. I stare after my father and once he's out of earshot, I reluctantly turn on my heels to find Alice standing dangerously close to me. Her face is blank, revealing nothing. I know she has to be pissed. Hell, normal Alice, the woman I met last night, seemed like she could've punched me in the throat and not given a shit. I can only imagine the thoughts that are swarming her brain now.

Though I have faith in the connection we had, regardless of how brief it was, part of me wonders if she's going to try and set me on fire for her troubles. You never know with witches.

She reaches out to skim her fingers over my metal chest plate, tracing the indentions of Cerberus, then her eyes meet mine. They instantly turn cold, menacing even, and she storms away from me toward my room. Or I guess it's *our* room now.

What the hell just happened?

I let out a groan and follow after her. Of course, she had to be a witch. If she's anything like her mother or half of the others I've encountered, I'll be needing to brush up on my *'Happy Wife Happy Life'* speech. With them, the temper comes in droves, and I prefer to keep my manhood attached to my body. It's either that, or just get in the habit of getting to my knees...I'd probably prefer that way. It's enjoyable for all parties and is less demeaning than having to beg a woman to forgive you when half the time, you don't even know what you're apologizing for.

Although, Alice doesn't seem like the kind of woman to just let it go, even if orgasms are involved. So, what do I do? How do you apologize to a woman for having to marry me? For uprooting her life to fight a war she didn't even know existed?

My teeth nip into the fleshy part of my cheek as I push open the door to the room. She's already cocooned herself into the blankets on the bed. Clearly, she's not in the mood to talk.

Having never been in a committed relationship, I'm shooting in the dark. My personal forte has always been to enjoy the finer things in life, which means no strings attached. The closest thing I've ever come to a relationship is having a fling with one of the maids, but it was only sex–once a week like clockwork. It's not that I'm incapable of the sort of thing that committed relationships or marriage entails. If I'm being honest, I'm looking forward to it, assuming all things go well, but this is uncharted territory.

I could buy her flowers… Women like that, right? My dad used to give them to my mom. It's one of the few memories I have from my childhood. He'd bring her yellow daisies every time he came back to the keep and put them in a vase for her. I remember the way her face lit up…

That's an option. Though, my mother was delicate, sweet, a homemaker who loved her life, her child and all this kingdom entailed. She loved dresses and knitting and choosing decorations for the parties that were held in the throne room. Alice is… not that. Not even close.

THE DEMON PRINCE

CHAPTER ELEVEN

Kai

I walk over to the bed and sit against the edge, tugging back the thick blanket. Slowly, her face comes into view and my heart quivers, seeing her reddened eyes and the streaks where her makeup has started to run with her tears.

"You want to talk about it?" I ask, rubbing the back of my neck.

"Why would I want to do that?" she says, her voice dripping with sarcasm as she stares at the ceiling.

"Because you look sad," I reach up to wipe at the blackened lines on her cheeks but her hand swats at mine, making a quick *snap* sound when our flesh collides.

"I'm not," she lies. "That's just my face."

I resist the urge to chuckle. She's so fucking stubborn it excites and infuriates me at the same time. Alice turns on her side to look away from me and pulls the blanket tighter around her body.

"Hmm… Resting bitch face. I think I've heard of that." Her shoulder twitches once like she got a kick out of it. It's a start.

I breathe out heavily as I reach over to tuck her hair behind her ear. My fingers linger, brushing through the thick red strands. She doesn't fight it but stays silent. Pushing up from the bed, I walk to the end and remove plate after plate of armor, setting it on the bench by the footboard.

Alice peeks at me, then darts her eyes away, no doubt drawn by the clink of metal, but my lips tip up into a lop-sided smirk when her cheeks flush. She might not know it but seeing her turn all shades of crimson is the only confirmation I need to know that I'm on the right track to getting her attention. We'll bond over the one thing we have already. *Lust*.

No yellow daisies, gifts, or sweet nothings are going to drag this hardheaded woman out of bed. Nor will they bring back the smile that I saw when we danced. So, I change plans. I was going to take off the armor and lay next to her until she was ready to talk, but this way will be much sweeter and way more satisfying.

With the last of my armor and boots off, I yank the shirt over my head and set it on the bench. The belt around my waist jingles as I pull it through the loops of my pants and she sneaks a peek again, but still doesn't get up. It's cute, how nervous she is, like she's worried about offending me.

"I don't mind if you look. I have nothing to be ashamed of. We're going to be married soon. Gawk all you want." I watch her but she doesn't dare to move her gaze away from the spot it's glued to on the bathroom door. "Or don't. I'll be in the bath if you want to join."

I unzip my pants and ball up my shirt, stealing one last look before throwing my shirt at her. It pegs her in the face, and she flails up, scowling at me. God, her eyes can drip venom… it's the sexiest, yet most terrifying thing I've seen in my life.

My tongue flicks across my lips, wetting them as her eyes soften, trailing over my body. She sucks in a shaky breath and when her eyes meet mine, the sheer need in them makes my pulse throb beneath my skin. I hesitate for a moment, then step toward her side of the bed. Her eyes track me, and when my hand reaches up to cup her face, she stays deathly still. I think that's the first time she's let me do anything since I met her without making some smart comment.

My thumb presses against her bottom lip, stroking the silky-smooth surface. "Or talk. Your choice," I say, my voice low, smooth, and sweet.

I'm not sure what it is about her that makes me crave her on a cellular level. It could be the fact that she's mine, whether she wants to be or not. Maybe it's because she's so fucking stubborn and fights every instinct she experiences and rejects anything good for her. Maybe it's because of the connection we had last night and how my body can sense the power that lurks within her, hidden from plain sight.

I'd never experienced anything like that before. It felt like the atoms that make up my being were stretching and pulling, even as our skin touched, begging me to be closer to her. They still do.

"I'd never take advantage of you, Alice. It's not who I am, and you have my word even if you don't trust it. I can't tell you that I won't do things you hate, but I can promise to never hurt you. And regardless of whatever you think of me, I do truly hope that you come to believe that one day."

Dropping my hand, I walk toward the bathroom. I pull the door shut behind me and leave her to stew on the idea then strip my remaining clothes and sink into the bath, letting the water ripple around me. It's warmed by Hellfire, the same green hued flames that float in the hearths around the keep. It never goes out.

My eyes close and my arms stretch out as I lean against the rock ledge, holding me up in the water. I let the steam and the sound of the waterfall overwhelm my senses, but when the sound of the door creaking open hits my ears, I snap my gaze toward it. Alice slowly steps into view and grabs the chair from the vanity, dragging the wooden chair legs across the marble to position herself on the other side of the glass wall.

She takes a seat and looks at me for a moment before speaking. "You look comfortable."

I arch an eyebrow, and my lips tilt into a smirk of triumph. "You could be too."

"Pass," she says shortly, leaning back into the chair.

"Suit yourself," I say, pushing off the edge and dipping below the surface. The water coats my skin like silk and when I come back up, I slick back my dripping wet hair and resume my place against the rock ledge. "So, are you going to–" My words cut off when I see her face. I've never seen someone look so hungry before. She swallows, like her mouth has been watering. "You okay?" I ask.

She ignores my question and instead, asks one of her own. "Why are you doing this?"

"Doing what? Bathing? Um, personal hygiene?"

She scoffs. "I mean, this. Me."

My eyebrow bounces. Believe me, if I was doing her, I wouldn't be so pent up right now. Though, it's not what she means. "I'm not answering questions unless you come in here."

I watch her chest deflate and for a second, I wonder if I was too forward, but then she pushes up from her chair and comes on the other side of the glass. She slides her boots off, along with her socks and my heart nearly stops.

Is she really going to…
Am I about to see her…

Before I can finish the thought, she sits on the edge of the stone and slips her feet into the water. Besides her shoes, she's stayed fully clothed and my lungs quiver from the strain of holding my breath.

I should've known it wouldn't be that easy, but a guy can dream, right?

"Happy?" she says, gesturing to all of her.

"Ecstatic." It's impossible to resist the urge to smile, not when she's this close. If I knew she wouldn't kick me in the throat, I'd wade over and slide my hands up her legs. I've always had a thing for skirts. Easy access. And I'd be lying to myself If I said my fingers didn't itch to touch her more. Her skin is so soft. So delicate. I have the oddest urge to lick it… but something tells me that wouldn't go over well. At least not now.

"Are you going to answer my question?" she asks. Jeez, she doesn't waste a minute, does she?

THE DEMON PRINCE

"I didn't agree to it at first. Believe it or not, I wasn't too crazy about the idea of marrying someone I didn't know either. It's why I went with Allister to Earth. I figured if I met you, maybe it would be easier."

I toss water over my pecs to warm them up, since they stick out above the water and Alice nearly drools from the gesture. It wasn't my intention, but I'll take it as a compliment.

"And was it? Easier?"

After a second, I nod. "It was."

CHAPTER TWELVE

Kai

She drags her hand down her face before she trains her eyes to the reflection in the glassy surface of the water. "I have one more–"

"Oh no, sweetheart," I say, smirking and sliding along the rocks until my arms cage her against the rock ledge and I'm floating in front of her legs. "It's a question for a question and that makes it my turn." She stills but doesn't argue so I take it as permission to go ahead.

I lift a hand to finger the unbuttoned hem of the shirt she's wearing. *My shirt.* It lays against the raised edge of her collar bone and in doing so, a bead of water drops onto her skin and sinks down, disappearing under the shirt. What I wouldn't give to follow it, but I promised her I'd behave. So, unless she gives me an indication that she wants me to follow it, I won't.

"I like this on you," I say, biting my lip and letting my eyes wander over the fabric.

"That's not a question." Alice tips my chin up with her finger so I have to meet her eyes.

"I'm pretty sure you were given your own clothes and I'm all for what's mine is yours, especially when it looks as good as you do, but why my shirt?"

"I'm not a prude," she says, trailing her fingers over the veins that have raised on my forearms. Goosebumps erupt across my skin, and I shiver.

"Never said you were."

"The dress your father gave me was too short for my liking. So, I improvised."

"Hmm." I push away from the edge, resuming my place on the other side of the water where I'm not so tempted to touch her. "Snarky and crafty."

She scrunches her nose at me. "Your father mentioned that God wasn't on his throne in Heaven…" Alice pauses, as if looking for the words to say.

"I think I get where you're going with that. In short, God got bored and left to do only he knows what. He put Michael in charge and said it was temporary, but it's been decades. From what I've been told, Michael has tried contacting him, but he never answers. He just disappeared."

Her mouth contorts so she can chew on the inside of her cheek. "Your turn."

Wow? No comment? Granted, after what she's been through in the last day, I guess it's to be expected.

"The man you were watching at the party... Who is he?"

Her eyes light up, almost as if she's excited by my question.

"Jealous are you?"

"Not even a little. You and I both know whoever that man was would never be enough for you."

"Why is that?"

"Because he's too subtle. He wouldn't know how to handle you, Alice. You'd eat him alive. He wouldn't demand your attention. There wouldn't be a spark. What you felt was an infatuation but the moment it became a reality, the moment you touched him, he wouldn't have been enough."

"What makes you think that I need someone who knows how to *handle me?* And what's wrong with normal? I've prayed to be like that. So, what makes you think that I wouldn't want that in a man, especially when I can't be normal myself?"

"Because we're two of the same. As Nephilim, we crave power. You might not know the extent of it yet, since you're still spell bound. Once that's gone and you come into your power, you'll understand."

I wade through the water, on an undetermined path, letting it pull me. "The way it hums in our veins, the way it crackles in the air around us, it's like a drug and you'll always crave more. It's what makes our kind so dangerous. But there's a difference between wanting it and taking it. We're not born evil, Alice, but we're more susceptible to becoming it."

"I still don't understand what this has to do with Cameron," she says, crossing her arms in front of her chest.

"The moment your spellbinding wears off, no human will be enough for you. No witch, vampire, wolf... Nothing Earthly or short of an archangel will be. Trust me. I know. Anything short of it just feels numb. You can will yourself to be with someone physically, but when they touch you, you'll feel nothing. Your body won't come alive beneath their fingers. The moment I stopped aging and my power grew stronger, no mortal could fill the void. I realized last night that it was different with you and that's why I agreed to my father's plan."

She doesn't speak, doesn't move, and when her eyes drop, losing all emotion, I know I've pushed her too far. I gave her too much information to chew. I worry my lip between my teeth desperate to come up with something to change the subject and when my brain draws a blank, I look around for something to jog an idea. Then my eyes land on her necklace. I noticed the ruins and recognized it as angelite on the day I met her.

"Do you have a question?" She shakes her head no. "Do you mind if I ask another then?" Alice doesn't say anything, but her eyes raise to meet mine. "Why do you wear angelite around your neck?"

Her fingers instantly go to it, rubbing the septagram. "My fa-uncle gave it to me the day I was brought here. I didn't realize what it was until I took a bath here. It made me see things when I was underwater. I'm not entirely sure why."

"It will only work when exposed to fire. This pool is heated by Hellfire and thus, infused with it. Normally, witches burn it, and they can scry through the flames, but in this pool, and most of the water in Hell, you can scry with it beneath the surface." She fidgets in place, and it makes me wonder what she saw.

"Is what it shows you true?" she asks, unclasping the necklace from behind her neck and holding the pendant in the palm of her hand.

"Yes. It should've been whatever was happening at the moment you did it." I wade over to her, perching on the stone ledge next to her. "That's enough learning for one day." She nods and I start to push up out of the water and Alice's hand immediately shoots up to cover her eyes. "If you don't want to see it, you might want to turn around."

Her legs kick out of the water, then she spins around and hugs her knees, looking down between them. I get out and wrap a towel around my waist, though it does little to conceal anything, but it will hopefully give her peace of mind.

"You can look now," I tell her, and she gets up to start walking toward the bathroom door. I grab her hand and spin her back until her other palm smacks against my chest, jolting her to a stop. "Don't leave yet."

I grip her shoulder lightly and spin her so her back is toward me, but she can see us in the mirror above the sink. My fingers unravel hers, retrieving the crystal necklace while my other hand reaches toward the front of her neck, gliding along the sensitive skin to move her hair to the other side. But when my fingers touch her throat she stiffens, inhaling sharply. I clasp her necklace and then pull her hair through, enjoying the way it feels against my palms.

She inadvertently grabs at the pendant and then turns around to face me. Her eyes flick from side to side, scanning mine as her lips part. She wants me to kiss her, or at least it seems like it. I lower my head, feeling my heart pick up pace. My eyelids begin to close but right before our lips meet, she takes a step back and shoves against my chest. I jerk upright.

Well, I definitely fucking read that wrong.

I curse under my breath.

"What are you doing?" she asks, her tone is sharp as she seethes through clenched teeth.

"I thought you wanted me to," I say, not really sure what to do or where to put my hands at the moment, so I run one through my wet hair to busy it.

"You thought I wanted the man that I'm being forced to marry to kiss me?"

Good lord, and here I thought we were making progress. Becoming friendly, even. It's like we're back to square one.

"You're not the only victim of this, you know. I just told you I didn't want to, either. We both are having to make sacrifices-" she cuts me off.

"Not the only one? You're not the one who got *mauled* by a fucking *monster dog* named after a

Disney prince's emotional support moose. Don't even get me started!"

"Allister did what he had to do. Your aunt made it clear that you weren't going to go anywhere willingly. He knew that was likely the easiest way to get you here so that we could explain everything."

"You're wrong. I would've gone had people not kept me in the dark. You didn't have to kidnap me." Her finger pokes into my chest and her hair starts to float. The tresses whip and swirl like snakes in the air.

I tilt my head and cross my arms at her, arching an eyebrow for dramatic effect. "You would've? Really?"

She pauses, contemplating it for a moment. "Okay, maybe not. Still, he didn't even offer and even then, it was not necessary to have his mutt claw the shit out of me."

"Want me to drag him here and beat him within an inch of the grave, fine I'll do it. Say the fucking word, princess." I lift my hand to snap but she grabs at my hand, pulling it down.

"Don't. I don't want to hurt him. It wasn't right but hurting him doesn't take it away. I just need a damn moment to wrap my head around everything and you trying to kiss me isn't helping. You flirting relentlessly with me, isn't either."

"I don't know what there is to figure out. You can't stay on Earth. Michael will kill you as soon as the spellbinding wears off. It can't be redone. And if you want to stay here, then we have to get married. If we don't, someone will try to hurt you. You're a pretty girl, Alice, in a land of monsters and beasts. If you walk outside the keep, saying your Lucifer's guest isn't going to cut it. People will think you're saying it to save your skin. Marrying me in public and becoming his daughter-in-law has a lot more of an impact." I take a step toward her, putting her face within an inch of mine.

"So, tell me, princess. If you can't stay on Earth without being hunted, if you refuse to marry me and can't stay in Hell without being slaughtered, where the fuck will you go?" She doesn't answer, but her eyes well up with tears and it makes me regret letting the words leave my mouth, but I refuse to show it. If this woman found any sign of weakness, I'm relatively certain that she'd try to eat me alive. My nostrils flare as I inhale and finally, her gaze breaks with mine, tearing to the floor. "That's what I thought."

I turn and head toward the closet to get dressed, leaving her there to stew with her thoughts.

THE DEMON PRINCE

CHAPTER THIRTEEN

Alice

Kai comes out of the closet in gray sweatpants, a girl's kryptonite, and shirtless, as if that makes looking at him any easier. It's hard to resist the urge to stare at his abs, the need to run my hands over his broad chest and trace his defined pecs.

I don't hate him… I want to, for being part of the reason I had to leave my home, my family, but it wasn't his fault. He didn't make me this way just as he didn't make the angels bloodthirsty. And he's right. I don't have anywhere else to go. I can't go back home without possibly endangering Elise and Pops, not to mention my own death being imminent, and if I'm going to stay here, then it means being with him. Still, it feels wrong to marry someone I just met. Even if they do seem like a decent person… most of the time.

My mind circles back to the way he got in my face, remembering how his tone changed, becoming more sinister. It commanded every cell in my body and left my fingers trembling... but yet, *I liked it.* I did want him to kiss me. God, my lips ached for it. It's been hard not to think about the electricity that coursed through my veins the last time he did. But just because I want it, doesn't mean that I should indulge, and if he had kissed me again, I'm not sure I would've ever come up for air.

I'd have let him consume me, along with all the sacred parts of my soul and straight down to the raw materials that make up my flesh. God, I'd have begged him to have his way and to do as he pleased, just to feel his hands scorch across my skin, just to feel that spark...

There was truth to what he said about no one else being enough after experiencing a taste of what he provided. I'm no saint, and I've had my share of lovers and not a single one could compare in the slightest. One of them I even thought I loved, and yet, I'd had sex with him and it didn't turn my core even half as tight as a simple kiss did with Kai.

The problem is, once I let him in, once I submit to this idea of being his bride, there's no going back and my heart doesn't want to accept this as my new reality. It doesn't mean it's not tempting though… I guess that holds true to the stories I've heard about Hell. It's chock full of temptation and the carnal urge to sin in the most delicious ways… and all of them involve the man ignoring me across the room.

We sit for hours, with him on the couch and me on the bed reading. We don't talk, we don't even interact beyond a few silent glances in each other's direction. It's not until a maid I don't recognize brings in a cart with food that either of us make an effort to break the silence. He waves me toward the living room as the smell of pasta bathed in basil and oregano hits my nose and it's then that I realize just how hungry I am.

The maid spreads out our plates on top of a small table for two that sits next to the windows while I do my best to stay out of her way. Once she's unloaded everything off the cart, Kai pulls out a seat and I reach for the other.

"What are you doing?" he asks before nodding toward the chair in his hand. I dip my head but take the seat he offers me.

"I'm not used to people doing that," I say, biting my lip between my teeth to steady the nerves that being so close to him ignites.

He sits across from me, sliding closer to the table. "It's how things work here," his voice is clipped and short. I know I should probably apologize for going off on him in the bathroom, but every time my mouth opens to do so, I can't force the words out. Saying sorry, almost feels like giving up, and I'm not sure I'm ready to do that.

There has to be another way. There always is… I just have to find it, but for now, I need to keep him happy at a distance. I look over my meal, mouthwatering, and the urge to scarf it down my throat rampages through me.

I pick up my fork, determined to be proper, but the second the first bite hits my tongue, any shot at that goes straight out the window. The mere taste of food sends a moan reverberating in my throat, and I shove a second bite in my mouth before I finish the first, craving more.

Elise is a fantastic cook, but it doesn't even come close to the explosion of flavors that glide across my tongue. Who knew something as simple as spaghetti could be so diverse? Before I know it, my plate is empty and I'm so full it hurts.

I sit back in my seat and look up to see Kai smiling at me. That fucking grin is enough to send butterflies spinning through my stomach and all the way down to my lady bits. My thighs squeeze together, and I immediately hope he doesn't pick up on my subtle movement, but the tongue that darts across to wet his lips, tells me he did… that he liked the reaction that just being around him elicited from me.

"I take it you like spaghetti," he says, twirling noodles around his fork. "Duly noted."

"It was amazing." I run a hand through my hair and arch my back toward the chair, staring at the ceiling, which I'm just now noticing is vaulted. My eyes flutter closed, and regret aimed at my choice to eat so much floods through me.

The wooden legs of his chair scrape against the marble floor and just as I'm about to sit up to see what he's doing, hands tangle into my hair holding me in place from behind my seat. My eyes flare open as I gasp, seeing his devilish smirk that makes my pulse throb in my veins. His thumb swipes at the corner of my mouth before going straight to his lips, where his tongue licks it clean.

"You missed a spot," he says.

My mouth gapes and I stay deathly still, forgetting how to think, let alone move. "Thank you," I say like a fucking idiot, mesmerized by the way his lips curve as his eyes search mine. He releases my hair, and my head snaps up, staring off at the plates on the table, and slightly afraid to move. I'm not scared of him, per se, but more of what my libido might make me do if I'm not careful.

Then his lips are at my ear. "Breathe, Alice." The dark chuckle that follows snaps me out of it. I push up out of my seat, brushing against him before gliding across the room to get my book. I'm desperate to pretend he doesn't exist, to calm my racing heart, but a knock on the door cuts my plan short.

Kai lets them in and suddenly, the room is swarmed by men carrying cardboard boxes, placing them down in the middle of the room to create a mountain of brown. Most of them, from what I can see, have my name written on the side in my aunt's handwriting. Kai comes over, which at first, I think is to stay out of the way as dozens of men filter in and out of the room on loop. However, once he speaks, I know his true intentions are to torment me. "Looks like you won't be needing to wear my shirts anymore. *Bummer.*"

The last of the men leave and I hop up, walking past him without so much as a glance and begin opening boxes. I shuffle through the things packed inside, and slowly start strewing my belongings around the room. Kai seems to busy himself while I do since he disappears. But a couple of minutes later, he comes out of the bathroom fully clothed and begins to slide his armor back on.

"I have to go take care of some things before the moons rise. Will you be okay here?" he asks like I have a choice in the matter. I nod yes. "Great. If you do need anything, there's a red button on the wall. It will patch you through to the maids. Please don't leave the room. You're not a prisoner, but it's very easy to get lost inside the keep and you shouldn't go outside of it without an escort… I'm trusting that you'll listen. Don't make me regret it."

"Yeah, yeah. Don't leave my prison cell. Got it," I say, pulling stuff out of the box in front of me.

"I'm serious, Alice." I hear his armor clink as he shuffles in place.

"So am I." Looking up, I find his mouth pressed into a flat line. A sure sign that he's not amused. "I won't go anywhere. Want me to pinky swear?"

"Your word is enough. No need to get *pinkies* involved." Then without another word, he's out the door and I'm left alone.

CHAPTER FOURTEEN
Alice

After what seems like hours of hanging up clothes and trying to find places for things, and a visit from the keep's seamstress, I see the sun, or at least what I'm assuming is the sun, begin to fade. The maids bring me dinner and I eat it at the small table in the company of Clamara, but she doesn't stay long. And by the time it's dark outside, Kai still hasn't returned.

I've unpacked so many boxes that my fingers feel bruised from tearing at tape, but I am incredibly grateful for my own clothes along with those the seamstress left me. There were carts of beautiful gowns that I got to pick through, along with regular outfits and satin pajama sets. One of which I plan to wear to bed tonight. I head into the closet, stripping naked and grabbing the black satin shorts and camisole, then slide the silky fabric over my body.

Before leaving, I grab the robe that the seamstress insisted that I have, saying it was fit for a princess. I took it to appease her, but it does look temptingly soft. It's mostly sheer but has fuzzy hems and I shrug it on before stepping into my slippers. I grab my book off the end table by the bed and debate on whether going to the sitting area would be considered wandering... Kai's only concern regarding me staying put was geared toward me getting lost, and with it being right down the hall, I think I'll manage to get back on my own. So, there's no harm in it right? Right.

I walk out of the room and start down the hall until I see a door that was closed earlier when I came through, now wide open. It's dimly lit, but from what I can tell, it looks like a library. The walls are lined with leather-bound books and the smell of paper and ink hit my nose. Yellow bulbed lamps paint everything in a dusty glow and a large reclining chair sits on the furthest wall. A floor light arches over it, making it the perfect reading spot.

Sitting in the chair, I snuggle into the plush cushions and start into another chapter, but after another hour or so, my eyelids feel heavy and I'm not sure when, but I fall asleep, dreaming for the first time that I can remember. It's not until the odd sensation of moving overcomes me that I wake to find Kai carrying my body, with my head snuggled into the crook of his neck

"Ah shit, I'm sorry. I must have dozed off," I say, rubbing my eyes as he sets me on the bed.

"It happens. It's easy to fall asleep in there."

I scan over him, while sliding beneath the covers, to find him in his own pjs, aka loose hanging sweatpants and no shirt. I'm starting to think that's the normal attire for him when he's not planning balls or slaying monsters in his shining armor… Or whatever the fuck he does in it.

He doesn't break a beat before sliding into the bed next to me in the darkly lit room.

"What are you doing?" I ask, arching a brow at him.

"Going to bed." He stills, freezing mid-motion. "Why? What does it look like I'm doing?"

"We're sharing a bed?"

He looks at me and cocks his head. "Um. Yeah? This is my room too."

"Oh no. That's not happening," I say, sitting up and getting ready to protest but he simply ignores me and lays down, snuggling into the pillows. "Hello. Did you hear me? We're not sleeping together."

He grumbles and turns on his back to look at me. "Go to bed, woman. It's not up for debate. This is my bed and by default, what's yours is mine, or at least it will be."

"I'm not sleeping in the same bed as you so your grubby paws can sneak over to my side and feel me up in my sleep. No. Find somewhere else," I say, leaning over to push at his body in a futile attempt to kick him out.

He grabs my waist and throws me back to my side without moving an inch. "No, and my hands are not *grubby*. If I wanted to feel you up, I wouldn't need to do it while you were asleep, either. Trust me, if I did it, you'd want me to. Hell, you might even beg me for it. So, enough. Go to sleep, Alice."

I drag in a deep breath and inflate my lungs. My pulse throbs in my neck and my heartbeat rings in my ears. My hands form into fists as my nails make crescent shaped cuts into my palms. I feel the veins around my eyes threatening to ripple and I know it will only be a matter of seconds before my eyes go black. I slowly release the air in my lungs, but what comes out of my nose is smoke, twirling and spinning around me.

Kai's eyes watch me as I steady myself. Part of me wants to let him see what I look like when I get mad. Maybe that will be enough to get him to move. My entire life I've had to stay in control. I've had to live by the book of rules Elise made and that meant keeping my emotions in check. I'm the only witch I know of whose eyes turn black when my control snaps. I've gotten better at controlling it, but when something, or rather someone, like Kai grates my last nerve, it makes it hard.

Elise never told me why it happens, and now that I know what I do about who my father was, it makes me wonder if it has to do with him. Does Kai have the same struggle? Is it a Nephilim thing? Or is

THE DEMON PRINCE

it something to do with the angel and witch side meshing? I want to ask him, but I'm too stubborn to let him have the satisfaction right now.

"You part dragon now?" he says in reference to the smoke, rolling from my nose with every exhale. My head snaps toward him and I don't need a mirror to know my control has gone out the window. His eyes grow for a moment then settle into an emotion I can't quite put my thumb on. Do my eyes *intrigue* him? His hand reaches out, gripping my hip and dragging my body toward his and in the same fluid motion, he lifts onto his side and props his body up with his elbow.

His hand moves from my hip to push me backward, then pulls my body against his, molding my back to his front. I'm too shocked to move; to protest. Instead, I go pliable in his hands, letting him do as he sees fit, and dear god, it scares me how much control I'm willing to give him.

There's a mirror on the wall I'm facing and though our forms are small, I can see my face. My obsidian eyes look hollow and tendrils of black stretch from them, reaching out in intricate swirls and tracks across my pale skin. Kai meets my gaze in the mirror as his hand pulls my hair away from my neck. Who is this man? Everyone, including Pops and Elise, were terrified when my face looked like this, so why does it seem to draw him closer? Unless he deals with the same thing and that means that it is due to being a nephilim.

My eyes flutter closed when his lips brush against my pulse and the warmth of his breath mixing with the coolness of my skin sends a shiver down my spine. He kisses the hollow behind my ear, and a moan escapes my lips. I feel his smile against me, as if he's pleased with the way my body bends for him. Then his teeth nip against my throat, making the room spin from both pain and pleasure before he kisses the same spot to soothe the ache.

I open my eyes to find him watching my reflection and I stiffen, going cold in his grasp. How do I keep losing control with him? Why do I keep letting him affect me this way? My eyes are back to normal though. It did accomplish that, but I don't want him to have the idea that the moment I argue, he can plant those sexy fucking lips against me and I'll submit.

"This doesn't change anything," I say, coldly and he chuckles against my ear.

"Doesn't it, though?" *No! It doesn't.* I unwrap his arms from my body and get up, grabbing my pillow and walking toward the living room.

"You're not sleeping on the couch," he says, sitting up in bed.

"Watch me, asshole," I say, plopping the pillow down and grabbing a throw blanket. I wrap it around my shoulders before laying on the soft cushions.

"I did, and I don't think it's *my grubby paws* you're worried about. Now come back to bed. I won't touch you again unless you ask, deal?"

"No," I say, staring at the arched windows and the moonlight shining through the curtains, painting the floor white. I hear the bed creak as he gets up, cursing under his breath.

"Why are you fighting this so hard?" he asks, coming to stand beside me. I don't answer. "You don't have to pretend or be ashamed that you're attracted to me. There's no one here to impress or save face with. It's just me and you're about to be my wife."

He tries to smooth the hair away from my face, but I smack at his hand, and he chuckles. "I'm not going to let my princess sleep on the couch. So, either let me soothe that ache between your thighs or stop being so damn stubborn and go to bed so I can sleep."

I could lie and say that I don't want him, that the sheer sight of the man doesn't spin lustful butterflies in my stomach, but he'd see right through it. Instead, I don't acknowledge his ultimatum, which only seems to make him want to prove his point more.

"Besides, I think it's safe to say that I'd kill to be buried in that sweet little cunt of yours until my name is branded on your insides. You'd be doing us both a favor and it doesn't have to mean anything."

My eyes flick up to his for a brief second, shocked by the crudeness of his words, and I nearly lick my lips at the promise they hold. He crouches down, hovering mere inches from my face.

"So, what's it going to be, princess?"

THE DEMON PRINCE

CHAPTER FIFTEEN

Alice

"I don't need you to do anything. If I wanted your dick, I would've had it already." I glare daggers into him, but he doesn't flinch away, as if it's a look he's seen a hundred times. Instead, his smile turns predatory, crooked, like if given the opportunity, he'd devour me.

Worrying my lip with my teeth, I watch as his eyes slide to my mouth, dripping with lust and desire, forcing me to tighten my hold on the blanket to steady myself. "We're in a fucking castle. I'm sure there's another bed you can sleep in and as for your concern for my *cunt*, I'm more than capable of *soothing it* myself, thank-"

"Do you even hear yourself right now?" he says, cutting me off. I scowl, tightening my face and giving him my best 'what the fuck' look.

"Of course, I do. Do you hear the words coming out of my mouth? I don't–"

"Quiet," he demands. My mouth snaps shut, and the room falls silent and that's when I hear it. The low rattle in my throat. Oh, my *fucking God*... Am I *purring?!* I gasp and my mouth shoots open as I jerk upright. No. *No, No.* This is *not* happening. Not again.

"What is—Do you do that?" I say, my hands flinging to my throat trying to hush it. It's only happened once before, and it was so short lived that I thought I'd imagined it.

His face stays frozen. His lips parted and pulled into that mischievous grin as he slowly shakes his head no. It's like he's in awe over the fact that I literally just went fucking *feral* over him. I slap my hands over my face, shaking my head, then lift it to shoot a murderous look his way as if it's his fault. He bites at his lip, trying to fight back his amusement, but it doesn't even attempt to hide it in his eyes.

"You were saying?" he taunts, and I chuck my pillow at him. It smacks him in the face but doesn't do much damage. He simply swats it away and it falls to the floor. I get up and storm toward my bedside table, where he's placed the book I was reading when he found me in the library. However, I hear footsteps growing closer behind me and I ditch the mission, deciding to make a break for it and find something else to read in the library.

"Where do you think you're going?" he asks.

"Anywhere you're not," I snap, reaching for the door handle only for him to grab my arm and whip me back around to face him. He continues walking toward me, pinning my frame against the wall.

"Oh no, sweetheart. You don't get to make sounds like that and just leave." He leans forward to rest his forehead against mine. I feel his hand trailing up my side. Honestly, I don't even think he actually touches me, just hovers, yet my body still arches toward him in a silent plea for more. "Come on, Alice. Just say the word."

I bite back a moan that pushes up my throat and force the word through gritted teeth. "Fine." I say, watching him cock an eyebrow like he's unsure of how to proceed.

There is no reason for my body to be revolting like this. I shouldn't be craving him with every fiber of my being. Kai can call it my primal need for power, but that's the understatement of the year. It feels like a goddamn mob made up of my insatiable vagina and my lonely heart holding pitchforks, with the spokes pointed toward my common sense. I've only been in Hell for a day and he's already making it hard to say no to the point that I want his lips on mine more than I want air.

Sliding to the right to squeeze around him, he turns to watch me walk toward my bedside table. I open the drawer and set my book inside it, and search through the contents, knowing what I'm looking for is in here somewhere.

"What are you doing?" he asks.

My hands find purchase and I yank it out, holding it up for him to gawk at–a purple vibrator that's shaped like a decently sized dick. "Taking care of it," I announce, spinning around to head toward the bathroom for some privacy, but he's there, snatching it out of my hand like some kind of lunatic and pulling the entire drawer out of the nightstand.

He throws it inside while his jaw ticks and his teeth grind, then storms into the bathroom and straight toward the closet.

I follow after him and stop cold in my tracks when I realize what he's about to do. Lunging forward and grabbing the drawer, I hang onto it for dear life. My book is in there and quite frankly, it's the only thing I can't live without right now. He lifts it up, taking me with it until my fingers lose grip and I drop to my feet. Kai slides it on to the top shelf, easily four feet above my reach, and my jaw falls open. *Asshole!* "Real mature. Get it down!" I demand.

"If you want it so bad, use your magic and get it yourself, little witch."

He watches me fail multiple times before he snorts and walks back toward the bedroom.

"Fuck you!" I yell, tired of his horse shit and tired in the literal sense. At this point, I'm surprised there isn't steam rolling out of my ears. "So what? You own my vagina now too? As if my life wasn't enough?" I glare at him and my face burns as rage rips through me. My hair begins to float, swirling around my head in the air like snakes, ready to strike.

"You're not going to torture me," he says, stopping to turn back and cross his arms over his chest. "If you need help, I'm right here, princess. Ready and waiting. But you're not going to lock yourself in the bathroom and make me listen to your battery-operated boyfriend."

"Gah! How many times do I have to say no before you get it through your thick ass skull? My body might want you, but I *don't*. Now, get it *down*," I say, walking toward him and poking a finger at his chest.

"You know, you seem awfully pissed off at losing your toy for someone who isn't needy."

My palms plant hard against his chest. "I'm not that hard up, asshole. My book was in that box, and I only have four chapters left."

Kai doesn't say anything, just grabs my waist and heaves me over his shoulder, carrying me back to the bed on a warpath.

"Put me down," I demand, slapping at his back but he doesn't waver, instead he tosses me down on the bed like a ragdoll or some sad war trophy he won from a village he plundered.

"Go to sleep. You have a long day tomorrow," he says, walking around to his side. I want to get up and storm back to the couch, but I'd be lying if I said my eyes didn't feel heavy. I'm exhausted. *He's* exhausting. I turn on my side, looking at my reflection in the mirror.

"I hate you," I mutter, quiet enough that he might not have heard it.

"No, you don't. Go to bed, Alice." Oh, we're on a first name basis again? And here I thought his use of *witch* was actually code for *bitch*, just without the regret.

***

Waking up to the bright light of the sun shining through the arched windows, I sigh, feeling the warmth pressed against my body. My hand reaches up to rub my eyes and rid them of the wish to return to my dream, which unfortunately, involved my dear fiancé.

As if sensing me thinking about him, I hear the man mumble, "Good morning," and my eyes shoot open wide, realizing my head is touching his meticulously defined chest. Slowly raking my gaze up his body, I find a grin so wide, it might split his face in two.

"Don't look at me, princess. You did this all on your own. I just wasn't going to stop you. Did you know you snore?" He tucks a chunk of my hair behind my ear, and I quickly reach up to smack his hand in a spastic motion which instead of deterring him, elicits a dark laugh from his lips. "It's kind of cute… you know, like snuggling with a grizzly bear."

"I'm still mad at you," I seethe.

"I know. You can be mad at me all you want." He gets up from the bed and stretches before turning back to me. "I have to leave today, but one of my men will be by to get you out of the room. He's going to take you to the market, get whatever you want. I thought some fresh air would do you good."

The air deflates from my lungs, almost like I had hoped it would be some sweet line about what he wanted to do to me, but I straighten my shoulders anyway and pull the blanket tighter around my body, realizing my camisole has shifted, revealing way too much.

When my eyes meet his, they dart away as if to play it off like he wasn't looking. "Thank you," I say, and he clears his throat and heads off to get ready. When he emerges again, he's dressed and clad in his golden armor.

"Clamara will be here soon with your breakfast," he says, pausing at the front door with his hand on the knob, "And Alice, behave please and when I get back, I'll get your book."

"No promises," I say, flopping back onto the bed.

THE DEMON PRINCE

CHAPTER SIXTEEN

Kai

I've never met someone so irritating in my life, yet I've already grown sort of fond of being around the woman. Walking down toward the keep's entrance, I find Finn eating a baguette slice and leaning against one of the stone pillars.

"Where to today, boss?" He says, falling into stride next to me as we descend the stairs toward the bottom where the rest of my men wait with horses.

"Sure, you want to know? You're not going to like it." Finn's body stills as we take step after step, slowing from the pace we've set.

"Well now I need to know." He's been my best friend and second hand for dozens of years and the man can read me like a fucking book, and I him. So, the face he gives me is a silent warning that he knows I'm up to something, but I know he'll stand by my side, even if it means going against my father.

"I'm meeting with the High King of the Realm of Monsters."

The color leaches from Finn's face, leaving it ghost white. "Why on earth would we go there? This is Lucifer's plan?"

"No. It's mine," I say as my foot collides with the graveled ground.

"What? You get a wife and now all of a sudden have the biggest balls in the seven realms of Hell?" I ignore his comment as my mouth contorts into a frown.

If my father had it his way, he would've shoved every soul there into glass jars, but sadly, our judgment system wasn't meant to lock away titans. Hence the realm. It's a prison world built for the monsters that were too vile to live amongst the rest of us.

"Kai, your father locked them away. You really think marching into the darkest corner of Hell, waving a white flag is a good idea? You might be the strongest in this realm, but there… You're not the only one of your kind and the nephilim locked away within it are the very definition of evil. They've been allowed to run rampant and who knows what they've created in the process," he argues, hoping to catch my attention and change my mind. He won't. It's already been made. When I don't answer fast enough, Finn continues, "Kai, no one that has gone in there, has ever come out."

"Well, it's a good thing that we're not going in then… at least not all the way. And regardless of how much they might hate us, an enemy of our enemy is our friend." My father acted on Michael's orders to banish a majority of them. Though we know it was with just cause, it doesn't mean they won't be willing to get revenge too. We need whoever is willing to fight. "The war won't be in Heaven again. This one will be here, on our turf, and I'd like to have a last resort wild card. Wouldn't you?"

"What do you mean? How can we negotiate without going in?" Finn asks as we mount our horses and make our way out of the keep's walls with the men in tow.

"I astral projected in a few weeks ago and the king agreed to a face-to-face meeting. He was rather

THE DEMON PRINCE

civil about it too. And if the nephilim are alive, I find it very odd that their king isn't one of them. All of those who were thrown in had been spellbound like Alice beforehand. My guess is something bigger killed them before it wore off." That seems to ease his nerves a bit.

"The king is going to set up a spot right next to the border. That's where I'll meet him, and I'll make a bubble on their side of the border. No one can go in without my permission, and no one besides me, will be able to get out on to our side. I can hold it. It will work."

"Are you trying to convince me of that? Or yourself?" Finn asks, rubbing his horse's neck.

Both. "Does it matter? We need this," I say.

"We have a solid plan. Michael doesn't even know about all the angels you walked out of the void. We have a wild card already. When they do come here, he's not going to expect us to have an army of winged-folk that are pissed at him, waiting in line to take their shot at fucking 'em up." Okay, he's right. But an army of winged-folk and an even bigger army of monsters sounds better.

"It will give me peace of mind to have a fail-safe. We can't lose. It's more important than ever, now."

Finn is quiet for a moment, staring at me as his body bobs from his horse's gait. "Oh please, don't give me some sob story about how it's not just your neck on the line anymore."

"It's not," I say, brushing off his hidden insult. "Should we lose, my father will get sent to the void. You and the rest of the demons that stood with us will too, but for me and Alice, it's not a nap in the dark. Michael will tear our souls to shreds. We'll cease to exist. I've accepted that fate. I wouldn't have agreed to this war if I hadn't, but I've also lived for hundreds of years. Alice… she's just barely getting started. For me to go into this war knowing what losing will rob her of, I need to know that I've crossed every T and dotted every I."

Finn closes his eyes for a moment then sighs. "Fine. I just hope you know what you're doing…. When do you two meet?"

"Two days from now." I cringe, waiting for him to blow up. That's pretty short notice for something this substantial.

His jaw falls open. "You realize that's the night before your wedding, right?"

"Yes. I do. That's the time he set and I'm not going to argue it. I'm honestly surprised he's been so civil about it to begin with."

"So, if you're not meeting until then, why are we going today?"

"I want to see where we're going to meet. I don't want to walk in blind, but it will be a quick trip. My father won't guess a thing and by the time we have to tell him about it, I'll have a peace treaty signed to hand him."

I grab the hilt of my dagger that is secured to my boot, pulling it out to carve a sigil into my palm. The blood beads and once enough has pooled into my hand, I hold it out like I'm going to blow a kiss, but instead, I blow against the crimson liquid and it turns to dust, scattering in the air. Slowly, it begins to ripple and turn as the portal opens. One after the other, the horses step through, vanishing into thin air. I'm the last one to enter and as I slide through the otherside, I take in the open field, looking for vantage points that we can use, as well as those that can be abused by their wicked king.

"What is the king going to do? Have a first supper on the prairie?" Finn asks.

I dismount and walk toward the hum of the field that contains creatures too abhorrent for our world. My hand cascades over it, feeling the static in the air. Pressing my palm harder, the view in front of me changes, and instead of it being a golden field for as far as the eye can see, it changes to jagged, rocked mountains and a forest that looks too whimsical to be ordinary. The trees move like they are animated as the wind whips around them. The yellow hue from our sun is absent there, cast in dark shadows and the white of the moons.

"The Field is an illusion," I mutter.

"Made by who?" Finn asks, but I shake my head. Did my father cast it when he ascended the wall, splitting their realm from ours? Or did they?

THE DEMON PRINCE

CHAPTER SEVENTEEN
Alice

Someone knocks on the door, and I barely hear the man's voice carry through the wood. "Princess, I've come on orders to take you through town."

I kick up from the couch, and go to let him in. When I open the door, baby blue eyes meet mine. He's about my age, clean shaven, and his blonde hair is short on one side, revealing intricate golden tattoos on his scalp. The longer hair on top lays to the other, but when he smiles at me, dimples divot his cheeks, showing off a boyish charm.

"I'm Ivar, I'll be your escort today, while the prince is gone. May I?" he asks, gesturing into the room. I step aside, allowing him in. "We can go whenever you're ready."

Great. My own personal tour guide. *Just what I wanted.*

Bending down to grab my boots off the floor by the bench at the footboard of the bed, I turn to take a seat, cinching them on my feet. The silence is eerie, and I turn to check on the boy, finding him wide eyed with his eyes glued to the ground.

"You okay, there?" I ask, but he just nods yes, not daring to remove his eyes off the floor. Shrugging it off, I step into the mirror to give myself one last once over, I smile, appeased and happy to be back in my own clothes.

I opted for black sheer tights, a pleated skirt that falls about mid-thigh and a sheer teddy, adorned with solid black swirls. My bra matches, and the lacey edge is visible through the sheer areas of my top, along with the tattoos that curve beneath my chest, ending at a point just above my belly button.

The design itself is simple, a full moon, surrounded by two crescents facing opposite ways, dressed in roses and draping lines. The sheer material of the shirt covers my arms, ending at my wrists. My curls are down and for the first time in a while, I actually spent time on my make up. I guess I had more time on my hands, since Kai took my book. My eyes are smokey and my lips match the same coppery red as my hair.

I pace back to the guard Kai sent me and grab his arm, swinging him around to follow me. "Let's go, big boy, show me this city." Flipping on my heels, I face him abruptly and he skids to a stop. "And don't call me princess. My name is Alice."

"Yes, mi lady," he says with a nod. Damn. That's more like it. Finally, a man listens to me. Kai could take some pointers from this dude.

He falls into step next to me, telling me about the areas of the keep we pass as we make our way to the bottom floor. When I step out of the front gate, the sun scorches across me and it feels so damn good, I nearly sigh.

I link my elbow with the guards, watching his pale cheeks blush from the contact and let him show me around. We walk around the keep before we head out the gate to the surrounding barricade wall, finding a vast market, filled with tents and huts, worked by street merchants. There aren't just humans, or human-looking creatures, but beasts that look like trolls, ogres, and hell hounds. There's a lady with green skin and horns, another with weird wings and dark amber lines scattered over what skin is exposed to us. It's a melting bowl of species and my eyes don't know where to look.

The vendors sell a plethora of things such as fur pelts, exotic food, dyed fabrics, jewelry, clothes–you name it, it's here. Ivar leads me toward a table, and nods for me to go look. "Maybe something blue?" I worry my lip, wishing that I could forget that I was going to be tying the knot with the man I woke up wrapped around like a fucking koala. It's not like I planned it, but it did feel good waking up wrapped in the warmth his body offered.

Skimming through the jewels, the silver and gold chains, I find a stunning pair of sapphire earrings and pick them up to look at them closer. Ivar studies me, watching my every move, and after I stare at them for a moment, I see him hand the merchant a sack of coins.

"They're yours, princess… Uh… *Alice.*"

I smile and take them off of the paper backing, and don't waste any time putting them on. The merchant takes the trash and we're off to the next row of tables.

"So, are you dead? Or just visiting?" I ask Ivar, and he laughs softly before answering.

"Dead. Been here a hot minute." His fingers touch my arm as he points toward the cart with large lizards speared on pikes, roasted and glazed. "You want to try it?"

I shake my head. "Not a chance, and spare me the 'it tastes like chicken' BS."

"Suit yourself," he says, looking over the crowd.

This place is almost like a flea market, if they were run by trolls. A cart pulled by two horses… not just horses, but zombie horses by the looks of it, strolls across the street and I gawk at it.

What the fuck did a horse do to earn a place in hell? Bite the hand that fed it?

Ivar's hand presses against the small of my back, leading me toward the next row. My lips pull into a frown. It's not that he touched me-quite frankly I could care less-and that was the problem. Had Kai done that, I would've leaned into him, I would've wanted his hand to wander. This guy is a hell of a

THE DEMON PRINCE

lot hotter than most of the men I know, to the point that I feel like all of the earthly references to the heat in Hell might be metaphorical and referring to the men. He's not Kai hot, but he should be enough, yet he isn't. It grinds my ever-lovin' gears.

He leans in to let me know he's going to get himself a reptile on a stick. I nod and busy myself looking at the tables. Walking down the next row, I don't really look for anything in particular, but soak in the craftsmanship that each of the merchants have to offer.

There's a painter who's canvases look so lifelike, that I have to double take to notice they're not real. Another woman sells bouquets of flowers, poppies mainly, and as I walk by, I lean in toward a bin of roses, closing my eyes, and inhaling deeply.

Hands wrap around my waist, retching me backward against a solid form. My eyes flick open as I look over my shoulder to see a man with sickening yellow eyes. A dead giveaway that he's not human, despite his body looking so.

"Put me down," I shout, my eyes darting toward Ivar, standing with his back toward me, oblivious to the man trying his best to drag me away. My elbows fly backward, jabbing into his ribs repeatedly, but he lifts me until my feet leave the ground taking away any leverage I have.

My body bucks against him, kicking, clawing, and yelling for someone to help me. No one even so much as turns their head or bats an eyelash. I look to Ivar again, praying that he turns around before my body disappears between the tents. He doesn't and it's too loud with the live musicians playing further down the row for him to hear me, even if I scream.

I kick my feet sideways, pushing off the tent post. It's enough to send us falling sideways, bringing the canopy to the tent I kicked off of with us. I pry at his meaty arms, trying to loosen their hold, but they only seem to constrict around me tighter like a snake.

Like a snake…

What in the name of *Shark Boy* and *Lava Girl*… There's fucking *snake people*?!

"Calm down, little girl, and I'll make it quick," the man groans as I feel something slither around my ankles and up my calf.

THE DEMON PRINCE

Oh, *fuck no*. My legs clench together, trying to shift my feet to dislodge whatever is on the hunt for my chamber of secrets but it merely slows it. My head swings back, slamming into the man's face as pain shoots through me. He loosens his arms enough for me to force them off.

I don't bother running the way we came through since the tents have collapsed, blocking the path. Instead, I run down between the long stretch of tents as fast as my legs will allow me until something whips around my ankle, yanking my feet out from underneath me. My chin slams into the ground sending a sharp wave of pain through my jaw and making my head ring from the impact.

God! I fucking hate this place.

My body is yanked backward, dragging against the shredded gravel, biting and digging into my skin until it's bloodied. I reach for whatever is wrapped around my leg, desperate to dislodge it. It looks like a snake's tail and stretches nearly ten feet to its owner, the yellow-eyed man. I look at the man quickly, seeing the appendage disappear beneath the hem of his tunic and I pray that this thing I'm fighting isn't his dick. My body would never recover.

My efforts prove futile as I come to a stop at his feet. The man reaches for me, and my leg kicks up, slamming into his cheek as I flip on to my stomach and push up with my hands. My feet move before the layers of my body are stacked up right, causing me to fall forward again and cry out as a rock embeds itself into my knee.

A hand yanks my hair backward and a knife's blade nips at my throat. I feel a bead of blood, rolling across my collar bone and my body stills. I see the man I had originally been fighting walk toward me rubbing his cheek. I feel part of him slither around my feet, solidifying my assumption that he's one of the same.

The man holding me drags his knife down my chest, scratching the tip of the blade down and slicing through my top before running over the pleats of my skirt. He goes down just low enough to slide beneath it with ease, angling the sharp edge against the fleshy part of my thigh.

My body trembles and my eyes look down while the man holds me by my throat against him. The one I kicked reaches me and the back of his hand collides with my face, sending a flood of crimson through my mouth. I know I bit my tongue deeply and I spit on the ground, chest heaving as I search for a way to escape. Unable to find one, I shout the only thing I can think of that might save me.

"I'm the princess! You don't want to hurt me!"

"Hell doesn't have a princess, girl," the man says, laughing at the way my voice cracks.

"It does now," I snap. "I'm to marry Prince Kai by the end of the week. I don't imagine killing me will go over well with him or Lucifer."

The man holding me, jerks me a little closer to him. "We aren't going to kill you, just make you wish we did."

"Well, that's reassuring," I say, letting the sarcasm dip my words.

"If you're engaged to the prince, where's your ring, hmm?" the guy I kicked in the face says.

I lift my hand, cursing under my breath, realizing I haven't been given one yet.

"Nice try, little girl," the man holding me says, digging the knife into my thigh a little more as something slithers up my leg, climbing higher and higher.

Something snaps within me, and I scream louder than I ever have. My hands, forearms and hair ignite in green flames and then the man holding me jerks backward and the knife slices deeply into my leg. He falls back, releasing a blood curdling scream as he burns with hellfire. A flame that never goes out. A wound that never heals.

The yellow-eyed man in front of me, the one who snatched me out of the street, stares in shock, mouth open. Then he shakes his head as his eyes narrow into slits. I can feel the veins in my face raising and sliding beneath my skin. The man opens his mouth to speak, but snaps it shut as he takes off running.

I turn back to the man who held me and as he sits shaking on the ground, but very much alive, despite his arms and face burning. Waving a hand, the embers extinguish along with the flames on my own body, which was a complete shot in the dark, but worked. My boot collides with his chest, spartan kicking and slamming him to the ground as I pick up his knife.

I'm the fucking princess of Hell and it's about time I start acting like it. I might not have been born here, like Kai, but his people will know my name and fear it before I lay victim to what just happened again. Moving to stand behind his head, I grab him by the hair, pulling him against my legs as the blade slices through his neck like butter.

Blood sprays, coating the ground in crimson and flooding my nose with the smell of copper. It streams down my arms as I throw the man forward, letting him die in the dirt.

My fingers won't release the blade. It's as if the damn hilt has become one with my body. In truth, it's the reality of killing a man, and knowing I made the lights go out in his ugly ass eyes. I don't step away, I don't even move as the puddle of blood beneath his body grows bigger by the second, threatening to get on my boots.

Someone calls my name. I don't look for it, but it grows closer until hands grip onto my shoulders, shaking me from my stupor. I flick my gaze up toward Ivar, but his voice sounds muffled by my own mind trying to wrap around what I've done and how good it felt to do it.

Closing my eyes and shaking my head, I pause before opening them again.

"Alice! Are you hurt," Ivar repeats, loud and clear.

I slowly shake my head no. "Nothing life threatening," I say.

His hand runs through his hair, whipping it to the side. "What the fuck happened?"

"He and his friend tried to rape me."

THE DEMON PRINCE

CHAPTER EIGHTEEN

Kai

"Let's get a barricade set up here," I say to one of my men. He scurries off and Finn comes up to grip my shoulder.

"For someone so sure that you're going to keep that boundary up, you're certainly being very cautious." I turn to him, scanning his face for any hint of a joke, but finding nothing.

"The bubble isn't failproof. It stretches our realm into theirs and I have to let the king cross through for it to work. It has to be perfect. One slip up and the king would be a fugitive in our world, and I can only imagine the chaos that would come with."

A raven squawks, gliding down to land on my arm. I hold it out for him and take the folded-up piece of paper from its beak.

Finn watches me suck in a breath and gasp as I read it and immediately asks what's wrong.

"We need to go back, now. Goddamnit!" I say, running a hand down my face. I should've never left her alone. I should've known she'd try some shit and that the guard I sent wouldn't be enough.

Finn's eyes search me for a moment before he whistles, to round up the men.

"Well, you're not leaving me here again, not this close to the border. So, open the portal back up," he demands, but I'm already ahead of him, carving the sigil into my already healed hand.

The portal opens and the group heads through leaving me to cross over last. My horse steps through and we land right in front of the castle where we started. I don't waste a moment telling Finn orders, nor does he need me to. He yells something toward the men and then dismounts to follow me inside the keep.

"Kai, what is going on?"

"Someone attacked Alice in the market. I don't know much of the details, but I fucked up, Finn. I shouldn't have arranged for her to go without me. I thought having a guard with her would be enough. After we married publicly, it probably would've been. They must've gotten separated, or Alice must've tried to lose the guard. I don't know."

"Jesus… is she okay?" Finn asks, completely ignoring everything else I've told him. I stop climbing the stairs to my floor and then turn back to search his face.

"I don't know." I continue the climb shaking my head. "What I do know is that woman will never leave my fucking sight after this until a ring is on her finger."

When we make it to the top, my father is waiting for me outside of the room pacing down the long hallway and chewing on his fingernails deep in thought. He hears our footsteps and stops as if to say something but decides against it and opens my bedroom door. As if showing me was the only thing that made sense.

Alice sits on the floor, leaning against my side of the bed. Her knees are pulled up and her arms rest against them, cradling her head.

The guard I assigned to her sits in the chair against the wall and I hear his armor plates sliding as he straightens his posture, seeing me.

"My prince—" he starts to say, but I hold up a hand to shush him.

Alice's head lifts and I see the streaks where her makeup has run down her cheeks and the blood stains on her smooth skin as if it's spewed from her mouth. Her arms unfold as she sits up, revealing that they're also caked in crimson that has dried against her fingernails. A dark crescent shadow blankets her cheek bone and nearly rips my heart from my chest.

She's had time to heal, and yet the bruise still remains? She won't heal as quickly as I do, not by a long shot, but after an hour or more, that discoloration should've been gone and it's telling of how hard that blow must've been.

My eyes skim lower, seeing the dried blood coating her thighs and it nearly brings me to my knees. Had she been raped? I'd never forgive myself if she had. Hell, I'm struggling trying not to lose it over the fact someone laid their hands on her at all.

The anger I felt before coming in here at the fact that she might have tried to shake her security detail leaves me and without thinking another thought, my hand moves up summoning my magic as the guard I assigned her gets jerked from the chair violently by an invisible force and he slides toward me until his throat is wrapped between my fingers.

My hand squeezes until the man's face turns purple, threatening to crush bone as I turn my gaze toward him. His hands claw at my own as my eyes go black with rage and I bring him inches from my face.

"How the fuck did this happen?" I ask, ignoring Alice's pleas to stop, to let him go.

I release my grip and the man drops to his knees gasping for air before turning his face up to me and answering my question between coughs.

"You left her alone for a fucking rodent on a stick?" I seethe as Finn's hand lands against my shoulder, calming me and preventing the need I have to tear this man limb from limb.

"Please," Alice says and I right myself. My back has been toward her, so she hasn't seen my face yet. I take a deep breath letting my eyes return to normal before looking at her.

"This man failed you, yet you protect him," I say, stepping toward her. "Why?"

"It was an accident. I told him I'd stay close, and I didn't realize how far I'd gotten away until it was too late. He doesn't deserve to die for something he's not responsible for."

I inhale until my lungs burn, unable to hold anymore, before letting it out slowly.

Finn ushers the man out of the room while I stare at her, drinking in what I allowed to happen.

"Leave us," I command, and Finn exits the room along with Clamara and my father, shutting the door behind them.

"Are you hurt? Is that your blood?" I ask, after falling to my knees in front of her. My head bows as I rub my palms against my face.

"No, not entirely," she says quietly.

"I need to know where, Alice." Her hands tremble in and I want to wrap her against my chest, to make it go away, to take back ever leaving the woman here without me. "Show me," I say, as she stares off toward the wall. Her bottom lip quivers and my hand reaches out to cup her face and my thumb presses against it.

"Tell me, please."

"He hit me in the face, and I bit my tongue," she says as my fingers skim over the bruise, watching it disappear beneath my touch as I heal the damaged skin. She sticks her tongue out and I watch the deep bash disappear before my eyes.

"Where else," I say, grabbing at her hand and searching the dried blood for a wound but find nothing.

"That's not mine," she says, and my eyes meet hers.

"Whose is it?"

"The man I killed," she says, not flinching away from the words as they roll off her lips. She's proud of it and I've never been more proud of her.

"Did he rape you?" I ask, letting my eyes shift down toward her bloody thighs.

"Tried… but no. I set him on fire before he could." Unable to stop myself, I smirk, happy that the prick got what he deserved. Had he faced me, I would've pulled him limb from limb and spread his body parts across the realm.

My head falls against her knee and my lips kiss the bloodied skin. Relief sweeps through me, and her hand reaches up to thread her fingers into my hair, sliding the mussed tresses back into place.

"I'm okay," she says, trying to soothe my pain from seeing her like this, when I'm supposed to be the one coddling her, making her forget any man ever touched her.

"Where's this from then?" I point to trails of dried blood on her knee that disappear beneath the fabric of her skirt.

"He held a knife... down there and when I set him on fire, it cut me. It's not deep, nor anything that won't heal."

My eyes flutter closed as I let out a shaky breath.

How am I supposed to protect this woman when I've let something like this happen so early on? When I could've prevented it had I just stayed here instead of going to the edge of the realms, seeking monsters... I should've been here to protect her from the ones we already have.

I start to lift the fabric of her skirt so that I can heal the wound but her hand shoots forward to stop me. Instead, I change course, noting that she still trembles even as she holds me still. The adrenaline coursing through her is still wearing off, making the nerves spark erratically and it pains me to know that she ever had to be that scared… she would've had to in order to release that much into her bloodstream, to still be shaking over an hour later.

Gathering her to me, I carry her into the bathroom and set her down on the rocks.

"Let's get you cleaned up," I say as my fingers work at the laces of her boots, squeezing each of her feet before placing them against the cool rock. "I don't want that man touching you anymore, even if all that's left of him is his blood."

I pick up her shoes and set them on the other side of the glass. "Do you want me to help you in?" I ask, but she shakes her head and I bow mine, turning away to give her privacy.

She throws her clothes toward the opening in the glass wall, and I hear the water disturb as she slips within its depths.

THE DEMON PRINCE

Only then, do I turn around. Her head bobs through the surface, slicking her hair backward with her hands. I let her swim around for a bit, until her skin is clean and resumes its porcelain shade. Removing my armor, I pull the vanity seat, watching her glide through the water with such grace, that it makes me question what she's more of, angel or demon.

It's hard to say which, since her father was falling when she was conceived and honestly, there's a lot about her I don't understand. Like the noise she made yesterday.

I've heard of witches taking on characteristics of their familiar before, but from what I understand, she doesn't have one to mimic. It's a mystery, but one I'm fond of. It's odd, yes, but knowing she purred for me made my dick harder than I ever thought possible.

When Alice is done, I grab a towel, walking toward the water and holding it outstretched with my arms and eyes closed. She gets out and wraps herself in it.

I open my eyes to find her staring at herself in the mirror, like she's looking for the bruises that I took away. Moving to stand behind her, my fingers reach to dance across her shoulder, but I wince, remembering that she probably doesn't want to be touched by anyone right now, especially me.

She watches me in the mirror, and I hear her snort, causing my gaze to meet hers in the reflection.

"I'm not broken," she says coldly.

"Never said you are." I stand deathly still unsure of where this conversation is going.

"You winced when you touched me. You didn't have to say anything." She holds my eyes, but they're almost hollow, and free of the snarky, strong willed, sassy woman's glare that I've grown so fond of.

"I figured you—I didn't think you wanted me to," I say, grabbing at the back of my neck.

"Because someone else did? Believe me, I know he won't ever again. I burned him alive before slitting his throat and watching his blood sizzle into a puddle, still warm from my flames. And as for his friend, well, I'd be surprised if he doesn't have nightmares for the rest of his pathetic life."

My eyes shoot wide for a second, letting her words soak in. "There were two? You let one live?"

She nods and I bite my lip. I leave her to get dressed and head out to the hallway where Finn still waits with the guard I assigned to her.

"One of the men who attacked her lives. Find him and tell my father that tomorrow's plans move to tonight," I command and they both nod, leaving to do just that.

CHAPTER NINETEEN

Alice

I walk out of the bathroom, cringing with each step as a sharp pain where the blade cut my thigh radiates through the fleshy part of my leg.

"Wow. A girl tells you one of her assailants is still alive and you don't waste a second, do you?" I smooth my hands over my loose, flowy dress. I don't even want to think about wearing pants right now, it would just rub against it.

"I won't have a rapist running around hell," he says, shutting the door and strolling toward me.

"So, this has nothing to do with you wanting revenge? It's simply for the greater good of the kingdom? I doubt that, not with how you made Ivar turn every color in the rainbow. If you're going to lie, at least try and be convincing." I sit on the bench at the end of the bed, and he kneels in front of me.

THE DEMON PRINCE

"Little lamb, to say I seek revenge against the man who hurt you is an understatement. I'd burn the kingdom to ash if I needed to, and I wouldn't stop until he's lying dead at your feet."

I smile at him, letting my eyes wander over his body. "Am I supposed to be impressed?"

His tongue swipes over his teeth before clicking and he stands up tall. "I see that attitude of yours is still as striking as ever." He steps toward me, and his hands grip around my waist, picking me up and placing me on the bed. He walks around to the side and swings my legs toward him.

"What are you doing?" I ask as my pulse quickens and my blood heats as it courses through my veins. My heart takes flight, beating erratically as his hands latch onto my knees, which are bent as I push up on my elbows from the bed.

"Let me see it, Alice," he says, his voice growing darker with each syllable. I try to scoot back so I can sit up, but his grip holds me still. "No. You don't need to. The wound will heal just fine on its own."

"How deep is it?" he asks, staring into my eyes like my gaze is the only thing keeping him in control.

"Not deep enough to endanger my life, I can tell you that much." My hands fling down toward my thigh defensively.

"Will it scar?" I don't answer. Swallowing the growing lump in my throat, his thumb swipes over the exposed skin just above my knee and I shudder as the raw need and desire to have him touch me more rips through my body. *What was that?* Jesus, he's sexy and the embodiment of sin, but that… Dear lord, his touch wasn't even remotely seductive, yet my hips just squirmed like a cat in heat. Uh, uh, fuck that noise. "Do you really want a permanent reminder of what happened?"

My mouth mushes into a flat line, and I look off to the side. I don't. But I also know that if my body responded that strongly to an innocent stroke across my knee, I can only imagine how it would react to him being that close to my center. Call it self-preservation.

"Goddammit woman, please don't be stubborn right now. Show me," he demands.

I force my knees together, ignoring the pain that shoots through my thigh when I do. "I don't want you anywhere near my hoo-hah. If it scars, so be it. Capeesh?"

"Well, how about we not call it that…" he says, trying to lift the hem of my dress over my knees and I shoo him away. He breathes out deeply and then cocks his head at me sighing. "I'm trying to help you."

"You criticize my nickname for it, but how about we not call it a cunt? Ever think about that?" I say, remembering the way he said given the chance, he'd bury himself so deep that I never forgot who I belong to and instantly, my insult backfires. My tongue licks across my lips, and he doesn't miss it. Kai's eyebrow cocks up while I debate on whether or not to give up the fight and let him ravish me.

Maybe I can go back to pretending to hate him tomorrow…

"Can we please stop the theatrics? Let me heal it. That's it. That's all I'm asking and all I plan to do. It could take weeks to heal on its own. Your spell binding has weakened since you've been here, but it's still not going to heal fast enough to not scar, so please, love. Let me help you forget."

Grumbling, I lay back, giving in as his fingers lift the hem of my dress and his hands spread my legs apart. I look up toward the mirror on the wall behind me and watch as his tongue darts across his lips. Kai's enjoying this way too much... I'm vulnerable, weak, and I could've died today, yet instead of getting to work and putting me out of my misery, he stares down at me. I can't tell if he's contemplating what I taste like, or if he's stunned–whether in a good or bad way, I don't know.

"Some warning would've been nice," he says as his fingers prod at my wounded thigh. I feel it tingle as his touch knits the wound closed.

"About what? Is my downstairs not to your liking, *your highness*." He glances up at me with a smirk. "Glad we got that out of the way. Hell, if I'd have known just flipping up my skirt would've deterred you, I would've done it ages ago. Maybe then, I wouldn't be so goddamn tired today. I mean shit, I've been dropping those energy shot things of yours I found into my coffee like Jager bombs all morning and it's barely made a dent."

Kai studies me for a moment. "What energy shots?" He stands opening his hand as a drink appears. Did his throat go that dry that he needed to summon a tall glass of water? God. What am I? Chopped liver? ... Well, right now I kind of feel like it.

He lifts his drink to his lips while I point to the one opened container on the coffee table, they kind of look like Keurig cups. Most of the writing on them was in some sort of weird language, but what I could make out was something along the lines of eight-hour energy. So, I winged it. No pun intended, since I'm still waiting for those bad boys to make an appearance.

Kai spits out his drink when his eyes lock on to the Keurig cups and laughter erupts out of him. I narrow my gaze, failing to see what's so goddamn funny. I'm exposed here. My legs begin to close together as I try to regain some of my dignity, but he stops me and props his hands on my knees. At this point, he might as well be my gynecologist. "That explains a lot," he says, his eyes dance over me with a level of amusement I have yet to see on him.

"What does?" I ask.

"Those aren't energy shots, Alice." He bites his lip, trying to fight back the urge to laugh at my expense again.

"Well then what the fuck are they? I drank three of them. They didn't taste bad."

He closes his eyes for a moment, like he's gathering the courage to tell me, and I hear the chuckle sound from deep within his throat as he snorts.

"Those are Hell's equivalent of Viagra."

My gaze flicks between the cups on the coffee table and him, repeatedly before I ask, "Well, why the fuck do you have them then? Do you need them?" My tone goes from angry to kind of concerned against my will, but the question is out there now, and I can't take it back.

"Orgies. They can be kind of... *tasking.*" I now understand why the bed is so big and it makes me nauseous to know I've slept here, like a baby mind you, curled up with the man who might as well be the embodiment of lust. "They can last days and sometimes you need a pick me up." He shrugs as if it's no big deal. It is *very much* a big deal. It is to me since three doses course in my veins.

"I Viagra'd myself?" I ask, saying it more to convince my mind of the raw reality than to him.

"Yes ma'am. They'll wear off. It's not as strong as Viagra, but same context… which explains why I probably could fucking wring out your panties right now." His thumbs stroke my knees before his hands slide up my thighs.

"Um, excuse me?" He looks up to meet my eyes. "That's an exaggeration if I've ever heard one. I think we're done here," I say, starting to close my legs again. His hands stop them, holding my knees apart and pushing them to the bed when he traps them under his weight.

"Want to bet?" I stare at him, unsure if I should go there. How would he prove it? Take off my panties and hand them to me? Is that worth winning a bet? "I'll tell you what," he says, "You win, I'll move into the room down the hall until further notice."

I don't even ask what he gets if I lose, instead, I just say, "Deal." I don't even care at this point. If it means getting a bed to myself and not having to deal with his heated gaze every time I turn around, I'm down.

"Fantastic," he says, as his hand slides up my thigh and his finger hooks under the bottom edge of the waistband of my panties. But instead of taking them off, like I expected his finger slides beneath the lacy fabric and strokes against my sex. My head falls back, and my arm flies up to shield my eyes from what I just got myself into, just as his finger slips inside me. My hips rock into him, wanting more and needing him deeper. "Fuck me," I say under my breath, hearing him chuckle.

"I intend to."

His finger slides out as two replace it, and he spreads them apart while they're deep inside, sliding against my walls and stretching me to his will. A moan escapes my lips as I rock into his movements, meeting him halfway. I don't even care anymore. At this point, I can feel the need to come building inside me and I chase it.

Kai's other hand trails up my leg, over my hip, and across my stomach, making my chest arch into his palm. He growls, finding the bra between us and cursing when he can't find the clasp to remove it.

My back arches and my legs begin to shake as I climb closer and just as I'm about to fall over the edge, just as my mouth opens to moan, he retreats and shoves his fingers between my lips. I jolt and look up at him, watching me as if he's excited to see what I'll do next. Slowly, my tongue swirls around his fingers, tasting myself on them and a breathy moan sounds from deep within his chest.

"Believe me now, princess," he says, and I nod. I'd tell the man anything he wants to hear as long as he continues. He removes his fingers from my mouth, smirking in triumph as his eyes skim over my body, like he's wondering what he should touch next.

"What did you win?" I ask, silently kicking myself for not seeing what the stakes were before agreeing to a deal with the Devil's son.

"A taste." His eyebrows bounce and my heart skips a beat, thumping against my ribs as his hands grip my thighs. Dragging me closer, he slides my panties off and his head dives between my legs and the moment his tongue hits my clit, I melt. My body gives in, submitting and letting him devour me as I rock my hips up, pleading for more.

He raises his head an inch and skims his wet lips up my thigh to my knee. "You're a greedy little witch, aren't you," he says, sending a shiver up my spine as his breath hits where his lips have trailed. He smiles against my thigh, before biting the tender flesh hard and quick, making me jolt toward him.

I wiggle my hips, begging him to return to his task and make me shatter to pieces. "Oh, sweet girl, I don't plan on coming up for air until you come on my tongue. Don't you worry," he says, staring up at me with those sexy-as-sin amber eyes. A dark laugh rumbles from his throat and their honey color turns to jet black as the veins darken and raise over his cheeks. Just. Like. *Mine*.

There's no doubt in my mind that I'm in over my head. This man literally plucked me from Earth and brought me to Hell like some sort of mail order bride, and here I am asking him to tongue fuck me harder.

My therapist was right. I am a hot mess… But I don't care. This man could lead me to my grave and ask me to get in it and as long as he promised to bury his face between my legs for the trouble, I'd have no regrets.

His fingers dip inside me as his tongue swirls until my legs convulse. My body explodes with a force so sweet, so satisfying, that I moan out a string of curse words. Kai nips at my clit, pulling gently as I come down and my legs tighten around his face, holding him there.

For the love of all that is holy… he can have me. All of me. I'll put that ring on my finger right this second if it means that this will happen again.

Kai sits back on his feet and wipes the sensitive skin of his wrist against his mouth, before licking his lips for one last taste. I roll forward, grabbing at his pants as my fingers fumble with the belt. His hands cuff my wrists, pulling them away.

"Woah. Easy, little witch. There will be plenty of time for that. The moment that ring goes on your finger you'll have all of me, to snuggle, to fuck, and eventually love, till death do us part. But first, we have to make it through our engagement party." My eyes slowly trail up his body as my lungs deflate. He tucks my hair behind my ear. "It was supposed to be tomorrow, but with what happened today, I moved it up."

I grumble, falling back on the bed and the asshole just chuckles as if this is the reaction he's been waiting for all along. "Tease," I groan and a smile spreads across his face, so wide I can probably count all of his teeth. But his eyes are amber again and I can't stop looking at them, knowing we truly are cut from the same cloth.

"I'm sorry. We don't have the time, love. And I want the time to get to know your body and find out what makes you tick. I want to savor it before I make your knees weak and fuck you so hard god blushes."

And this is the man I'm marrying. Lord, help us all.

THE DEMON PRINCE

CHAPTER TWENTY

Alice

"How am I supposed to pretend to be your fiancé if I've never seen it," I ask, sitting up from the bed.

"You don't need to see my dick to look at me all doe-eyed and even if you're spewing curse words at me all night, they'll see the way you melt when I touch you. No one will question whether you like me because it's written all over your face, sweetheart."

Narrowing my eyes, I watch him grin triumphantly. "I barely know you. I don't even like you. I just don't hate you, and you're pretty to look at." It's a flat out lie. I'm definitely starting to like him, but I don't want to inflate his ego any more than it already is.

He snorts, crossing his arms in front of his chest. "Keep telling yourself that. Regardless, people have arranged marriages all the time, on Earth and in

Hell. You know enough... but if it makes you feel better about it, ask me anything," he says, laying down next to me on the bed.

I turn on my side to face him. "Favorite color."

"Green." He reaches over to cup my face, tracing his thumb over the structures of my cheek and lips like he's making sure the bruise is really gone. "Next."

"Favorite food."

His lips pull up into a smirk as his fingertips trail down my neck and over the curve of my chest. "Does it have to be a food?"

I scowl. "Yes."

"Probably tacos." A smile breaks out across my face as I stifle the urge to laugh. "What's so bad about tacos?" he asks.

"Oh, you were serious? I thought... never mind. I just can't imagine the prince of Hell going to a place like Chipotle and asking for extra guac."

"Well, assuming that's a restaurant, we don't have Chipotle here, but I do like guac," he says, letting his hand travel over the dip in my side and the arch of my hip. "Who knows. Maybe under different circumstances, I would've taken you on a date to one."

"Oh please. If we had met differently, you wouldn't have given me the light of day."

"Woman, I would've ripped my heart out of my chest and handed it to you with a pretty little bow if you'd have asked me to. From the moment you cursed at me at that damn frat party, you've had me wrapped around your finger. So, stop with that nonsense."

My mouth gapes as he leans forward to hover above me, and I roll onto my back. His knee slips between my legs, way, *way* too close to my center, and my hips rock up to grind against him.

He brushes his lips gently against mine and butterflies erupt in my stomach. I feel his hand slip beneath me, pulling against my lower back before he lifts up, taking my body with him so he can sit on his heels. Straddling one of Kai's bent legs, he peppers kisses across my jaw, down my neck and chest and my body arches toward him, needing to be closer.

"Do you know how hard it is to not touch you?" he asks, before carrying on his mission.

"Enlighten me." My hands weave into his hair, holding him closer.

He trails his lips back up to claim mine and I moan against them. "It's excruciating... But we need to get ready. So, why don't you tell me what's really bothering you." I lean back, settling my arms around his neck. "I highly doubt it's not knowing what my favorite color is, or the food I like to indulge in."

I stare at his chest, chewing on the inside of my cheek. *Don't do it, Alice. Don't look.* My eyes flick down to the front of his pants and back up. *Fuck! You looked.* Cringing, I meet his gaze as his gaping mouth snaps shut and he blinks in shock.

"You're worried about *that*?" he asks, tilting his head and pressing his lips together to hide the amusement that pulls at his reddening cheeks. *Is he blushing?* "What could possibly be scary about it? Unless..."

"Sorry to bust your bubble but I'm definitely *not* a virgin. So, don't even get that in your head," I say as his eyebrows lift in silent question. "I just feel like I need to see it first... What if someone asks about it, you know?"

He squints and looks off to the room behind me. "Well, first off, no one is going to ask about my dick at our engagement party."

"Okay, let me rephrase. Does it look weird?"

He smiles wickedly. "No. It doesn't look weird, and no one has complained about it yet."

"I think I still need to see it," I say, biting my lip and when I release it, his eyes drop to look at the impressions my teeth made.

Kai sighs as he drags a hand down his face. "Jesus, woman. Is anything sacred?" He stands up, dragging me to the end up of the bed before unzipping his leather pants. He shrugs as he reaches in and whips it out, then pumps twice as he steps closer. Kai lets go, holding his hands out to either side of him, like a silent, *'Are you happy now?'*

My mouth falls open and my cheeks flush hot as my eyes track up his body to meet his heated gaze before returning to stare at it again. It's fucking *huge*.

"Go ahead. Touch it," he says.

My fingers reach out to do just that, but I pause, and he grabs my hands wrapping them around him. "It's yours… If you keep your mouth open like that, though, we might be late to our own party." I snap it shut and swallow hard, running my hands along the length of him. His head tips back slightly and a low groan sounds from his throat.

"Will it… um, Will I…" I trail off, trying to form a sentence without it coming out like gibberish.

"Will it fit?" he asks, tipping my head up with his finger, forcing me to meet his eyes, and I nod. "Trust me. It'll fit and you'll take every fucking inch like a good little princess."

My body shivers and I'm not sure if fear or anticipation causes it, but he notices, shooting me a wicked grin and lowering his mouth to mine for a kiss. Then as if on cue, someone knocks on the door, and he fixes himself before they come in.

Clamara and three other women come and shoo Kai from the room.

"Mi lord, we'll bring your stuff to the guest room," she commands, pushing him toward the door. He looks over his shoulder smiling at me as he's kicked out by the small French woman.

For the next two hours, I'm poked and prodded as the women ready me for my engagement party, which is looking more and more like a ball by the minute.

"You'll wear these. King's orders," Clamara says as she turns toward me, holding up a dress bag. Lucifer is deciding what I wear now? That's shitty. I gawk at the heels in her other hand, praying that I won't break my ankle before the night is over. The women curl my already curly hair, but instead of it being an unruly mayhem, now it's mostly straight and hangs in delicate wide curls at the bottom of the strands.

Next, they shove me into a black dress that has a high slit in the front so the poof of it slips to the side when I walk. The top is form fitting with corset strings in the back to cinch it even tighter. It has see through lace sleeves and a deep plunging V in the front. Satin laces, similar to what ties in the back, stretch through the V leaving holes that my tattoo peeps through.

It's gorgeous. More revealing than I'd like, but at least I don't have to worry about flashing people, like the last dress Lucifer chose. Clamara does my makeup, lining my eyes like a cat's with gold accents, and finishing it off with a natural-looking lipstick. She stands up, dusting her hands on her apron.

"Next is shoes and you're ready to go," she says.

What? No crown? What a rip off. I stand and walk toward where I left my boots.

"No. Mi lady. Not tonight. You'll wear these, the—"

"King's orders. Got it," I say, cutting her off and scrunching my lips. It was worth a shot. "I'd rather stick to my boots." She smacks at my hand when I reach for them again and I sit up giving her a look that could kill.

"Don't worry, I'll make sure she wears them." Kai's voice hits my ears and for the first time, I realize I actually missed his absence. My gaze shoots to where he stands in the doorway, and my mouth drops open.

Holy mother of God…

My mouth waters as I look him up and down. *He's gorgeous,* like he was chiseled from stone to be the embodiment of my dreams, or the prince fairy tales are told about. A black suit covers his body, beneath it a pristine dress shirt the same color with a black tie covered in gold swirls. His dark hair is slicked to the side beneath a beautiful golden crown, without a hair out of place. The dude knows how to clean up.

His head tilts, trailing his gaze over me, and his chest inflates as he drags in a deep breath. A noise escapes from his throat, something between a moan and a growl, as he presses his lips together to contain it. He takes a step toward me, running a hand down his face.

"You going to say anything?" A wicked smirk creeps across my face. "Or are you just going to keep eye fucking me?" I mock him. It's nice to have the tables turned, and him to be the one to lose control for once.

Clamara walks toward me with my heels, but Kai holds out a hand. "I'll get those. Thank you," he says. She nods, handing them to him before exiting the room, along with the others. Lucifer steps inside as soon as they're gone and gives me a devilish smile.

"You look lovely, Alice."

"I'm glad someone thinks so," I tease, earning me a sharp, but playful, glare from Kai.

"Oh, I'm sure he's just trying to catch his breath."

Kai talks to his father without taking his eyes off me, "We'll be down in a moment."

Lucifer laughs darkly before unbuttoning his suit jacket and taking a seat in the chair by the door. "Not a chance. If I leave, I fear you two will never make it downstairs. So, I'm chaperoning. Deal with it."

Another man comes into the room with shorter dirty blonde hair and a chiseled jaw but dimples that give him a mischievous vibe. His amber eyes pop wide as they rake over my body.

"Holy... *God*, you get to marry that?" Kai turns to glare at him, and the man shrinks with a playful grin. "Sorry, princess, that was rude of me." He turns his gaze back to Kai watching him like an animal about to pounce as he scoots closer and holds a hand out. "Finn. Pleasure to meet you. I'm this behemoth's best friend."

"Alice," I say as he backs away like Kai will kill him if he lingers any longer.

He gives me a toothy smile before turning to Lucifer. "I can watch these two delinquents if you'd like to go downstairs. Belphegor was looking for you about the elephant in the room."

Lucifer stares off at the ground for a moment before standing. "Okay, yeah. I should probably go." He turns to Kai as he walks past him. "Behave."

"When have I ever done that," he says, making me smile. So, he isn't always the prim-and-proper prince... *Interesting.*

Lucifer leaves the room and Finn looks out the doorway, signaling when he's out of view before stepping out into the hall. "You've got five minutes. Make it good," he says as he closes the door.

"Five minutes for what?" I ask Kai as he walks toward me with wide pupils and the look in his eye that tells me he likes what he sees way more than he's letting on.

"To be alone," he says as his arm loops around my waist, drawing me to him. "To do whatever we want... You look absolutely delicious."

He squats and picks me up, throwing me over his shoulder and it tears a laugh from me. "You can't just carry me off like a caveman every time you want me to move." Kai sets me down on the bench. "You could just ask."

He shakes his head no. "I'll throw you over my shoulder if I want to," he says, shooting me a wink before crouching down and grabbing my foot, holding it up toward his chest. He slips the heel on and secures the clasp then leans forward and kisses the top of my foot. Then repeats the process with the other.

When he's done, he stands and holds a hand out toward me. I grab it and rise to my feet, getting my bearings before taking a step toward him. "You know, you look incredibly handsome yourself," I say, lifting up to place a kiss on his cheek, and remembering I have lipstick on. Luckily it doesn't seem to leave a mark behind... it must be a good brand.

"Five minutes is up," Finn says as he creaks open the door holding a hand over his eyes. "Is everyone clothed?" He doesn't even wait for an answer before spreading his fingers to peek, then stands a little taller as he drops his hand. "Perfect. Let's go before your dad takes my balls."

THE DEMON PRINCE

CHAPTER TWENTY-ONE
Alice

My arm is linked with Kai's when we walk through the keep, down to the bottom floor that's decorated in blacks and golds, glass and stone. Hundreds are gathered, talking and holding champagne flutes as they move about the massive throne room. Lucifer sits on a raised platform on the far side in a chair made from a monstrous-sized skull. What creature is that large? I'd like to avoid it.

Kai's hand reaches across the front of his body to grab mine, the one around his elbow. "Breathe, Alice."

"I'm fine," I say, knowing it's a lie. I haven't been able to breathe normally since he walked in dressed like that... and I'm the farthest thing from a people person, so the crowd does not help matters.

He snorts. "I can hear your heartbeat from here, love. It's going to be okay."

Maybe for you. The moment people begin to notice us, the room hushes and they clear a path toward Lucifer.

"What are they doing?" I ask, my eyes darting back and forth toward the crowd on either side of us. They all kneel as we pass.

"Showing respect." Kai gives my hand a reassuring squeeze. "When we get to my father, you'll need to curtsey. It's part of our custom." I nod, singing my ABC's backward in my head to calm my racing heart.

When we reach the opening in front of Lucifer's throne, he smiles at me with his eyes and Kai bows. I do the same, bending at the waist and I hear the man beside me chuckle… *Shit.* This is starting out well. Both of us stand back up along with Lucifer, who holds a wooden box in his hand. He steps down from the platform and walks toward us.

"We're gathered here today to celebrate the engagement of my son, Malakai, and the daughter of Azazel and Celeste Whittaker, Alice. May you welcome her with open arms as she dons the crown of my late wife, Persephone. A crown fit for a princess that will soon be your queen. A crown fit for a woman that will help lead us into battle against Heaven when we reclaim our right to free will. Our right to love. Our right to happiness. Please help me, honor my wife today as I place this crown upon a woman worthy of her spirit and the protection it brings."

Lucifer steps off the platform and Kai whispers to me, "Bow your head."

I do and when the Devil reaches me, he places the crown on top of it and the cool metal makes me shiver. It's heavier than I expected, physically, not metaphorically, though I'm sure that's coming, especially since Kai left out the part of becoming Queen... Granted, I should've probably seen that coming, considering he's the prince. But with immortals, who knows when someone is going to kick the bucket, especially someone as significant as the Devil.

Kai squeezes my hand and I stand back up straight, adjusting the crown that's just slightly to the right. Lucifer smiles and leans forward to kiss my forehead before turning to the man beside me.

"I believe you have something to give her," Lucifer says.

Kai nods and swallows the lump in his throat. He turns toward me, and I face him, as he reaches into his pocket and pulls out a velvet box. For a moment, he doesn't seem to want to let go of my hand, but I trace my thumb over his fingers, and it seems to give him the encouragement he needs. Kai kneels, holding out the box to open it, revealing two beautiful gold rings. One is a princess-cut diamond and the other a gold band, but both have intricate details along the band that when pushed together, create an image of Cerberus.

"Alice... You're the only woman I know that can stare me in the eye and call me an asshole. Just as I know that there's never been a woman, I'd destroy a kingdom to save. Nor a woman I'd build one for, just so she could call it home. Not until you. In the short amount of time you've been here, I've already felt like you've become a part of me, like I finally found the other half of my mold. So, let my happiness be yours, and your sadness become mine. Accept more than a crown. Accept my heart, and do me the honor of calling you my wife."

My heart pounds in my chest, listening to him speak. It sounds so genuine, so *normal*, and up to now, I've wanted to accept his proposal to save my family, to survive. But standing here, literally in front of everyone and their mother, I *want* to accept it. Not so much because I'm ready to run down an aisle, but because I do like him, and I want more of it–of this.

If I had to go home right now, my heart would ache for a man I met days ago, and it scares the living shit out of me. Not that I wouldn't eventually recover… just it's enough to make me see the promise that a real relationship with him might hold.

"Yes," I say, giving him my left hand. He exhales as if he's been holding his breath, sliding the diamond ring on my finger and kissing the top of my hand.

The crowd erupts with claps, whistles, and bystanders yelling in excitement.

Jeesh. How long has it been since they've seen a wedding? Someone get these people some rom coms.

Kai stands up, handing me his ring and then holding his hand out so I can return the favor. His hands are warm, clammy even, giving away how nervous he is to do this. It's the first time I've seen him out of his element.

Looking up to smile at him, I'm greeted with his lips against mine as he wraps his arms around me and drags me into a heated kiss that sends butterflies rampaging through my stomach.

The crowd cheers again and Lucifer's voice chimes, "Okay, okay. Save it for the wedding night."

Kai pulls away before grabbing my hand and raising it above my head to the crowd. Lucifer calms the crowd to start the festivities.

"Whatever you do, don't drink the punch," Kai whispers.

"Why?"

"Just trust me. Don't do it," he says, leading me across the room and waving to people that address him.

He introduces me to a couple people. Achilles, a literal walking piece of history. Leonardo Da vinci. Lust, who is an actual person by the way. The moment the man's hand touched mine I swear my pussy quivered, and Kai didn't even break a sweat when he shook his hand, though I felt his reaction press against my back. The control this man has is godly.

"One more, okay? I promise you'll want to meet him. Stay here," Kai says before taking off through the crowd. I do as he asks, and when he returns, a middle-aged man follows him. His blonde hair is slightly gray, and the crow's feet around his eyes say he's definitely seen some shit.

"I'd like you to meet your great grandfather," Kai says, gesturing for me to shake his hand. I do but the man ignores it and hugs me anyway. I go stiff in his arms looking at Kai.

"Grandfather?"

"Yes, this is Belphegor. He was an original watcher angel like your father."

"Yes, yes. We are–*were* best friends actually. It's so lovely to meet you, Alice. I've been wanting to come by since you arrived, but Lucifer wanted to give you a moment to adjust before we bombarded you."

"The pleasure is mine," I say with a smile even though I'm internally screaming. As if sensing my unease, Kai steps behind me to hold onto my shoulders, rubbing small circles with his thumb. "So, you're my great grandfather on my father's side then, right? I didn't know angels had parents like that."

"Oh no. Your mother was my granddaughter," he says.

My entire body hits the pause button. That would make me… more than half nephilim, because my mother would've been a quarter. Right? Right. Well, how the fuck did they get to stay on Earth? Not that I'm regretting my decision to stay here, but they made it seem like if I stepped back on Earth, I'd be gonzo.

"I want you to know that I'm incredibly proud of you. It's not easy growing up the way you did. I'm very impressed at how you managed to persevere in a world that is so wicked. I know if your parents were here today, they would be too. Regardless, I know they both love you very much and would give anything to walk you down that aisle."

Tears sting my eyes, but I try to blink them away to not ruin my makeup.

"Would you allow me the honor to give you away at your wedding?" Seeing as I don't have anyone else here to even contest his offer, I nod yes, and he gives me a cheeky smile. "Great!"

"If you don't mind me asking, and I don't mean this in a bad way, but my mother lived on Earth. So did my grandparents. If they were part angel, wouldn't they have to leave like I did?"

"No... I had already become a demon when me and Bessie conceived your grandfather. So, since I didn't have grace in my blood, since he hadn't been to Heaven, nothing ever activated his angelic side. And that's how Michael tracks them. He had no idea that me and Bessie were together, let alone pregnant because he thought I was in the Void. However, with you, your father hadn't fallen yet, which means you inherited some of his grace and it runs in your veins. It might not be a lot, considering he was in the process of depleting it, but it's enough that Michael can track you topside... I'm sorry. I know leaving your home has to be hard."

"It is, but I'm starting to realize that sometimes there are things bigger than me." Belphegor smiles, but it's not as bright as when he first came over... like I've brought up some kind of painful memory.

"Well, I'll leave you two alone, but I'll see you again really soon, Alice. Congratulations."

"Thank you," I say, and he turns on his heels and disappears into the crowd. I look at Kai. "Why do I feel like he doesn't like me?"

"Why do you say that?" he counters.

"Because his entire face fell. I should've waited to ask my question and just asked you instead."

Kai walks in front of me and tips my face toward his. "It's not that. That man has been bugging the hell out of me to meet you. But like most here, they've had a past, and your family is a part of that." He releases me and takes my hand as we walk around the throne room.

"What happened?" I ask.

"He fell in love with a witch."

I narrow my eyes at him. "Are you going to elaborate on that? Or are you throwing secret punches at me, because I'm one too?"

"Both," he says with a wink. "Back in the day of the original watchers, they didn't know that the longer you were on Earth, grace wanes and that's everything to an Angel. When you go to Heaven, over time it will recharge, but like a battery, after it drains so many times or is left empty for so long, it never holds a charge like it used to. Grace links the angels to God, to an extent. It keeps them from feeling strong emotions like love, hate, and sadness." He pauses to study my face.

Where is he going with this?

"So, after time, the angels lost their grace and started to feel things and love humans. Your great grandfather was one of them. He loved a woman so much that they had a child named Agnes. The archangels found out and descended on Earth, fearing that the child would become too powerful. They shredded the baby's soul to make a point and shoved Belphegor into the void."

I gasp and he pulls me a little closer, throwing his arm around my shoulder possessively. Having never been to this part of the keep, I look around, adoring the obsidian stone and moss-covered floors. It helps take my mind off the eyes that watch me and Kai, though innocent, they make my skin crawl.

He continues, "The woman, Bessie, was killed but her soul was just put back into the pool so it can be reincarnated. Years later, my parents had me, but they managed to keep me hidden from Michael and the other archangels until I was about six. They killed my mother and made Lucifer throw me into the void himself. He must've sat in that hallway for hours... At some point, I just walked out, and we realized that it couldn't hold me. So, my father asked me to pull as many angels as I could from the void, and Belphegor was one of them."

My heart aches for him–for both of them. I lost my mother as a kid, but to have known her twice as long and have to live with the memories of losing her... I'm lucky to not remember. I nuzzle closer to him, hoping my nearness will provide comfort, or the sympathy that my words can't. I wouldn't even know where to begin.

"How long was he in there?" I ask.

"I'm not sure, but it was a long time. He immediately went looking for Bessie's jar. They hold souls while they're transported or stored, he found it just in time for her to be reincarnated. So, he went to Earth as a demon, hence why he's aged so much compared to my father, or me. He found her, running the academy he started when he was a watcher, from before he fell, with the theory that if he could teach the paranormal how to control themselves, he wouldn't have to rid the world of so many for his job. It worked, and this woman who he had loved centuries before, was now the head of it. That's when he had your grandfather. He came back to Hell as soon as he found out she was pregnant though. He didn't want to risk the angels killing her again or learning about the baby. They never did. Not until you."

"Whatever happened to her? Did she pass on to Heaven? Is she here with him now?"

He stops and turns toward me. "Belphegor wanted her to know peace, so she stayed for a while, but as the war effort ramped up, he wanted to know she was safe, if…"

"If we fail," I say, finishing the sentence for him.

Kai nods in confirmation. "I'm sure he'll join her though, should we win."

"Where are my parents then? If the angels killed my father, did they send him to the void? Did they shred his soul? My mother's too, since she was nephilim?"

He hesitates as if he's not at liberty to say but continues nonetheless, "They're together and at peace. My father found a way to give them a Heaven of sorts. They stayed in Limbo for a while, until we managed to find a loophole."

"And I can't see them in Heaven without Michael killing me for what I am…" It's more of a statement than a question.

"Yes… but I promise, as soon as the war is over, I'll take you to meet them. We wanted to keep them here so you could, but Michael had sniffed around, and we couldn't risk him finding them."

He licks his lips, letting his eyes wander down my throat and chest, he grabs the satin laces on the front of my dress and pretends to be adjusting them, when in reality, we both know it's just an excuse to touch me. "Now. No more history lessons tonight. Tonight, is about having fun."

THE DEMON PRINCE

CHAPTER TWENTY-TWO

Kai

"Come on, pretty girl, let's go eat," I say, pressing my palm against her back and leading her toward our table.

Her eyes flick over to me, as if she's trying to figure out if I mean food, or her. Then comes a gesture I'll never miss. My eyes track it *every… fucking…* time she does it. Her chest lifts as she breathes in deep, running the tip of her tongue over her teeth before worrying that gorgeous, oh so bitable lip between them. I love when she does that…I love knowing what I do to her, even if she won't admit it.

"Remembering something?" I tease, hoping her mind has traveled back to me between her thighs.

Her pupils blow as her eyes skirt down my body. She reaches toward me and lets her fingers follow her gaze until they cup the front of my pants,

and her palm rubs over the length of me. "Maybe."
Good god, this woman. My jaw tenses as I try like hell to keep my composure.

It takes every ounce of restraint I have to not steal her away. If it weren't for the fact that we haven't crossed that line yet, I would in a heartbeat. There's a supply closet down the hall that I'm already fantasizing about bending her ass over in. I bite my lip hard enough to taste copper in an attempt to suppress the mental images. *There will be plenty of time for that later...*

My tongue toys with my incisor as I lean in close to her, letting the back of my fingers trail down her neck and chest, until I cup her breast in my hand and squeeze. "Careful what you ask for, love."

"And what exactly am I asking for?" she fishes, wanting me to say it out loud. Thank God she's kinky...I'd be vanilla if she wanted me to, but knowing that with her, I'll get to enjoy all of the flavors, that makes my heart stutter. It makes me greedy with the urge to ravish her...My cock jerks against her hand that's still pressed dangerously against my crotch and her eyes light up like a Christmas tree.

I weave my hand behind her neck, and I yank her close until my lips ghost over hers. "You're asking for me to make you scream, princess. Am I wrong?" I ask, feeling her hand tighten as fuck me eyes stare at me. "Jesus," I say under my breath before I grab her arm and we teleport into the supply closet down the hall. Before she's able to catch her bearings, I flip her around, pressing her against the wall and kick her feet apart, spreading her for me as I drag her ass up until it's level with my hips.

This woman evokes the seven deadly sins from me like it's her job.

My lips become *greedy* the moment she gets close. I'm *gluttonous* for more and tantalized by her fruity scent, her sweet taste, the way her round ass feels in the palm of my hands. What's worse, is that I'm way too fucking *prideful* to admit out loud that I'm falling for her, but no woman has ever made me this ravenous and I've certainly never wanted to snuggle with one. I've always been a stickler for doing the deed and nothing more. I don't even kiss the women I fuck, yet this woman…

I *lust* after every damn piece of her to the point that it's physically painful to hold back. Part of me is worried about what our first time will be like. If I can't rein myself in, I'll fucking break her in two, and she's way to pretty to be treated like an expendable toy. But my body craves to be buried again and again, as deep as I possibly can go. I want to touch her fucking soul. I want to hear her scream my name as her fingers grasp at my satin sheets.

I'm *envious* of every man who has touched her before me, so much so that I'd love to feel their neck snap in my hands. I'm supposed to be the white knight, the one who saves the damn day and dropkicks Michael off his illegitimate throne. Yet this woman makes me want to become the villain, to murder for my own enjoyment.

She wiggles her hips, and I swallow hard, brought back to the sexy-as-sin view in front of me. I slide a finger slowly, down her spine, and she shivers. Goosebumps raise, pebbling the surface of her skin and I bend down to bite her ass, trying like hell to control the monster in me that begs to rip her apart.

She's so fucking responsive.

I press my body closer, causing Alice to stand up against the wall as I rope her hair to the side. My lips connect with her pulse, the only sound in the room being the shuffle of fabric, as our bodies itch to be closer, and our breath. There's no doubt that she can feel how much I want her pressed against her back. It's hard to hide, but she rocks her hips into me, rubbing so softly, yet just enough to make my knees weak and my heart to beat wildly in my chest.

"I need you woman," I groan, nipping at her ear and breathing her in. "You have no fucking idea how bad I need this, but if I sink inside you, I won't be able to stop." She pouts, letting her forehead fall forward as she leans against the stone wall. "I'll fuck up your hair, I'll ripe that gorgeous dress, and I'll make your make up run down that beautiful face of yours. We still have a whole night to get through. You look like a queen and I'm not about to leave you to face the entire kingdom a mess because I couldn't wait a few hours." I swallow and my stomach muscles clench as she teases me. It's hard to think straight, let alone talk when her ass is rubbing against me.

My hand snakes around her, sliding through the slit of her dress and finding her bare. *I swear to fucking god, this woman...*She has no idea what she does to me, and if she does, she's maniacal.

"You're going to want to scream, but you have to promise me you'll stay quiet. I don't want anyone to hear you. Your moans are mine and mine alone, do you understand?"

She nods, as my hand slides over her sex, and I groan against her shoulder, trying to resist the urge to rock my hips against her ass. "God, your fucking soaked," I growl, letting my fingers sink inside of her. Her hips buckle forward, pushing them deeper as a whimper sounds through her pressed lips. I love the way her body molds against mine. *But that moan...*Holy fucking hell...That moan is everything I've ever wanted and more.

At this moment, it doesn't matter that we're rushing into marriage. It doesn't matter that there is a fucking war brewing; one we both might die in. It doesn't matter that the fate of Hell and the demons that dwell within it are depending on us to bring Heaven to its knees. All that matters is that I'm a man and she's the woman I'm falling in love with.

Alice's fingers grab onto the stone as I pick up a rhythm, swirling my thumb against her clit as my fingers pump in and out of her. Her hands shake as they flex off the stone surface and I link the hand holding me up with the adjacent of hers.

Curling my fingers inside of her and adding a third, she gasps. "Fuck me," she says under her breath and my lips tip up into a smirk as I kiss her shoulder, watching her every move. Her body goes pliable in my hands and her pussy clenches around me. *G-spot? I think, yes.*

I kiss her neck, feeling her pulse thump against my lips, and hearing the magic sing in her veins. Her eyes are closed and her head lolls back against me as her thighs start to shut. I pull my fingers out of her and hold them over her sex as it clasps at the air, so fucking close to coming, so fucking needy that it's started to have a mind of its own.

"Spread your legs, love, or I'll stop," I say, pulling her body back against mine and I drop her hand to snake mine around her throat; not squeezing, but the sheer threat of it being there is all she needs. Her thighs settle apart again and I circle my fingers over her clit for a moment before sinking them back inside. Alice arches toward me as she starts to get close.

"That's it, little witch," I whisper and her pussy clenches around my fingers. My heart skips, realizing that she likes it when I talk dirty way more than I anticipated. *Such a dirty girl…* "Come for me. I want to taste you on my fingers." Her eyes flutter shut as she bites at her lip. She's so fucking hot…

When her lips part and her pussy clamps down on my fingers, I slide my hand up from her throat to cover her mouth and muffle the moan that leaves it and as if on cue, her body lurches forward and she shatters to pieces. I continue to slide my fingers through her slit, playing with the wetness that coats me before bringing them to my mouth and sucking them clean.

"You drive me mad, you know that?"

She doesn't answer. She's still trying to catch her breath, but her eyes find mine over her shoulder.

I kiss her cheek, grinning like a schoolboy as I try to fix her dress.

"That was amazing," she says, her eyes hooded and satiated as she drags in a deep breath, like she's trying to slow her speeding heart.

"There's more where that came from," I say, pulling her face to mine and kissing her deeply. "Now come on, princess. People are going to start wondering where we are."

I reach in my pants, trying to adjust my throbbing dick that threatens to bust the seams of my pants, then open the door to find Finn walking through the hall. He stills mid-step before turning to us, standing in the open doorway. His jaw bounces off the floor and Alice's cheeks turn bright red.

THE DEMON PRINCE

CHAPTER TWENTY-THREE
Kai

Having let Alice wander around the room so that I could continue making my rounds and saying hello to friendly faces, I circle back in an attempt to find her. The music plays, rattling my eardrum, and shits already started to get crazy. If there's one thing Hell is known for, it's that everyone loves a good party, and the people here will find dumb excuses to have them. So, when the opportunity comes to celebrate something that's actually worth the effort, things get wild.

And without fail, Lust spikes the punch every single time there's a gathering. His *essence*... excuse me while I cringe at that word, is a massive aphrodisiac that makes *energy shots* look like kiddy drinks and my father always throws a tantrum when orgies break out after a dozen or so drink it. It's done nothing but egg him on to hit all the gatherings in

THE DEMON PRINCE

Hell Hold. Surprisingly enough, it's actually how I lost my virginity.

I'm not against orgies, obviously, but I am when it involves my soon to be wife. I've yet to have her to myself, so I'm not even condoning the idea of sharing her. As is, I wish we could've stayed in the bubble of our room. At least there, we can pretend the rest of the world doesn't exist and I can tease her, without worrying about wandering eyes.

I've already left Alice alone for too long, but it's relatively safe now for her to be, at least within the keep and even though people are about to be horny as hell, no one will dare hurt her here. Now that the kingdom knows she's mine, they know I'll personally escort anyone who thinks otherwise to their grave.

Though I'm currently regretting my decision, I thought she would appreciate a few minutes of freedom. And I didn't leave her entirely alone, Finn stayed with her and if there's anyone I trusted with my life, or my soon to be wife's, it's him. He might talk shit, but the man worships women. All she has to do is bat her eyelashes and he'd commit murder for her.

A circle has formed in the middle of the keep, causing my heart to quicken. It's starting and I still haven't found her. I weave through the rows of people toward the center and as the last few move out of the way; an image comes into view that I'll never be able to get out of my head. Alice and Finn are dancing on top of a table pretending to be rockstars. She's singing into the wooden ladle from the punch bowl and he's on his knees, playing air guitar.

My mouth gapes as I watch her, easily the happiest I've seen the woman since bringing her here. She jumps around, red hair flying in every which way, singing *'Things I hate about you'* by Leah Kate. It could easily be worse. I fight the urge to laugh when Finn accidentally slides off the table only to jump up from the ground and the crowd to enthusiastically screams.

He doesn't skip a beat, and I know she's managed to get him shitfaced–and yes, I say her, because there's no way he would've done so without her asking. He would've wanted to be sober to protect her. I cover my mouth with my hand as her eyes meet mine and she swivels her hips getting lower to the table until she's crouched so Finn can occasionally share her *microphone* and belt out the chorus.

He holds the ladle for her so she can flip her hair and for the fucking life of me, I can't look away. If she looks this fucking sexy clothed and in front of this many people, I can only image the way she'd look when we're finally alone… and unsupervised.

The song ends and their faces land dangerously close. I watch as her eyes go from shock to excitement. Finn gives her his fuck-me-eyes and I know without a shadow of a doubt what comes next. So, I walk into the circle and grab her off the table, caveman style. Her body bends over my shoulder as I snag her crown off the table and walk away, heading toward our room. There's no way in hell I'm going to let that continue anymore, even if she did drink the punch and can't help but be attracted to anything with a dick.

She's mine.

Finn's chest heaves from dancing and singing as he holds his hands up in a *'what the hell man'* gesture but I ignore it, heading toward an open area to teleport us into the room. I toss her down on the bed and legs go every which way.

"What the hell?" she asks, sitting up to glare at me as I put her crown on my nightstand. "So what? I have fun for the first time since coming here and you get jealous?"

"I'm not jealous. Hell, you want a third, then say the word and I'll go get Finn. It wouldn't be the first time. But I specifically told you *not* to drink the punch." She opens her mouth to protest but I raise my eyebrows, propping my hands on my hips like a soccer mom telling little Timmy to share. "You literally have the evidence in your hand."

"Okay, so I drank the punch... but Finn did it first," she says, and I can't help but let the laugh roll from my lips.

"What does him going first change? He *wants* to drink the punch. He's usually the one who starts the orgies. God, woman," I scrub a hand down my face trying to resist the urge to pace back and forth.

THE DEMON PRINCE

"Orgies?" she asks, and I close my eyes.

"Yes. Lust spikes the punch every time there's a gathering and it always ends in an orgy. I wouldn't be surprised if the castle starts shaking in about ten minutes, when my dad finds out. Last time, he yelled so loud for people to stop that it busted out the windows in the keep."

When I open my eyes again, she's standing in front of me, way too close for comfort. Anyone else in Hell Hold, sure, let's go. They know what drinking the punch consents to. Hell, I might've even been okay with giving Alice whatever she's about to ask for, if she had known beforehand... if she hadn't just killed a man for trying to take advantage of her. I won't be the next.

The look she gives me goes straight to my dick, and when she bites that perfect fucking lip, it makes me want to take it between my teeth and never let go. She stands up on her tippy toes and that's when I realize she's lost her heels somewhere. Her lips brush against mine and I cup her face, drawing her to me, tasting the wine and cherry that coats her mouth and tongue.

I ditched my suit jacket and tie a long time ago, but her fingers begin unbuttoning my shirt, pulling it out of where it's tucked into my pants.

"Please," she begs and my dick throbs. Her lips trail down my neck to my chest and abs and when she tries to unbutton my pants, I grab her hair and pull her up to her feet.

"No," I say, closing my eyes to try and avoid seeing the hurt in hers. When I open them, she's still licking her lips and I match every step she takes toward me with one backward.

A small puff of air escapes the confines of my quivering lungs as I try not to think about her perfect lips being wrapped around my dick and how I'd love nothing more than to fuck them until they're raw and swollen. My fingers tremble, trying not to picture the way my hands slid over her smooth thighs hours ago. How good it felt to spread them for me and only me… The way she tastes.

Look at me. I'm a fucking mess. I don't ever get this worked up, not even when I've had the punch, but now I understand why people sell their soul to the crossroads demons for their significant others.

She's an addiction and with addictions, one taste is never enough.

"You know, I've been meaning to ask you. Where are your wings?" I cock my head at her. "I saw them at the party before you brought me here, but they're not there now and haven't been since."

"They're there. Just not out." She scrunches her eyebrows together confused so I shrug and pop them free, letting them stretch to their full length so she can gawk at them. My wingspan is well above average, so I have to take a step away from the bed to not hit anything. Alice walks over in awe, seeing them in the light for the first time and running her fingers over the feathers. She bites her lip hard enough to leave teeth marks.

"Hmmm," I say.

"What?"

"For some girls, it's the abs that get them hot and bothered, but for you, it's the wings. Are you going to purr for me, princess?" She scowls at me, and I swear she's the cutest angry person I've ever seen. It's like looking at an angry baby kitten. They bite and it hurts, but you still want to play with them, even though you know they'll do it again.

Shrugging my shoulders again, my wings disappear. Her mouth gapes. "Stop…" Is that aimed toward my comment or is it a reaction to my wings disappearing?

Maybe making her angry will keep her from jumping my bones. At this rate, I'm going to have to sleep with one eye open… or in full armor. Maybe I can just tie myself to the bed and let her do what *she wants*. Can I claim negligence? I'd never forgive myself if she regretted it though.

"Are you shocked or embarrassed?" I ask. "I can't tell."

"Oh please, don't flatter yourself, I'm not embarrassed and you're not the first person I've *purred* for," she says, rolling her eyes and walking away from me.

Yes. It's working. Maybe a bit too well… I arch my eyebrows and cross my arms. I could've gone my entire life not knowing that detail.

Her shoulders slump forward, and she groans. "Because it's weird! People don't purr."

"Maybe to you, but to me, it's easily the sexiest sound I've heard you make."

Okay, hindsight, probably not the best thing to say when I'm supposed to be taking down the woman, but it's the truth.

She starts undoing the laces in the V of her dress and my tongue darts across my lips trying not to swoon. Then a noise comes from my throat that I don't recognize. Something primal. Something all man, that nothing will satiate but her. Her touch. Feeling her beneath me. Her saying my name as I educate her on the ways a real man should treat her. I want her *everything* until there's not a single inch of her body I haven't caressed, kissed, or fucked into submission.

Closing my eyes again, I suck in a deep breath.

Be good, be good, be good.

Be a good fucking fiancé, even if it goes against everything you stand for.

Dead puppies, inside-out socks, upside-down toilet paper rolls.

Usually, thinking about random things I hate makes my cock calm down instantly, but she pulls the last of the lace free and I see her tattoo. Fuck, I want to trace every line with my tongue. A lopsided grin flashes at me as she walks toward me and I make a leap toward the living room, hoping to put more distance between me and her. She follows me tracing her fingers over the wooden top of the small dining table as she walks past it.

Uh uh. She can't get closer. I won't be able to stop myself from touching her soft skin, breathing her in, and making my dreams come to life. I take another step back, keeping the same pace as her.

"What are you doing, Alice?" I growl.

"What does it look like? Don't you want to?"

"*Yes...* I mean, no. Yes. *Shit.*" I drag my hand down my face, squishing my eyes together. It's a feeble attempt to get the look she's giving me out of my head, but I've already committed it to memory. It's seared in there and will take years of torture to remove it. "You drank the punch."

"Yeah, so?" She shrugs.

"I told you not to. So, I'm sorry, but I can't," I say, flopping my head back, hating the words as they roll off my lips and sending up a silent prayer.

"Yeah, well you're also not my Daddy, but I'll call you that if you'd like." My dick pulses as my head falls back forward and I stare at her with wide eyes. Jesus Christ... She talks dirty, too? I swear she came from Heaven. I didn't even know that was *my thing* but the way she says it... *yes, please.*

"No. You don't understand–" I try to reason, but she cuts me off with a hand.

"I'm well over the legal age–if that's even a thing here. I can drink alcohol if I want to just as I can ask you to fuck me until I forget my name. Now, are you going to strip or what?" She moves closer and I physically can't bring myself to step away. "Choose carefully, sweetheart," she taunts, "this determines whether I'll be a satisfied fiancé, or one who fills the void with porn."

For fuck's sake. "It's not spiked with alcohol, Alice," I say through gritted teeth when her hand slides down over the length of me through my pants.

She stops her prowling motion, and her face goes blank. "What's it spiked with?"

I shake my head. "You don't want to know, but let's just say they call him Lust for a reason."

Please tell me that killed the mood... I could tell her that it's the essence of his tears and not what she's thinking, but I'm hoping it will deter her from trying to seduce me any further. The threads of my restraint are snapping.

Alice smiles and any hope of that goes out the window. "Is it consent you're worried about? That I'm not fully sober? If that's the case, relax. I've found you rather..." She trails her eyes up and down my body. "*Fuckable* since I met you. So, what other excuses are plaguing that handsome head of yours?"

"How about the fact that I've killed people. I'm dangerous," I say. "Too dangerous to bang."

"I don't think you would without reason, and ironically, so have I." She undoes the button on my pants and tears the zipper open.

"Okay. I'm old. *Hundreds* of years old," I say, letting my head fall back. My fists grab on to the extra fabric of my pants to resist touching her.

"Experienced... and you don't exactly look your age."

"I'm possessive," I say, flexing my jaw.

"I call that sexy," she counters, pushing my dress shirt from my shoulders and letting her hands linger. "Plus, it kind of turns me on."

"Alice…" I enjoy the way her name rolls off my tongue a little too much. Her lips twitch into a come-get-me-grin, but that's not what makes me come unglued. "We should wai—" I feel her fingertips trail down my chest, oh so lightly, and then dip beneath the waistband of my pants. She circles her hand around my cock. "Fuck me…" I say under my breath.

"Yes?" she whispers, leaning closer as her other hand pushes the waistband of my pants down until it's free of the confining fabric. "Come on, baby. Let me taste you." My hand cups the side of her face, making her eyes meet mine. Then, my lips claim her, hungrily. Her hand's feel so goddamn good as they bury into my hair, pushing my crown off my head. It clangs as it bounces off the floor.

Fuck it. I'll get it later.

My hands grip her hips hard, lifting so she can wrap her legs around my waist. I drop to my knees against the marble floor, holding her against me, as my tongue sweeps inside her mouth, claiming it as mine. She moans against my lips and my hand slides beneath her dress. I slide my fingers inside her with ease since she's still not wearing panties. She's fucking dripping for me still…

No. *No.* I shouldn't be doing this.

Standing up from the ground with her kissing my neck, I carry her over to the bed and set her down. Pushing her back with my palm to her chest. I shove my dick into my pants, buttoning and zipping them. Walking over to my shirt, I slide my arms through it only to look back and find her glaring hard enough to melt my soul.

"I'm sorry, we should probably have some space tonight. The punch will wear off in an hour and if you still want to, I'll fuck you as hard as you'll let me. I promise. Until then, I can't. I don't want you to regret it. Not for our first time."

"I thought you were the prince of Hell. Aren't you supposed to take what you want? Unless you just changed your mind and don't want me…"

I grind my teeth, flexing my jaw beneath the taunt skin. "Are you serious right now? I've daydreamed of this since you got here. I want you so bad that I'm pretty sure circulation is being cut off to my dick right now, but I don't want you to hate me tomorrow."

She stands up, sliding off the bed and her eyes go black. Her hands fly out and my body goes sailing like I weigh as much as a paperclip, and I crash through the wooden door of the room. I collide with the stone wall in the hallway of the keep, knocking the air from my lungs. I shake my head, and drywall dust falls from my hair.

Well, that's fucking new.

"Okay, I deserve that," I say, waving a white flag and dusting the wood splints off my shirt, still sitting against the floor.

"Fuck you!" she screams back at me, then the feeling like someone is watching crawls over my skin. I turn my head, looking down the hall to see Finn, frozen mid-step with wide eyes.

I button my shirt, trying to gather my dignity and Finn says, "I was just coming to make sure she was okay… clearly, I should be asking you that question instead."

"Don't lie, you came to see if you could tap in," I seethe.

He holds a finger up, opening his mouth to speak before shutting it again… "Okay, yeah, maybe. Not the only reason though. But just so we're clear, if she asks me to…" he trails off.

"You'll keep your *grubby paws* to yourself." I take a page out of Alice's book of insults and he nods, setting her heels inside the door and stealing a look inside the room.

THE DEMON PRINCE

CHAPTER TWENTY-FOUR

Kai

"Okay, I saw that coming, but it was worth a shot," Finn says, holding a hand to me and I take it as he pulls me up. I'll give him credit where it's due. I've always been open to sharing in the past and so has he, but Alice is different.

"Oh," he says, holding up a finger again. "Ivar found the guy from the market."

"Well, why are we here then?" I say, peering into the room and immediately ducking as she throws one of her boots at me. I wave my hand, magically locking her inside. No one in. No one out until I get back.

Her other boot collides with the boundary and bounces to the floor inside, it doesn't stop me from ducking though.

"You want to leave your engagement party to go arrest some douche canoe?" he says, squinting at me. "Why aren't you in there?"

"Yes. That douche canoe tried to rape my wife and as for the second part, it's none of your business."

"Fiancé," he corrects. "I'm still holding out on the idea that she might like me more. You never know, she might decide to rethink whose ankle she shackles her ball and chain to and mine will be open, ready, and waiting. I mean I didn't see you playing air guitar. Just saying," he says, walking down the hall the way he came backwards and holding his arms out.

I follow after him, buttoning my shirt as we go.

"So, tomorrows the meeting with the... *he who shall not be named,*" Finn says. Obviously, he's watched way too much *Harry Potter*.

"Yeah, and?" I say, securing the last button.

"What are you going to do with Alice? I mean... I don't want to grate you or anything, but if someone has to volunteer to stay behind and make sure she's taken care of, I gladly would volunteer as tribute. It's a much better way to spend a Tuesday than walking into certain death," he says.

"Enough, Finn. You're not touching my girl." We start stepping downstairs two at a time.

Running a hand through his hair. "I'm just saying you can't leave her here. It might be safer, but if one of us isn't going to stay, you should probably bring her. After what happened with Ivar, I wouldn't trust anyone else."

"Oh, hell no," I say, stopping to turn around. Finn slides to a stop and even though he's two steps up, we're still eye level. "I'm *not taking her* to meet him. For one, she would be the one to say some snarky ass comment to set him off. Two, if it goes south, it would terrify her. And lastly, I'm not even sure I'll be able to sleep in my own bed because she's high and trying to jump me. I just got thrown through a door because I told her no. She's the most infuriating woman I've ever met in my life and with her coming into her powers, all it takes is one thing to piss her off and I'll be handing back the monster realm their rotisserie fried king, so crispy, they might not be able to identify dental records. Pass!"

The minute the last word rolls off my tongue, I notice just how much she's rubbed on me... Finn's mouth tips up in the corner and something mischievous dances behind his eyes. "She sounds perfect."

My hand reaches up to pinch my nose. "Where's Ivar?"

"He said they're at Ripplie's Bar." I grab onto his arm and teleport us there, finding Ivar waiting by the door.

"You know, having her there might be good for you. She's Nephilim and even though she's spellbound, I can taste the power rolling off her. It's like taking a supercell battery with you. Might work out well in your favor." Finn raises one hand and lowers the other. "Two Nephilim... One Nephilim... I think the math is easy."

When we reach Ivar, he snaps to attention. "My prince, he's inside." I nod and walk through the door, spotting the Serpentman at the bar, downing a beer and chatting with a woman.

"On the brightside," Finn whispers to me. "You're out of your love nest for the night. I don't think I've ever seen you spend so much time in your room."

We take a seat next to the man we're here for at the bar and order a drink.

"*Love...* don't even get me started. Love is fucked and just because we're getting married doesn't mean we've crossed that bridge. But to keep it simple, a week ago, I was good. Now, my fucking back hurts, my dick hurts more, I'm pretty sure the woman has given me high blood pressure, and I'm–"

"Whipped?" Finn says, trying to complete my sentence, leaning his elbow on the bar and propping his face up.

"I am *not* whipped."

"Yeah, you are, and I don't blame you. Fuck I'd be whipped too. I think I might be already, and I don't even get anything out of it but to *look at her*–" he cuts off, seeing my eyes narrow. "I mean, *serve her every need*," he says, pretending to cough. "That didn't come out much better."

The man next to me turns in his seat, double taking at me and Finn, who's waving like *Forrest Gump* on the shrimp boat.

"You," the man growls.

"Me," I say, letting my eyes grow wide with the syllable.

The man takes off running, knocking over the bar stool and leaving his date at the bar, gaping. "See," I say to Finn. "I'm doing you a favor. Love is so fucking fickle."

I snap my fingers and the man's head spins in a circle, snapping his neck, and killing him on the spot. His body falls to the ground with a *thump* in the middle of the bar. People gasp and the woman the guy was drinking with starts screaming. I pick up my beer that the bartender dropped off and down it. Getting up and turning to her, I snap my fingers again, but this time, instead of killing her too, the woman's vocal chords go silent.

"Don't worry, it will wear off," Finn says to her, peeking up over my shoulder as she continues to silently scream.

I look at the crowd who are all staring at me. "You might want to leave. If you think that was bad. It's about to get a whole lot worse."

"That's right, ladies and gents," Finn says, getting up and adjusting his belt. "Don't fuck with my princess." I glare at him over my shoulder, and he grabs his neck pretending to stretch. "*His*... His princess." He clears his throat, looking everywhere but at me.

I tell Finn to make sure the guy gets jarred in Limbo, and he takes off, leaving me alone with the man's body. Everyone else cleared out of the bar except the woman. She swats at my arm, trying to get me to turn her voice back on.

"Are you going to scream?" I ask. She shakes her head no and I snap. Her hand flies up to her throat then she runs out of the bar like the others.

I kick the dude's boot. "WWAD... What would Alice do?"

***

When I return to the keep, blood splatter covers my shirt and a massive snake-like piece of flesh drapes around my neck. My father is waiting by the door, seeing people out as I walk up, not giving a shit about who's watching.

"Where have you been and... *What happened?*" His eyes scan over my body, staring at me like I have a dick on my head... I don't. I just have one around my neck. No big deal.

"We found the guy that hurt Alice." I point to the boa constrictor worthy piece of meat around my neck. "Wedding gift."

He furrows his eyebrows. "No. Don't give her that..."

"Oh, I'm going to. If not for her, then for me. She threw a boot at my head and put my body through a four-inch thick, wooden door. So, if it makes her happy, I win. If it pisses her off, *I still win*. Now, if you'll excuse me." I try to squeeze past him, and he rolls his eyes.

"Where is she? She's not still at the party alone, right?"

"Calm your tits. She's upstairs locked in her tower until she goes back to being the nice witch, or at the very least, ditches her broomstick."

He mushes his mouth. "Piece of advice?"

"Is it optional?" I ask, seeing him shake his head no.

"Just apologize. It doesn't matter if you did anything wrong or not. Just save yourself some trouble and say sorry."

"Okay," I say, stepping up the stairwell toward our room. *Not a chance in hell.*

When I get to the room, she's laying down on the couch, but otherwise seems calm and nothing like the feral beast I left in here. I wave my hand and the boundary goes down.

"Come to check on your prisoner?" she asks. "No, I'm not having fun. Yes, I'm still pissed, asshole." A smile stretches across my face. It's impossible to be mad at her.

"Actually, I brought a present… and I was going to make sure someone brought *my prisoner* something to eat… or see if she still wanted to be eaten."

She sits up, looking over the couch arm toward where I stand. Her mouth drops open, drinking in the sight of me.

"What the fuck happened to you?" She pauses, squinting at me. "Is that what I think it is?"

"His dick? Yeah," I say, walking up to drop it on the coffee table. She stares at it for a moment before looking back up at me with a scowl.

"Have you ever had a cat?" she asks. I shake my head no, wiping the blood off my knife before putting it back into the holder on my boot.

"Well, not entirely true. I think we had one, why?" I say, stripping out of my shirt and trying to dab at the blood spots on my chest and soak it up with the fabric. It doesn't work as well as I thought it would.

"Well, they're notorious at killing birds and bringing them inside through the dog door and leaving them for their owners. Apparently, it's because they think we can't hunt for ourselves–"

"Are you comparing me to a feline?" I ask and she nods, biting her lip. "I thought you would want proof that he's gone or a trophy. Maybe we can make a snakeskin scarf or boots out of it."

"I'm not putting a dick, or a scarf made from one anywhere near my head."

"Is mine the exception?" I ask, undoing my belt and sliding my pants down onto the floor before stepping out them and my shoes.

"Not right now. You missed your window. And we don't have a door. Anyone could walk by."

"Well, whose fault is that?" *Certainly not my backside. It was a victim.* Pressing my lips together, I toss my knife down and the point sticks in the table. "I'm going to shower."

THE DEMON PRINCE

CHAPTER TWENTY-FIVE
Alice

I change, getting ready for bed, throwing on a band t-shirt that's about three sizes too big, so it hangs like a dress on me. Opting for no pants, like I always did before coming to Hell, I cross through the bathroom, and attempt not to look at the naked man swimming around in the obsidian water. It's almost annoying how fucking perfect he is. No. Scratch that. It *is* annoying. Annoying in the most delicious way…

It's almost painful at this point. I want him. I crave his touch, but I hate it at the same time. It's maddening that one man can have so much influence over me and all it takes is for him to smile or so much as breathe and my body itches to be closer.

I might've had punch intoxicating my brain earlier, but when we came up here, I was determined to just fuck him out of my system. It wasn't a spur of the moment thought. Before the party, I was debating on whether that was an option, but didn't want to give him the satisfaction if it didn't work. *If once wasn't enough.*

Thinking that maybe if I just gave in to the temptation, then my body would stop betraying me and I could think straight again. It was a dumb plan. Once would never be enough. Not with Kai. Not if I am to *live* with him, to *marry* him… and honestly, that last part should justify my urges. But every time I convince myself that it would be okay to fall for him, to like him, he gets cocky, and it lights an inferno inside of me that causes my teeth to grind.

Am I proud of my behavior? *No.*

Do I regret it? *A little.*

Will I do it again? *God, I hope not.*

Hanging out with Finn was a blast, even if it involved me drinking punch laced with… I shiver, not wanting to admit it to myself. I would've never let go and had fun like that on Earth. I couldn't and follow my aunt's rules. But tonight, felt so good to just dance like no one is watching and be spontaneous for once.

Did I know the punch was going to make me horny to the point that my ribs ached? No... Finn conveniently left that out when we agreed to drink it and say fuck the rules. And honestly, the only thing I would've changed about that decision, is if Kai had just decided to let go and have fun. Even if it was just to dance with me and live a little. It never had to go anywhere, though I wish it had.

The punch allowed me to move past my pride and I gave it a shot... and he fucking said no. I get his reasoning; I just don't believe it. It's more fitting for him to try and tease me with rejection, because I've been doing it to him. Not intentionally. I'm not trying to encourage him, but my mouth says no while my body comes alive under his gaze. It beckons him to bend me over and to give us what we both want. It doesn't take a genius to see that. He knows how hard it is for me to resist. Hell, it intrigues him.

Lust's drug put my pride in the back seat while my desire took the wheel. And now, after saying things that sober me wouldn't have let become anything more than thoughts, I can't bring myself to jump his bones now. Even when he asked me if I still wanted to, after dropping a dick on the table like a barbarian, I couldn't. It felt like he was pitying me...

The punch provided an excuse for my need, my words, my actions, for my plan that probably would've failed anyway. It allowed me to maintain some dignity and for that I'm grateful. If I try to fuck him out of my system now or give in, telling him to do as he pleased, Kai would know it wasn't entirely the punch talking and I won't pop my pride's life raft. As is, it's losing the battle against the current and sinking by the minute.

The man is a walking power trip. It's hot as hell to fight with him and watching him take blow for blow in the ring only to come back harder, is impressive. I'm tempted to just give in and let him win, just for a day, just once, but I won't do it. I won't cave again until he's the one who's come unglued. I want him to beg for it the way I did. Only then will I allow myself to revisit the idea.

Walking through the bathroom, I do my best to go as quickly and quietly as I can to not disturb the beast in the pool, like a burglar stealing some artifact from a museum. And in my attempt to do so, I realize I'd make a shitty thief.

I'm about halfway to the bedroom door when the brute of a man, steaming in the tub, if you can call it that, clears his throat. I freeze, perching on my tippy toes and shrinking at the noise. Slowly, I crane my head toward Kai, who's arms are stretched against the rocks. He takes in the sight of me, and I swear I can feel his gaze spill over my body, soaking through my skin from head to toe.

"I'm sorry," he says, and my throat goes dry. *Well, that was unexpected.* "I should've been more forthcoming about the punch thing, and I probably shouldn't have brought you the serpent man's dick... I don't want to go to bed mad and I hope now that you're sober, you'll understand that I said no because I was trying to be respectful."

Wiggling my bare toes against the floor, I pick at my t-shirt's hem, unsure of how to respond. So, I offer the same. "I'm sorry, too. I should've listened." He doesn't say anything back, just nods, and the anger I held toward him disappears. His apology felt *genuine*, not like he'd said *'no'* just to tease me. This man is an enigma.

I leave the bathroom, folding back the blanket and climbing into bed. It's not long after that Kai comes out. Assuming I'm asleep, he comes over to my side of the bed, pushing my hair out of my face and kisses my cheek gently, then climbs in on his. It was such a small gesture yet meant more than anything else he's done so far. Part of me hates how big this bed is. I want him beside me where I can bask in the warmth of his body, and the comfort it provides… but he's way the fuck over there.

I grunt, sitting up to crawl toward him. His eyes shoot wide, and he freezes in place, trying to figure out what I'm doing. I lift his arm and he lets me manipulate it so I snuggle up against his side, setting my leg over him so it can slide between both of his, and I don't miss the smile that hints on his lips as I lay down.

"Don't make a big deal about it," I say, listening to the sound of his heartbeat and letting it lull me to sleep.

"I wouldn't dream of it, princess."

***

I woke up this morning in the same position I fell asleep in with his fingers tracing circles on my back. It was pure bliss, even if it was short lived, and something that I could easily get used to experiencing every morning.

It was a compromise… well, internally for me. From here on out, I'll allow myself the reins to touch him, but that's it. There will be no permittance into my chamber of secrets.

After breakfast, the maids bring in a bag from the seamstress and open it up to reveal leather pants, and a jacket of the same material that when zipped, shows the decorative design that's on Kai's armor. A golden Cerberus.

"What is this?" I ask, looking at Kai, who's watching my every move like a hawk.

"We had this made for you when you first got here, and I have to go to a meeting today to negotiate with an… *indifferent* king and I'd rather not leave you here alone." He steps toward me and then dismisses the maids, declaring he'll help me.

Of course, he will. As if my lady bits would have a fighting chance against that...

"There's more than one king in Hell?" I ask, contorting my face.

"There are seven realms within Hell, and we rule over all of them, but they're all delegated to lords, with the exception of Hell Hold, the one we're in now. The seventh though, has a king instead of a lord, but it's kind of allowed to do its own thing."

"You can't have multiple monarchies in one land, so do we rule it or does he?" I ask.

Kai looks away and bites his lip. "He does. It's a prison world, so they've developed their own system, but my father still holds the key to the barrier that traps them inside. It's a sort of gray area."

"And you want me to go with you? To a *prison world*?" I ask, running my fingers over the leather embossing. "That doesn't exactly have a good ring to it."

"Yes… but should you *choose* to go, there will be rules. I'm not trying to be a prick, but you're not used to our customs." He walks up and takes the outfit out of the garment bag. "It won't always be that way. Once you understand how things work, I want you to have an opinion and a say, but for now…" he trails off.

He doesn't need to explain. He's right. I don't know the beginning of their customs, let alone how to be even remotely in charge of a realm… or *realms*. "I can live with that," I say, taking the clothes from him and watching his chest deflate, as if he's relieved by my acceptance to go. *I'm missing something.* "Why do you want me to go? Wouldn't it be easier, *safer*, to leave me here?"

"After what happened at the market, I don't trust anyone to guard you besides my father, myself, or Finn. My father has a meeting with Michael today, he has one every month to give him the numbers on deaths, and new lives that come in and out of Limbo. If they don't monitor it, Heaven can become flooded and that's just bad for everyone. So, he won't be in Hell Hold today and I need Finn to come with me. So, it's either hang out on this floor of the keep or go on an adventure. Which would you rather do?"

I squint at him, holding up the pants from the outfit. "Well, that's an easy choice. Although, I'm relatively certain you just want to see my ass in leather. I'm coming. It's barely been a couple days, but I'm stir crazy. It feels like I've been here for two weeks and only have been outside once."

His hand rubs against the back of his neck. "It probably feels that way because it has." My gaze snaps to his face. *What? How?* "In Hell, you won't have to sleep or eat as often. Basically, what you need for one day on Earth, is the same for three here. We have three moons, and they all have to eclipse The Flame for it to get dark outside, and that only happens once every three days." My eyes slowly trail off to the floor. God Elise and Noah must be so worried, and Charlie is never going to forgive me for missing her birthday. I close my eyes and exhale heavily, trying to bring peace to my soul, while it aches for those I love, those I left behind.

His finger tips my chin up and I open my eyes to look into his. "What's wrong?" he asks.

"It's nothing, I just didn't realize I'd been gone that long." Stepping away from his touch, I slip my shirt up and over my head and start getting ready to go. I don't react when his gaze sears over my body, realizing he hasn't exactly seen me entirely naked and besides my panties, I am. He doesn't look away like he did when I bathed in front of him, but he doesn't make an advance either. I'm thankful for it, because my heart feels too heavy to go there. Upon getting the ensemble on, I step into my shoes and then head to the bathroom to finish.

A little while later, I'm standing in the mirror by our bed while Kai gets ready. He walks up, right as I finish fixing my hair that has somehow managed to stay decent since the maids fixed it yesterday… or was that two or three days ago? Fuck if I know, but it is nice to be able to actually brush my hair and not look like a poodle. He's dressed in a similar outfit as me, and his crown is on his head. That fucking crown… Why is it so hot?

Maybe he's right. I do have a thing for power. I'm not a gold digger. I couldn't give a shit less about his money or the finer things, but when he walks into the room, the air even seems to bend to his will, and that excites me on a cellular level that I can't even begin to explain.

He twirls something in his hands and my eyes drop to find my crown between his fingers. "Come here," he says. I step toward him as he places it on my head then tips my chin up so he can look at me. His eyes search over my face for a moment before he speaks again. "I've never seen someone look as heavenly as you do right now."

A smile tugs at my face as my cheeks tighten and flush red hot. "Are you trying to suck up to me?" I ask.

Kai's eyes fall to my lips, still holding my face hostage as his tongue plays with the point of his incisor. "A little." I stifle a laugh in my throat. "It's true though."

My hands reach out to wrap around his waist and pull him closer. I breathe in, smelling his cologne; it's a smokey and warm scent. It makes every nerve in my body calm. Then standing up on my tippy toes, I kiss him. He gently cups my face, locking me to him as he kisses me, so hard, yet so softly that goosebumps erupt across my skin, and butterflies flutter through my insides. He tastes of wine as I drag his bottom lips between my teeth, sliding the tip of my tongue across it, wanting more.

The man himself is an assault to my senses and sends my mind reeling, but when he kisses me like this, time could stop, the world could cease to spin, and I'd be okay with it. He's a savage who knows how to seduce and infuriate me with his words one moment and can make me feel like I'm the only person in the realm that matters, the next.

Someone clears their throat and I tear away from Kai, who doesn't even seem to give a shit, to find Finn standing in the open doorway to the hall. He shoots us a grin that looks like a kid who got away with sneaking a cookie out of the jar without his mother knowing and then whistles. "Hot damn… I'd say get a room but–"

"Not now, Finn," Kai says, moving to stand behind me and trails kisses down my neck. He doesn't even look at Finn, but I can't do anything beyond standing there wide-eyed staring at the man in the hall who's struggling to look away too. His jaw flexes as his eyes slip over me from head to toe and for some reason, I feel like I've been thrown into the middle of a pissing match.

His arm wraps around my waist and he nips my ear making me jolt. What is this man doing? We're on full display, and we haven't even done the deed yet, but it feels like he's on a warpath to make it happen, bystanders be damned. Is Kai trying to prove a point because of last night or is shit about to get weird?

"Um. The men are downstairs. We're ready to go when you are," Finn says, swallowing hard.

"Not. Now," Kai growls, and I can feel the command in his tone, causing my spine to straighten.

"Fine then," Finn seethes. "I can see you're in a fantastic mood. You could at least let a man watch, *shit*."

Kai stops his pursuit, then flicks his hand, sending the chair by the door straight under Finn's legs, forcing him to sit on it. The chair goes sailing down through the open doorway and down the hall. I hear Finn yelling at him but can't really make out much of what he says since he's moving with such velocity.

"Where were we?" he asks. Grabbing a lock of my hair and twisting it around his finger.

"Leaving. We were leaving." He visibly pouts and it makes my heart sing. He might be winning the battle, by making me like him, but I'm winning the fucking war on who wears the pants in this relationship, come Hell or high water.

THE DEMON PRINCE

CHAPTER TWENTY-SIX

Kai

Fucking Finn… I love the dude but right now, I wish he was anywhere else. I told him to meet us at high-noon, not first thing in the damn morning.

That kiss could've gone on forever had the asshole not interrupted. It was Earth shattering to say the least. The kind of kiss that wars are fought for; two people putting everything on the line and stripping down to their bare bones. I've never been kissed like that in my life, and if there was even an inkling of doubt in my mind that she doesn't like me, it's vanished now.

Alice and I make our way downstairs to find Finn's scalding glare. Okay, maybe kicking him out of the place via an enchanted armchair wasn't the nicest thing to do, but that doesn't mean he has to be shitty about it. He could've walked in, seen that we were preoccupied and gave us space, but no. He had to make a damn scene.

It takes me a moment to see that Alice isn't still beside me and when I look back, she's standing at the top of the steps that lead to the keep's gate. Her eyes are bugged wide, and she stares blankly at the horses. Maybe I should've prepared her... I turn back to the steads, most of which are reined in by men, except two. Finn's and mine. Their eyes are white, clouded over like a blind man's. Their skin is pale and glows a ghoulish green. They're nothing like the horses she's used to seeing.

I hold out my hand. "Alice. Are you coming?"

She swallows, shaking her head slightly to clear her mind and then trots down the stairs. Ignoring my hand, she walks straight up to the horses and slowly sets hers against the middle of my horse's face. He nuzzles against her palm and her lips tip up into a smile.

"They're beautiful," she says, scratching the hollow behind his ears until his foot thrashes against the ground. Nyx, my horse, hates everyone. He's usually the first to bite and ask questions later. Yet, he just shook his leg like a domestic dog getting his belly scratched.

Finn's hand clamps on my shoulder and he leans in so that he can say something for my ears only. "It looks like you're not the only one who's whipped." I draw my lip between my teeth to keep them from grinding, but it doesn't hide the tick in my jaw.

Alice turns around, searching through the group for something. "There's only two."

I stutter for a moment before saying, "I figured you'd just ride with me."

Her mouth forms a weird sideways frown before her eyes meet mine again. Then, I plant my hands on her waist to pick her up, but she removes them.

"I grew up on a farm. I don't need help getting on a horse. Thank you." She slides her boot into the stirrup and hoists herself up and over until she's in the saddle.

Okay then.

Sliding her foot out of the stirrup, I start to climb up to sit behind her, but before my boot can fully get into the stirrup, Nyx side steps, and I struggle to catch my balance. Did the fucker just choose her over me? What, because I didn't scratch his head?

Finn's laughter rings in my ears and I look over to find him bent over, propping his hands on his knees, and cackling like a schoolboy. He stands, wipes his hand over his eyes to remove the tears that have leaked down his cheeks, and then points at one of the men.

"You. Stay here. Let me have your horse so the prince can take mine," he says. As Finn walks past me to go retrieve his new ride, he pulls out a carrot from his pocket, making a pitstop to give it to his horse before handing me the reins. "Should've brought carrots," he says.

I shouldn't need them.

Once we're on our horses, I head toward the front of the pack and open a portal, slicing the ruin into my palm and blowing until my blood becomes dust. Alice watches me, then looks at her own, as if she wants to try it. The air ripples in front of us, and I let the men walk through, followed by Finn, before me and Alice bring our horses across together.

Finn cocks an eyebrow at me as his horse turns circles, waiting for us. "We're walking? I figured we'd just pop in by the barrier like last time," he says.

"Since someone decided to start out at the ass crack of dawn, I figured we'd take the long way, weave west, then circle back up so that Alice can see the titans." He glares at me but otherwise accepts my plan and moves to the front, giving me and Alice some privacy. *I wish he would've been that forthcoming at the damn keep.*

"I have questions," she says, riding beside me and looking around at the clearing we stepped into just past the forest that surrounds Hell Hold. Tall grass covers the ground and Nyx leans forward to steal a chunk before walking farther.

"Would you be you if you didn't?" I tease, but it doesn't earn a smile. What is going on with her? One second, she's shoving her tongue down my throat, and the next, she's scoffing at me for trying to help her on a horse...

"What's that big ass tree for?" she asks, pointing toward the massive elder tree in the middle of the clearing. Its leaves are made of copper that acts as a conductor of magic with a twisted trunk that puts most skyscrapers to shame.

"That's the tree of life, it holds most of Hell's magic and it's actually nine trees all bound together, one of each of the sacred woods. The trunks wrap around and support one another and live symbiotically. Without one, it would crumble under its own weight. And below it, is a cavern full of crystals that would make your witchy heart race." She turns to look at me in awe. "Don't worry, princess. I plan to stop there, too." Nyx keeps pace beside me, which is good, seeing as Alice is preoccupied with taking in the world around us.

"I'd like that," she says, "a lot." I whistle to Finn, and point at the tree, silently telling him to head that way. He turns his horse, and the men follow suit. It's quiet for a beat as Alice repeatedly turns her hand over, palm up, searching it. I smirk, knowing the questions coming, but I'm growing tired of waiting for her to ask it.

"What's on your mind?" I ask, looking off toward the tree in the distance.

"Why did you do the hand thing? Could we not walk here if we're taking the long way? Are we far away from the keep? My aunt is a time spinner, so she can teleport and open portals, but she's never had to cut herself to open one."

"It's blood magic. I can teleport without it, but only with one other person, anything more than that gets risky. By myself, it's cake, but I wouldn't try it with a horse. So, by using the magic in my blood, I can open up a portal and take more people along. So can you. You have to visualize the place you're going first, but otherwise it's pretty straight forward."

She nods, still wearing a poker face that hides any and all emotion behind a wall and I want to know why. It's the same look I saw when she realized how long she had been here this morning. When we kissed, she was normal, the same Alice I've come to know, but the moment it was over, the walls went back up and it bothers me on a cellular level. Is she homesick? Missing her aunt and uncle? If that was it, why hasn't she scryed home again?

"As for the keep, it's just past the woods behind us," I continue, hoping that maybe, seeing Hell and the beauty it holds will keep her demons at bay. "I'd just rather not go through them if I can avoid it. It's The Forest of Lost Souls, haunted by the ghosts of creatures who used to live here before us. For the most part, they stick to themselves, but the deeper you go, the creepier it gets. If you want, we can ride through on the way back. We just can't make any pit stops."

The forest is not my friend, but we've managed to keep it under control. It used to be ruled by Pan, one of the lesser gods before my father banished him to The Realm of Monsters. He collected souls from those who died before my father came back to remodel Hell.

There wasn't a place to store souls or reincarnate them then, so when people died their souls just wandered through the realms. Pan collected them, turning the ghosts into children who did wicked, unholy things to those who entered the woods. Even now that he's gone, the children won't find peace, we've tried to help them pass over, but nothing worked.

Now, every once and awhile, one gets a wild hair, but instead of playing pranks, they can get ruthless and bloodthirsty. When we find them, we try to suck them off into jars and send them to Limbo to be judged, but it's easier said than done.

"There were creatures who lived here before you? You mean it wasn't just Hell to start?" she asks, watching me. I squint against the onslaught of light, beaming in my eye.

"Yeah. Hell was God's first attempt at Earth, and the civilization you know. He created a group of people, much like angels, but they all had different strengths. They looked like humans, but some could wield lightning, others could create life from the dirt. Your people call them Greek or Norse gods. There were twelve of them originally. Zeus, Hera, the whole lot. But when God made them, he used a piece of his soul, just like he did when he created the angels, but they quickly realized they could tap into his power, and he couldn't control them. The only one who stayed by his side and obeyed him, was my father. So, he took Lucifer, who went by Hades back then, along with the few regular humans he had, and built a world around what we call Hell, trapping the lesser gods inside Earth's core and starting over with your world."

"So, if he trapped them before this became Hell, are they still here?" she asks, scrunching her eyebrows. I love that face. The confusion in it... Yet, you can see the gears turning, trying to connect the dots. She's such an intuitive woman.

"He made them mortal and left them here. They had children, and their power lives on through them, but they're gone now."

I eye her. She hasn't stopped looking at me since I began talking, but her gaze feels different. Formal... like you'd look at someone you barely knew out of respect. It doesn't belong to the stubborn woman who wants me but refuses to allow herself to, that is until I tease her enough to make her let her guard down. This look belongs to someone quiet, sweet. Someone who wouldn't think about insulting me every chance she got, and I don't like it.

There's something seriously wrong, but I don't want to push her to tell me until she's ready.

As we near, The Tree of Life's shadow casts over us and Alice cranes her neck up to try and see the top. It's an impossible task, but she tries anyway, shifting to try and get a better angle.

"I've heard stories about the Greek gods, or Hell, but none of them fully match up with what you're saying. It makes me wonder how humanity got it so wrong," she says.

"It's like a giant game of telephone. Where the stories originated, it's true, but by the time it reaches the other end of the line and spreads by word of mouth, agendas are inserted and the story itself is never repeated the same."

She grabs at her neck, wiping the sweat beading on it and gathers her curls into a ponytail before snapping a rubber band around it. *I'll enjoy taking that down later.*

THE DEMON PRINCE

CHAPTER TWENTY-SEVEN

Alice

We stop the horses at the bottom of the tree, staring at its gnarled roots that reach out, clawing at the ground. They're wide enough to stand three horses in, side by side. Below it, is a cave partially obscured by a webbing of roots and vines and made out of the same obsidian stone that's in our bedroom.

Kai dismounts and walks around to hold his hand out to me. Stopping my horse and against my better judgment, I take it, hating the way his touch sends shockwaves rippling through my arm. The man's an inferno that threatens to burn me alive and level me to ash, but I'm drawn to it like a stupid-ass moth.

I want to care. I want to give in, especially when he shelves his alpha attitude and is gentle with me.

when he looks at me like I'm his world. He shouldn't do that, it's not fair. It makes me forget about the people waiting for me back home... the people I love more than anything else and that I itch to see again.

It's so hard to keep my head on straight, to keep my heart shielded from the man that throws a sledgehammer against every wall I've built to keep him out. I know I can't go home until after the war is won... if I did, I could be putting those I love in the crosshairs of Michael's vendetta to kill me. Yet, I'm still holding out hope that once he's out of the way and the storm calms, that maybe I can return to Earth and my family. That I can return to my normal life.

When Kai touches me, when my heart sings, I lose sight of that and forget about everything else and everyone. If I let myself fall for him, I won't be able to return to my home because I won't be able to bring myself to walk away from him. I can't let that happen. It already physically hurts to think about leaving and it could take years before the war is over. How close can you get to someone within that time? Too close for comfort, that's for sure.

The moment my feet touch the ground, I can feel the pull of the power. It trickles up my legs and sinks into my bones. He wasn't kidding when he said this thing held most of Hell's power. Kai takes the opportunity to lean toward me and kiss the side of my head while I gawk at the way the trunks of the trees have meshed into one.

"Come with me," he whispers before taking my hand and leading me toward the base of the tree. My head swivels, trying to take everything in and the men dismount and make themselves comfortable.

Kai pushes open the vines that cover the cave, and the sound of tearing roots hits my ears. I walk inside and my mouth falls to the ground. It's *beautiful...* and well beyond anything I could've imagined. My fingers reach to skim over the amethyst walls that glow to either side of me on the mouth of the cave. The crystal sends power through my fingertips, bathing me in a wave of calm.

"Keep going. It gets better," Kai says. I can hear the amusement in his tone, and I do as he asks. After about fifteen feet, the cave walls open up into a massive cavern in the middle of the bound tree trunks and lined with crystal pillars of various kinds that are outrageously huge. Like the size of my car, *huge*. Looking up, I can see a small circle opening that basks the stone altar in the middle of the cavern with light. Next to it, is a smaller flat piece of blood-stained stone, likely used for sacrificing to *something or someone*. It makes me wonder whose veins it once heated.

I turn, walking around the walls of the cavern. Water gently falls over the crystals, reflecting the light and they too, glow painting the room like a stained-glass window would. I glance up, trying to see where it came from but it's impossible to tell. Below and in the cracks of the crystals are patches of green moss, cementing them together, and various kinds of mushrooms and herbs. He wasn't kidding. To a witch, this place is Heaven…

"These are the largest crystals I've ever seen," I say, trailing my fingers over the rough weathered surface of one made of black tourmaline. It's ironic to find the precious stone here, being that it's supposed to ward you from demons... I'm assuming that's another thing that fell victim to the telephone game. It's more likely to ward off negative energies.

"They're probably the oldest in existence," Kai says, coming to stand behind me and rest his hands on my hips, holding me to him. He leans down to place a chaste kiss on my shoulder.

Walking further, there's a stone I've never seen before that catches my eye. I reach out my hand in an attempt to skim my fingers over it, wondering what power it can hold, but Kai's voice stops me short.

"Don't touch that," he says.

I turn toward him and hug my hand to my chest. "Why? What does it do?"

"There's a fertility temple dedicated to Aphrodite in The Realm of Monsters. My father knew it would be trapped on the other side of the boundary so, he broke off a chunk of the main crystal that the temple guards as a present to my mother. She in turn, placed it here and it continued to grow. And as much as it pains me to say it, the crystal itself is incredibly powerful and pieces are given to women to wear as necklaces and jewelry because it... uh, has a pheromonal effect..."

Cocking my eyebrow, my lips tease into a smirk. "Pheromonal?" He stays statue-still with the exception of the slight nod he gives me. "Like, if I touch it, you're going to *want me* pheromonal?"

He clears his throat. "Yes, but even a small crystal is incredibly potent, and as you can see, that one is massive, so it—" My hand collides with the smooth surface, and I watch him as the words cut off in his throat. I lift my hand and he drags in a deep breath, closing his eyes.

"I see..." I say, biting my lip to hide the wicked grin that's spreading across my face.

"That was uncalled f—" I touch it again, enjoying the way his eyes flick black as his demonic side comes out to play, then release it as he rolls his shoulders and neck, likely trying to stay in control.

"Potent indeed." He grumbles under his breath, low enough that I don't understand what he says, but I don't need to know. Watching him react is enough entertainment. His eyes slowly come back up to mine, returning their normal smokey amber color.

"You're a tease," he says.

My chest jerks as a laugh tears from my throat. *"I'm* the tease? So, what do you call you telling me you can help me 'self-soothe,' hmm?" I chuckle again, spinning around to continue looking around the cavern. My voice drops low as I try to mimic his. "Mr. *'Come here puppet, let me pull your strings.'*" I look over my shoulder to find him smiling.

"Well, first, I'd never say something like that… It's cheesy. Secondly, I'd never tease you. I make promises. You just choose not to accept my offers… most of the time," he says, licking his lips as if he's remembering the way I tasted on them.

"Hmmm," I say, admiring the pale-green, marble-like stone ground in the cave, but it's untouched by the water that simply sinks between the moss filled cracks. "I wonder," I start, turning around to face Kai. "I want to try something."

"Princess, you don't ever have to ask permission," he says, his words oozing temptation, making my cheeks flush hot at their hidden meaning. "You can try whatever you'd like." He trails a fingertip down my neck and I push against his chest, making him take a step backward.

I don't tell him what I'm doing on purpose. He can reel from his own dirty thoughts. *It sucks to suck.* I get onto my knees in front of him, looking up to meet his lust filled eyes. His mouth snaps shut, making me smirk as I trail my hands down his legs, only to sit back and fold my legs crisscross applesauce on the pale-green, crystalline stone floor. *You wish, asshole.* Reaching behind me, I wet my hands in the water running down the crystal and plant one hand against the floor while the other wraps around the pendant on my necklace. Instantly, I feel the power surge through me, igniting every nerve in my body.

My eyes close and my head tips back as I mumble a spell for intuition, hoping it will tell me when the fuck my spellbinding will wear off so I can be *a real girl*. More importantly, a real fucking witch. I'm tired of being helpless and it's about time to take Hell by the balls and get my life back. They need my power to start the war, so the sooner I have it, the faster I get to go home.

I'm incredibly aware of Kai watching me. His gaze scorches across my skin, but he lets me do the spell without interrupting. My vision floods white, telling me it's working, that the power in this cave is enough to override my lack thereof, or access to. The baby hairs that have pulled loose from my ponytail whip around my face and images flicker before my eyes until I'm no longer mentally in the cave. Much like being submerged in the pool in our bathroom, I'm transported elsewhere while my body remains.

Cool air rushes over my skin, as I sprint through the dark woods, heart pounding profusely in my chest, threatening to break ribs. So hard, I fear it might tear out of my chest. My blood stings as it shoots through my veins, and my lungs heave as I stop and turn around.

Searching the forest, whatever I'm looking for is absent, but I'm somewhere I don't recognize. I curse under my breath and my feet take off toward the way I came. As I break through the brush and trees, I ignore the way it thrashes against my skin, pelting me with twigs that feel like whips. Holding my arms up, I simply swipe them away and continue my pursuit.

I guess that's a plus side to the leather outfit.

Kai comes into view, or rather his backside, but I could identify that ass in a line up if I needed to. He prowls around a man, sword drawn, but the man doesn't seem to care much for the glistening blade that's prepared to strike him dead. He doesn't even flinch when it slices toward him. Instead, he simply lifts his hand and the metal clatters to the ground.

The next blow goes straight to Kai's gut as the man tosses magic at him, sending him sliding backward until his feet catch something hidden in the leaves, allowing him to get his footing. Kai summons a sword made from the green flames, Hell fire, as the man rushes toward him. Dark magic surges through the air as they clash and oily shadows separate themselves from the man's body, circling around them as they battle.

Kai juts forward, but the man dodges again, giving him a smile so wicked, so fearless, that it mocks his entire existence. I watch while the sickening feeling of black magic slides over my skin, making my stomach turn and threaten to lose what little food it holds. Then as Kai spins to try and slice at the man again, the guy's hand flies up to block it with magic before his other slams into Kai's side.

I yelp, hoping that nothing was in it, and it was just a punch. He could survive that. Kai loses focus, turning to look at me just as the man's fingernails morph into long, knife-like claws, they shred through the air, slicing across Kai's chest and his eyes grow big as he falls to the ground.

The scream that tears from me is unlike anything I've ever heard before. It causes goosebumps to rise across my skin, my lungs to burn, and my throat to bleed. The sound disappears from the world around me, turning into a ringing that nearly busts my eardrums. I fall forward and my hands connect with the dirt, igniting it in Hell fire that scorches the ground and engulfs the men in flames.

A blood curdling scream tears through the air but it's short lived and when it stops, the sound doesn't come back, not immediately. I stare at the blackened dirt in front of my face and suck in air as something shatters to pieces within me. I gasp as the power floods every pore, every cell in my body, blinding me with the white-hot pain it causes. My mouth opens, but I can't speak, can't scream. Something deep inside me tingles like a limb that's been bound until the circulation has cut off, has blood flow again. I know without a shadow of a doubt that the spellbinding broke. That the pain is from me becoming whole… but at what cost? And even with the part of me restored, the part of me that had been taken and locked away freed, I know I won't ever feel whole again.

My head snaps up as the trance ends and I gasp like I've been deprived of air. My eyes shoot open wide as I look around, frantically, to find Kai sitting to my right and my body calms in relief.

"Scrying is a bitch, huh?" he asks, and the smirk that spreads across his face brings tears to my eyes as I throw myself forward and hug him. "Woah. Hey. Are you okay? What did you see?"

"I saw when my spell binding breaks… Promise me we won't go through the forest on the way home." I try to calm my quickening heart. "*Promise me*," I demand as his eyes search mine and his hand cups my face. Then, he slowly nods and pulls me against his chest.

"I promise, princess. No forests."

CHAPTER TWENTY-EIGHT

Alice

We don't stay. After seeing Kai possibly die in the vision the crystals gave me, I didn't want to. He doesn't ask again or push for me to tell him what I saw and I'm thankful for it, because experiencing that and feeling the way it will tear my heart out in the future, I'd rather just pretend it never happened.

I wasn't sure if it would work, but it did… and now I wish it hadn't. I had been unsure if I could even draw enough power to combine the angelite and crystalline to get my answers, but I was able to. Which means my spellbinding is loosening, and the ribbons that bind my soul are fraying at the seams and will soon tear. But that vision did more than simply tell me I'd get my powers, it solidified my worst fear.

That I'm going to fall hard enough to never want to leave.

Even worse, I'm going to be the reason this freaking god of a man dies, and I don't want to have that on my conscience. Maybe if I react sooner when it does happen, I might be able to prevent it. Without my magic though? It seems the only time I can do anything is if I'm scared for my life or Kai's. So, how the fuck am I supposed to keep it from happening? Stand there and look pretty? How am I supposed to tell this man that I just saw him die, because of me? I can't. He might kick me out of Hell to fend for myself if he knew I'd be his death sentence just to try and prevent it. All I can do is stay away from fucking forests and pray… although, I don't even know who would answer my prayers with the big guy gone.

I was wearing the same clothes as I am now and it's incredibly hard to believe that in a matter of hours, I'd feel strongly enough to not just weep for the man but burn an entire enchanted forest down. I mean, I'd gladly save him if I needed to, or at least I'd try. I'm not an asshole…but the way my heart bled for him, the way every cell in my body screamed as magic pulled from the ground...*I'm so fucked.*

That's the kind of love that Hercules felt when he faced Cereberus to bring Helen back from the dead. I can't go through that. So, as much as I'd love to break this fucking binding...*Thanks Mom*...I'll be avoiding the forest at all costs.

We ride in silence, up and down green luscious hills until massive, obsidian, stone statues of men covered in moss, come into view. My mouth opens in awe at them, wondering how the hell someone carved something that large. The men are dressed in armor. One holds a sword, another an ax. They look as if they were frozen mid-fight.

"What the hell are those?" I say, and Kai chuckles beside me.

"Those are what's left of the titans. Despite popular belief, God actually made them to try and provide order over the lesser gods he created. Thinking if he made an army of something larger and more powerful, to rule over them like parents, he could gain back control. Instead, Zeus along with the others, turned them to stone. Now, they're nothing more than giant yard ornaments, like garden gnomes."

"Jesus... No wonder God trapped them here. No one should have that kind of power," I say, looking over the land, filled with the stone giants. God forbid one was to fall... We'd be crushed.

"Alice... We do. We have that sort of power. But just because we can use it, doesn't mean we should. Using that much power warps your mind. The difference between us and them is that they flaunted their gift, used it, all of it, siphoning off as much as they could. We use what we need and no more."

"And should we use more?" I ask, remembering the way I blew the fuck out the forest in my vision.

"You won't be able to stop. We're not the only nephilim to be brought into existence, Alice. Granted, they likely aren't alive... There have been others who went rogue, went dark, and my father's spell bound them and threw them into The Realm of Monsters. They were powerless and likely didn't survive a night, but if you could've seen the way it consumed them... It was unlike anything I ever witnessed and entirely irreversible."

Great... How much is too much? Am I going to go dark, now? Wouldn't that be a shitty turn of events. I didn't feel dark... I can't let that vision come true.

"How did your father conquer Hell, anyway? Wouldn't it have been better to create a new world for Hell than getting rid of the gods? Zeus doesn't exactly look like the man anyone wants to mess with. Not if he did this to the titans," I ask.

"After losing The War in Heaven, my father, along with the other angels who fought with him, were banished here. There wasn't a choice in the matter. The void didn't exist yet. So, God said if they survived then they could fix the judgment system and live here, but they wouldn't be welcome in Heaven again. It was a death sentence. By then, the gods were mortal, but they were still here and had their power."

Jesus... How could a God who spoke of love and forgiveness, be so brutal? I play with my horse's mane while we ride, trying to ignore the pained faces on the statues. Kai continues on like he's been through this field thousands of times. Hell, for all I know, he has.

"My father and the other angels managed to trick them into a corner of Hell and bound them to the land with a barrier spell conjured with blood magic. Those who accepted his rule got to stay and were warned not to go, but everyone else went into the prison world and couldn't get out. By the time the war ended, the original gods had all died, and Zeus' son held the throne. Still does. It's who we're meeting today," he says, like the bomb he just dropped meant nothing.

Great... We're meeting the son of the man who used to kidnap pretty girls and force them to carry his babies... That's just fucking fantastic. Please tell me the apple fell *very* far from the tree.

"We're meeting him?" I ask, the nerves slipping over my body, blanketing me in a wave of unease. *"Zeus's son?* If they were mortal years ago, how could he still be king?"

"He's their High King. Just because they were mortal, didn't mean they lost their power. They just grew old. The king's ability is to duplicate another's power by touching them. So, when my father tried to barter peace, to end the war that had killed so many, the man shook his hand and became immortal, like Lucifer. He's been running The Realm of Monsters since," Kai says. I know he's probably told the story a thousand times, but it doesn't make the reality of it any easier to swallow.

Mountains come into view as we crest the last of the rolling hills.

"We're almost there," he says, and I can see the dome of the barrier come into view, cresting in the sky with a light blue hue.

"Have you met the High King before?" I ask and Kai falls silent for a moment, chewing the inside of his cheek.

"Not really. I astral projected in to set up the meeting but that was it."

My eyebrows draw together as I try to connect the dots. "Why are we meeting him? Doesn't he hate us for trapping him in there?"

"Yes, but I want a last resort. Should we start to lose, I'd rather unleash a bunch of monsters with the same enemy, than die... The barrier was brought up with my father's blood, so, I should be able to manipulate it so we can talk formally. The High King wouldn't give me the time of day as a projection. He likely saw it as us still being scared, so I'm willing to do it the old fashion way. I'll create a second barrier for the king and a select few to come into as well as us and a few of our men. He won't be able to step on our side without me escorting him, but his side will be open for him to come through."

We pull the horses to a halt and the men get to work, setting up a barricade. I reach down to brush my hands across the horse's sweaty neck, but Kai's voice draws my attention back to him.

"You don't have to go in if you don't want to," he says. "I won't force you."

"Oh, hell no. You didn't just drag my ass across Hell to sideline me. I'm not leaving your side."

Lord help us all.

If this shit goes south, we're toast, but if it goes well, and should we start to lose the war, we might be able to unite the realms and kick Michael's good for nothing ass.

CHAPTER TWENTY-NINE

Alice

I swing off of my horse and walk up the barrier, feeling the hum from the see-through, domed wall in front of me. The power from it slithers across my skin as I admire its blue hue. Honestly, the color is the only thing that makes it visible, without it, someone could walk in and never know what in the hell they just stepped into. No pun intended.

Kai's men continue dragging barricades into place that they must've prepared ahead of time, as I stare at a group of men on the other side of the barrier, dressed in silver plated armor. Three horsemen carry blood red flags with black lions on them and when they step aside, a man with a crown that looks like it was carved from some sort of bone, steps forward. An unnerving smile slides across his face, like he's sizing me up. He looks to be middle-aged, with blonde hair that falls to his shoulders, but beyond everything else appearing average, something about him seems anything but it. Like his face is a charade, and a monster lurks within his shadow.

Maybe it's just me, because I know who he is, what he's the spawn of.

An arm wraps around my waist and I jump, turning to see Kai and the moment his ocean eyes meet mine; I feel safe. I'm still aware of the High King watching me, and even with the barrier between us, I can feel his magic beneath my skin, crawling around, trying to find secrets. *Weaknesses.*

"Breathe, Alice," Kai says.

I drag in a breath, not realizing my lungs ached for it, and he leads me away from the barrier. Stealing a glance over my shoulder at the king, his lips part as his smile spreads wider, revealing serrated teeth and I gasp. I try to stifle my reaction. Showing any kind of fear when making deals with monsters is undoubtedly a bad idea, but Kai notices and squeezes my hand.

Turning my attention back to him, I see him swallow and when his eyes meet mine again, it's the first time I've ever seen him visibly scared. To someone else, he might seem guarded, but I've spent enough time with him to recognize that he's not comfortable with what comes next. And seeing the man who's supposed to be the biggest, baddest asshole in Hell shrink, makes my heart hammer.

Something doesn't feel right about this.

"Why would Lucifer not be here for this? Wouldn't he want to meet with him on a day that he's in Hell?" I ask. "With how important this is to go right; I would think he wouldn't just delegate a meeting of this stature to you." The color runs out of Kai's face, but he almost recoils as if my comment bit him. I didn't mean it in a bad way, but maybe I should've worded it differently.

Kai huffs out a breath before answering, "he doesn't know. I tried to get him to meet with the king and he shot it down, not wanting to risk it."

My mouth drops open and I stop dead in my tracks. "Don't you think it would be best to listen to the man who has met the prick? Who's faced off with him? This doesn't feel right, Kai. Maybe we shouldn't go."

"Don't you understand, me and you are the only two who will face the ultimate death should Michael win. Everyone else gets to take a nap in The Void, we cease to exist. I'm doing this for us, to give us a chance should things go south. I won't go into this war without a backup plan. My father lost a war and paid the price. I won't, the risk is too high. He only had himself to fight for, and every angel who stood by him did the same when they fell. He risked his own life, and I would've been willing to do the same now, but that changed the moment you got here, princess."

My breath catches in my throat, and I can hear my blood sing at the idea that he cares. I shouldn't enjoy the feeling, but I can't help the way my heart flutters, even if it is over something as sinister as dying. He steps closer, brushing his fingers across my cheek.

"Now, it's not just my soul that will be put through a paper shredder. I won't take the risk if there's another way... You know, when Finn suggested bringing you, I didn't want to. Now, I don't know if I can do this without you beside me. I wouldn't be able to focus." *Because I'm your weakness... I'm your distraction.*

He leans forward to brush his lips against mine and my heart skips a beat. "But if you don't want to go, you can stay out here. I won't force you to do something you don't want to."

But if I don't go, you might be distracted, you might slip up, worried about where I'm at... That's just as bad as me yelping during his battle. "I'm going," I say.

He drops his hand and I start walking toward Finn, who's waving us over, but when he doesn't follow, I turn back to see him staring at the High King through the barrier.

"And just so you know, if I die today, you're still an asshole," I say, seeing the corner of his mouth tip up as he inhales deeply through his nose.

***

The men have set up a canopy with a table under it, ready to serve a king. On the other side, servants wait with plates in hand, since apparently, we're letting the beasts cater... My stomach turns just thinking of what could be under those silver domed covers.

Kai moves toward the barrier and drags his knife across his wrist, splitting the skin until blood seeps through the wound. He doesn't even flinch. Once it begins to roll off the side of his arm, he begins to walk in a half circle around the canopy and connects the blood drip to the barrier on the opposite side of it. I watch as the trail begins to glow blue. His lips move, whispering words but I can't hear them over the hum.

The wind picks up, swirling around the circle until it turns translucent blue and smooths to look like glass. By the time he's done, the wound from his blade has healed and he steps up to the barrier where me and Finn are. His hand sinks through the glass as he pulls three of his men through, before looking at me and Finn. I start to walk forward, prepared to take his hand, but Finns grabs at my wrist.

"Wait. Take this," he says, crouching down to strap a dagger around my thigh. I let him and when he stands back up, he squeezes my hand. "Just in case." His eyes are hollow, watery almost, like he truly doesn't think we'll come back through and that sends a shot of adrenaline through my veins.

I nod and swipe a hand over my mouth before turning to grab Kai's hand. His eyes are dark, but he doesn't say anything, just stares at Finn like he should be ashamed for touching me. They're murderous and I hope he saves some of that energy for the man we're meeting because I do not feel like dying today.

"Down boy," I say as he pulls me through the barrier.

It earns me a snort as he tears his eyes away from the barrier and leads me toward the table. I take a seat, surveying the area. It looks more like we're having a BBQ with fancy china than a war meeting... maybe he really does need a woman's touch. I'm not the Jackie Kennedy type, but I can at least match dinnerware.

He walks over to the wall of the original barrier, and signals for the High King and his three servants to cross through. The man walks up to the glass, holding his hand out and slowly letting it sink inside before he gives it a go.

"Your majesty, thank you for meeting me," Kai says, bowing. Immediately, I get up and curtsey to the man, finding it a bit odd since I don't have a dress. I pretend that I do.

I see we're starting this off as if he has a real crown to stand on... *noted.*

"The pleasure is mine," he says, shooting Kai a smile. "So, you wanted to discuss a treaty for a war, is that right?"

"I'm here on Lucifer's behalf. We're planning to go to war with the archangel, Michael, along with the rest of Heaven, the people who ordered for you to be put into a prison world. I'd like to think we can put our differences aside and fight a common enemy."

"I know who you are, boy. Believe me. I know who all of my enemies are. And the last I checked; your father was the one who put us inside a barrier not whoever this Michael-"

"Acting on Heaven's orders, yes," Kai interrupts, and suddenly, I wish I had popcorn. The tension in the air is so thick I can taste it.

One of the servants puts a plate in front of me and removes the lid. I peer down at something that looks oddly like a squirrel, but with wings and three eyeballs, charbroiled and glazed.

Fuck no. I'm not eating that.

The king is quiet for a moment, before clasping his hands together, making me jump. "Let's talk over food, shall we?" he says, turning his gaze on me. I can feel his eyes slide over my person and I try not to hurl at the intrusion. The smog of testosterone in the room is smothering right now.

"Who do we have here?" the king asks, as a servant pulls out a chair for him. Kai comes around to stand next to me and my nerves almost entirely settle the moment he puts his hand on my back.

"This is my soon to be wife and princess, Alice Whittaker." The king nods to me and I awkwardly do it back, before sitting back down.

"Well, aren't you a beaut. I see my grandson has good taste," he says, and I nearly choke on air.

Grandson? Does this man have any more fucking secret ancestors I should know about? First, he seduces me at a party, only for me to find out that he's Lucifer's son, and now Zeus's great *grandson?* Good heavens.

"Sorry, love. I didn't mean to embarrass you," the king says, sending me a smile that almost appears charming... if you can get past the tooth collection between his lips.

"Oh no, just unexpected is all," I respond, slowly turning my head toward Kai who's staring at me with wide eyes. Did he not know, or did he just not plan on filling me in on that detail?

The king turns his attention to Kai. "How is my sweet Persephone these days? I swear it was impossible to separate her and Lucifer, even if we were at war, but it was nice to know she had a son. I knew the moment I saw you, when we set up this meeting. You look so much like her."

Kai's jaw clenches and his eyes drop to the table. "She's been gone awhile. Michael killed her for having me."

The king's face softens as he leans back in his seat. "Well, that's unfortunate." He's quiet for a moment before popping his eyebrows up. "Another one down."

My mouth drops open. How heartless is this man? That was his daughter, and he just shrugs it off like Kai said he squished a bug. I see Kai's head slowly tip up and his glare is bloodthirsty enough to level a city.

Reaching my hand under the table to set it on his thigh, I hope the gesture will ease the anger boiling beneath his skin. His knuckles turn ghost white as his hands ball into fists on the table and I can hear his teeth grind together, hard enough to chip enamel.

"Oh, don't get upset, kid, she's just a woman. You'll learn that soon enough. One day when you become king, you'll be forced to have a successor and the best way to do that is to have a bunch of children. I don't even know half of my daughter's names, but it's the price you pay when boys are so hard to come by. Persephone was my first child, and she was a good one and taught me a good lesson.

THE DEMON PRINCE

Don't trust a whore. She's the reason we're locked up here. She's the one who tricked me. My own daughter. On the bright side, at least she gave you good genes." The man gestures to himself as if he's the origin of everything pure in the world.

I see the apple didn't even fall from the tree. He's just as wicked as Zeus. There's no negotiating with a man like him.

The room falls silent, and the king removes his plate cover and begins peeling the meat off the small creature with his teeth, then uses the bones as toothpicks. Neither me nor Kai touch our plates. I'm not about to possibly eat something poisonous or that can look at me from every angle while I go to chow town.

"Have you thought about my proposition since I reached out? Are you willing to fight if we loosen the restrictions on you?" Kai asks, bringing the meeting back around to business and away from the personal issues.

"I have. Are you going to eat? Perhaps a toast to new beginnings," the king says.

"No thank you," I say, remembering that I'm not supposed to speak. *Oops.*

"You should really put some meat on your bones, dear. Men like women that won't snap like a twig the moment things get rough…" *Fuck this prick.*

I run my tongue over my teeth before making eye contact with the king and holding it. "Well, I haven't had any complaints, ass–*sir,* and I'm a vegetarian." *That's a lie if I've ever heard one. I'm so far from being a vegetarian it's not even funny.*

"Stubborn too," he turns to look at Kai. "Keep this one around." *Oh, trust me, he will.* "What exactly are you anyway, sweetheart. I can sense your power, but I can't tell its origin."

I look to Kai for permission, but he answers for me. "She's Nephilim from both sides of her lineage. Trust me, you don't want to piss her off. She threw me through a door less than twenty-four hours ago."

The king laughs, leaning back to release a belly chuckle, but when it dies, the look he gives me sends a shiver down my spine. "Well, isn't that something. I'll tell you what, sweetheart, when you're done playing with half breeds, you know where to find me. And maybe if you promise to be really good, I'll let you live, huh?"

"Excuse me?" Kai says, and I can see his teeth grind together with every syllable. His words drip venom while something growls behind me. Craning my head, I find that the man who served me dinner is dropping to all fours and shifting into something a hell of a lot more sinister than Allister's hell hounds. I swallow down the fear in my throat as I reach out for Kai, the air turning stale as the beast's breath dances across my skin. My fingertips grip into his leg, but he is too busy glaring at the king. I can't breathe or take my eyes off it, even as the other server in my peripheral slowly drops on all fours and starts to shift. My eyes bulge and the adrenaline shooting through my veins causes my body to shake.

"Oh, come on, son. You didn't really believe that I'd wage war with you, right? Or maybe you did. How else would you have been stupid enough to open up a hole in the barrier."

CHAPTER THIRTY

Kai

The blood drains from my face. How could I be so stupid? How could my dad not tell me that the High King is *blood?* God, I just hope he doesn't realize he can get through the barrier... Since he's part of my bloodline, he'll be able to cross without my help and if that happens, we're all screwed.

I can handle everything else, but that.

A growl sounds behind me, and I look over to find Alice, staring into the eyes of a creature I've never seen before. My fists clench and my knuckles flash white as I watch the other two servants morph. The sickening sound of bones cracking hits my ears as their body shifts until what it becomes resembles nothing of a man. Teeth cut through their gums like canines but sharp enough to tear through limbs; large enough to sever bones with one bite.

These were creatures that should've never been created, and they put our hell hounds to shame. Looking over my shoulder, I signal to Finn, and he catches it, and starts barking orders, readying the men for battle. Whatever we do, the king can't leave this boundary. The dogs, I could give a shit less about. We can take care of them, though it might take some work, but the king? I have no interest in adding another war to my list.

The men who came with us have their swords drawn, ready to engage as they step between us and the wolves at our back. I shove Alice backward, sending her chair falling to the floor as I unsheathe my sword and slice it toward the creature. It dodges, then circles us, snarling and snapping at the air, while the two behind me engage with my men.

The king throws his napkin on top of his plate. "You see... Nephilim are powerless within this bubble, your words, not mine. I'm not sure how exactly you managed to add that party gift to the boundary, but it works in my favor. Being Nephilim, you both are powerless too, but my dire wolves, not so much. They're going to enjoy this," he says, turning his attention to Alice who peaks up above the table on the ground. He lets his eyes wander too long and I can feel the intent behind them. It makes me want to tear his fucking throat out and my own flash black in warning. "Don't worry, love. I won't let them kill you. I have something special in mind for you," he says.

The fuck you do.

The king winks at her and I lose it. My sword swings, stopping just as the point touches his throat. "Call off your dogs," I demand, "Look at her again and I'll break every bone in your body and feed what's left of you to your pets."

He laughs and it causes my blood to boil, turning my ears hot. "Strong threats for a man who can't keep them. Bit of grandfatherly advice? Love is weakness. She will be the reason you fail. You can't protect her and yourself, son. You should be thanking me for teaching you that lesson," the king says, walking into my blade. It sinks into his being, but he doesn't bleed. My breath catches in my throat.

He's astral projecting…

It's both good and bad news all wrapped into one asshole burrito.

Good, because it means he can't leave the boundary and the only enemies I need to worry about are his wolves. Bad, because I don't know what his plan is and that could prove to be lethal.

I flip around as the wolf who's been stalking us lunges toward me and I slice the blade across its stomach and heave the creature through the air until it bounces off the boundary wall. Turning my attention toward Alice, I help her to her feet, ready to throw her outside with Finn, but the wolf gets up and continues his pursuit as if a chunk of its stomach isn't hanging on by a thread and its entrails aren't dragging across the ground.

The sound of metal scrapping metal comes from behind me as the men fight off the other two beasts. The third prowls in front of me as the king stands by, watching his plan unfold.

"You see, son. I might not be able to cross through to your side alone, but I can use you as bait to get your father to lower the shield. And tell me, do you think he'd hand over the crown for his only son? I do," he says, laughing. "So, my beasts will either kill you, and the shield you hold will fall, leaving a breach in the barrier, or we can take you prisoner and barter your life to have it brought down. Either way I win…" he pauses, letting the degree of how much I fucked up sink in. "But you bringing a woman, something we're in drastically short supply of these days; you trying to withhold information regarding what she really is… That was just pure stupidity. I can smell a witch a mile away. She might be Nephilim, but she can pull magic from more than just God's soul, and that… I'll be keeping. You really did me a favor by popping in here, boy."

His eyes flare wide as if he's excited about taking everything from me and it makes my heart thump harder in my chest. I need to get Alice out of here. *Now.* Jerking my eyes to where she sat seconds ago, I find nothing but an empty wooden chair, torn by claws as if the beast has stepped over it somehow without me noticing.

I took my eyes off her for two seconds…

My head swivels until I find Alice, backing away as the beast that stalks toward her on the other side of the table. She must've crawled under. Only now, she's two steps away from the boundary, the open side and if she crosses it, it will be a bitch to get her out. The way the spell was written, the moment you left the bubble, you can't get back in unless it's recast, and it can only be recast from the outside, assuming it's still strong enough to be breached again. If it's not, the entire fucking thing could crash down, unleashing the monsters it contains on the realms of Hell.

Fuck. I shouldn't have brought her. I shouldn't have risked this...

I turn back toward the king, but he's gone. He pulled himself out of the projection and left us to our fate. The air fills with the sound of metal clashing, teeth snapping, and primal snarls as the creature in front of Alice rolls its lips back, showing off its pearly whites. There's no time to think things through, hell, I can't even breathe. Screams flood the air as one of the men behind me is ripped apart. His head rolls across the grass at my feet and still, I can't take my eyes away from Alice.

Come on. Use your magic.

We might not be able to use our Nephilim side, but she's a witch. She can cast, but God, she has to try. All she needs to do is give me a window, just enough time to get her to our side and shove her through. That's it.

She turns to look behind her, her body arching away from the hum of the barrier. *Their* side of the barrier. *His side...* I could try and run, to rush the creature, but I'll never make it in time. I can't even teleport in here and it won't be long until her pretty throat is between its jaws, and it carries her off to only God knows where.

Lifting my sword over my head, I do the only thing I can. I pop the bubble and the walls fall as power floods my system. My sword erupts in hellfire, the element in which my father was forged in, and I throw it with everything I have. It stabs into the creature just as it lunges forward. Blood spews from its mouth and splatters across her face as it falls to the ground, but not before its head slams into her chest, knocking her through the translucent blue wall, and trapping her inside of the Realm of Monsters. *Fuck me.*

The last two of my men scream as flesh is torn from bone and I turn, as I hold my hand out, and one of the discarded swords on the ground flies into it. It feels light in my palm, telling me I'll have to swing that much harder. Body parts clad in armor rain from the air as the two wolves tear through limbs of the two men, who are long dead. As if sensing me, the wolves stop, the men between their teeth no longer providing the chase they crave.

I flip the sword in my hand, then spin to gain momentum and slash through one's carotid as it aims for my throat. The wolf recoils, coming after me again even as blood pours from the wound. My eyes go black as the demon in me comes out to play. My fingers blacken as my nails turn thicker and sharpen into blades within seconds.

The second the beast lunges, my free hand grips it by its open jaw, throwing my shoulder and slamming its bloodied body to the ground. I shove my sword through its neck, slicing through what meat remains. My eyes lock with the last one as it circles me, marking me as its prey. It wishes.

Finn and the other man close in, barricading it against the barrier, swords in hand and ready to attack should it try and run. It won't. It lives for this, and wolves are too prideful to back down from a fight. It's a predator, but so the fuck am I.

The air falls silent with the exception of our breathing and the erratic thumping against the barrier that surrounds The Realm of Monsters as Alice slams herself into it, hoping to cross, hoping to overpower the blue veil that separates us. She won't. No one can. The only way she's getting back across is by me poking another hole. She's just going to have to be patient.

Lurking around me, the wolf bares its teeth, threatening me before it snaps, testing my instincts. When it finally makes the first move, I crouch below it, flipping around to slice through the creature from below, splitting it into two. Blood rains, spraying across the ground and me as metal tears through flesh.

My chest heaves as I try to catch my breath, standing up wiping a hand down my face, which only seems to spread the crimson mess more. The sound of Alice beating against the barrier brings me back to the present and I don't waste a second before walking up to it and she stills.

"Are you okay?" I ask, my eyes searching over her and looking for any injuries she may have sustained, finding nothing notable. Satisfied, I bring my gaze up to search the clearing she's standing in, a forest wall. Nothing moves. She's alone.

"Alice," I say. She still hasn't answered me. Tears stream down her cheeks and air rips in and out of her lungs as she tries to calm herself. "Alice, look at me. Breathe." Her eyes find mine the moment they do, she drags in a deep breath through her nose and closes her eyes for a second. "Are you okay?"

She swallows down a sob. "I think so," she says calmly. Then her disposition changes on the drop of a dime and her eyes flick black as flames lick from the tresses of her hair and across the skin of her arms and hands.

I suck in a breath, physically stopping myself from stepping back. My eyes go wide as they hover over her figure. *Jesus Christ...* Is that how she looked when she fought the serpent man? *Shit.* I'd have run, too. "If being trapped in a fucking *prison world* is your version of okay!" she snaps, pacing back and forth along the barrier before taking a couple steps back and charging it again. Her body slams into the translucent wall, turning where she hit red.

Rushing over before she does it again, I say, "We will get you out, but you have to be patient."

"Patient?!" she yells, the flames glowing brighter. "You're the reason I'm trapped in this fucking mess to begin with. So, I'm sorry for not trusting a damn word that comes out of your mouth right now." She slams into it again and the spot gets bigger.

"You have to stop! If you slam into it again, it might break the barrier. It's already weakened from the bubble. It won't hold up for much longer if you keep assaulting it. Hate me, if you want. But neither of us want to unleash a prison world on Hell."

"I couldn't give a shit less about Hell right now—" she starts to protest gearing up to hit it again.

"You're not hearing me, Alice. There are families here. There aren't just demons here… There are creatures who haven't ever hurt anyone, and you'd be unleashing a king and monsters that would slaughter them without blinking. We're different, Alice. *Please.*"

CHAPTER THIRTY-ONE

Alice

Fuck him. Fuck Hell. Fuck everything about my situation right now.

I blow out the breath in my lungs through my nose, smirking as it rolls out as smoke. "Fine. But make it quick," I say and Kai nods awkwardly, unable to meet my eyes.

He turns to the men, looking over Finn whose mouth hangs open, staring at me. "You heard the woman. Let's test the barrier so we can get her out. Move."

I fold my arms across my chest, taking in the area around me. Tall grass brushes against my legs, but the barrier is only about twenty feet to the sparse wood line. It's not a forest per se, not like my vision, but it's definitely not a damn field. It makes my stomach turn just thinking about the vision.

There's a rock patch that sits about halfway between, so I head toward it, taking a seat on the black obsidian stone and bury my face in my hands. I should've stayed at the keep. I should've said "No, I don't want to join you in your fucking bubble." But no. I volunteered as tribute.

This month just keeps getting worse. I've been here… What? Two weeks, now? In that time, I was chased by a hell hound, brought to Hell, almost raped by a snake man, Viagra'd myself having drank spiked juice, and now, locked inside of a prison world? Can it get worse? I shouldn't ask that question… According to my vision, it definitely can and as much as I want to wrap my hands around Kai's throat right now, I don't want the fucker to die.

I close my eyes, running a hand down my face and when I open them, Kai is staring in my direction, frozen on the other side of the barrier. His eyes are wide with terror as they slide from looking above my head to meet my gaze.

What? Did I grow horns now? Who knows what's going to happen at this rate. I already can set myself on fire and he apparently has claws. Am I going to get a tail next?

I reach my hand on top of my head, finding nothing unusual. My shoulders shrug in a silent 'what are you looking at?' His finger extends pointing at something at the same time I feel something breathe against my back.

My blood runs cold and the breath catches in my lungs as I slowly crane my head around to peer behind me. Teeth meet my eyes, and I don't dare to turn farther until I launch myself off the rock and spin to face the beast that I don't even know how to begin describing.

You've gotta be kidding me.

It has horns like a rhino, a mouth full of blade-like teeth, and a body like a lion but bigger and a fluffy tail. It almost seems playful, past the blood red eyes that stalk me and the crimson-tinged, porcelain teeth. The jury is out on what possibly stained them bad boys... not really. I know *exactly* what stained them. As it lowers and cocks its head. Even on all fours, it's easily three times as tall as me.

It must've been drawn by the sound of me hitting the barrier... Fuck. That was a bad idea.

"Good kitty..." I hold my hands out, palms parallel to the ground and slowly start to step back. "I promise you don't want to eat me," I say, trying to sweet talk it. That's pretty pointless considering its an animal and they can't understand shit. "I don't taste like catnip... probably really burnt, charred chicken at best."

It hunkers down like a cat ready to pounce and its pupils blow as it's butt swishes in the air. Okay, cat. Maybe it likes red lights too. I swallow the nerves that make me want to scream and take a deep breath, continuing to circle toward the forest. There's no way I'd make it far in the open. That's for sure.

Trying to steady my magic, which is almost futile. I try to make a light ball in my hand, thinking maybe if I throw it, it will follow it, versus chase me when I run. Lightning sparks at my fingers and it turns its head the other way, watching it. Slowly, as sweat breaks out on my forehead, the lightning forms into a small ball the size of a marble.

I toss it and its eyes follow it for a second and I hear Kai cuss on the other side of the barrier. His men start hitting the barrier with their hands, trying to draw the creature toward them, but it's fixated.

Slowly, I breathe in. Maybe I have wings... I worry my lip between my teeth and dare shrugging my shoulders like he did when he whipped them out, and the creature jumps. Nothing happens, so I try once more and it causes its tail to swish, like it thinks we're playing a game.

I steal a look at Kai, knowing it's about to be my last and then bolt. My boots fly across the ground and my heart races as I leap over obstacles that lay on the forest floor. The ground shakes beneath my feet from the beast bounding behind me, no longer trying to be stealthy. I duck under a branch and scan for anything to hide in... because that worked so well last time. But what choice do I have? I can't run forever, and something tells me the creature has more stamina than I do.

My heart leaps in my throat as it starts to catch up to me, and I feel the air disturb as it snaps. I jump, changing direction and causing it to scrap against the ground as it slides on its side. It barely slows the creature though.

I gulp air with every breath as my lungs heave and my airways tighten and sting from the onslaught. Adrenaline floods my body, overcoming the fear of being eaten so that I can push harder and run faster until my skin feels like it's on fire and it reddens from the pulse forcing its way through my veins.

The beat of my heart smothers out the sound around me, hammering in my ears so when I finally do hear the sound of crashing water, it's too late. I break through the trees and the ground is ripped out from beneath my feet as I sprint over the edge of a cliff. Suddenly, I'm weightless and the panic sets in as I fall. I can't even see the bottom, I'm so high up, that the clouds obscure the land below from view.

A scream tears through my throat, echoing off the stone cliff and through the valley below. My limbs flail, reaching for something, anything, but only grab air. I close my eyes, unable to open them against the rush of wind whipping my hair around my face, and my stomach flips, lurching into my throat and cutting off my scream.

My body rolls in the open air, falling faster as I turn on my stomach. I try to breathe, but the air is rushing too fast for me to suck in a breath let alone open my eyes again. It's for the better. I don't want to see the ground coming. Then something snatches me, linking around my stomach and the force causes me to fold in half. My eyes shoot wide as I glide over the valley below. I jerk my head up and back until amber eyes meet mine.

The smirk on his face... I hate it, yet I want to kiss it right now.

Kai's wings slice through the air, slowly circling above the water, lowering us down to the valley below, until something slams against him, and he drops me. I point my toes, hitting the water hard. It feels like I hit a brick wall as pain erupts through my body and the lights go out.

When I wake up, I'm underwater but I'm not. The necklace around my neck transports my mind somewhere else. Home. I see Elise and Pops eating dinner, smiling at one another as if I never left and it tears holes through my heart. I should be happy for them. I should be glad that they're not complete wrecks, especially since I won't be returning home anytime soon, if at all. Yet, it pains me to know life is just carrying on without me.

My lungs burn, needing air and threaten to implode as I yank the necklace off of my neck, breaking the chain and the world around me returns. The obsidian water blacks out the view around me beyond the light reflecting at the top of the water above. I scrounge for it, kicking my legs and wading my arms to rise toward the top. My chest is so tight, I fear it might collapse, but when my head crests the water, I drag in a breath and relief floods over me.

My eyes search through the misty fog that hovers over the water, spotting what looks like the coast of the lake in the distance. I swim toward it and the closer I get, the more the rocky land comes into view. Something black and decent sized, disturbs the rippling edge of the water, bouncing off the shore.

What the fuck is that?

I wade toward it, as the water becomes shallow, and I regret wearing this damn leather outfit. If I thought swamp ass was an issue, imagine leather rubbing against damp skin *everywhere*. Up to and including my lady bits.

As I approach the mass, more characteristics come into view, including shredded feathers and torn flesh of wings.

THE DEMON PRINCE

CHAPTER THIRTY-TWO

Alice

"No," the single word leaves my trembling lips. "No, no, no, no," I say, no longer wading, but running through the water toward the mass.

Tears leak from my eyes and my heart quivers like someone has put it into a vice grip. I can't breathe. I've used up all the air and I can't convince my lungs to inflate again. It hurts too much.

Right before I reach it, I trip in the water and fall to my knees, catching myself with my hands and not caring about the sharp rocks that rip holes in my skin and shoot pain through my knees and palms. I crawl toward Kai, hesitating to touch him. His wing is clearly broken in more ways than one and if he's alive I don't want to hurt him more.

My hands shake as I bite back the sob that pushes up my throat, and slowly, I lift the wing, holding it together as I roll him on his back. It's dead weight, and that fact alone allows the sob to tear free as my fingers press against his pulse, searching for any sign of life, but unable to find one.

I let my hands roam, looking for anything else that might be broken or hurt beyond his wing. There's a decent amount of blood that trickles from a gash on his head, but it doesn't look terrible. Not like something his ability to heal won't fix, but why isn't he breathing? Why doesn't he have a pulse?

Climbing on top of him, I try to shake him awake, begging and pleading that it's because I've never had to take someone's pulse before and not the obvious reason... We're immortal. We're not supposed to be able to die, but I don't know where the line is drawn. Obviously, angels and demons *can* die at some point, since my father did, but the circumstances are unclear. What determines it?

What if this barrier makes us mortal? The gods still had their magic, their abilities... it wouldn't explain how the king has managed to get around it and live as long as he has, since his immortality comes from what he absorbed from Lucifer, but it would at least explain why Kai isn't breathing right now.

"You're not dying today. You can't leave me here," I say, unzipping my leather jacket and peeling it off the wet shirt I have underneath. I toss it to the side and start CPR. I don't know how long I go for, flipping between pumping my palms against his chest and breathing air into his lungs, but it's enough that I know it's not going to work. He needs a freaking hospital. *A doctor.* Not some pathetic witch who can't control her own magic, let alone protect herself. If I wasn't this way, if I wasn't spellbound, maybe he would be breathing right now. He wouldn't have had to dart into a prison world to save me.

I slam my fists into his chest. "Wake up, dammit!" I scream, repeating my assault between every insult. "You cocky… pain in my ass… son of a *fucking* bitch. Wake up!"

Wiping at the tears that slide down my face with the palm of my hand, my stomach flips as I lean forward, resting my forehead against his chest. My body shakes and goes weak. My muscles stop working and my heart feels heavy, like an anvil in my chest. I gasp for the air my lungs crave as sobs continue to tear through my body, leaving me shattered and raw.

I press my lips together, trying to still them and take a deep breath. Abs ache from crying, my body is battered from being hurled over a freaking cliff, and my legs feel like Jell-O from running but none of that compares to the void that has opened inside my chest. It's numbing, lonely, but even if it's not a physical pain, it hurts more than anything else.

"I hate you so much," I say, my voice barely a whisper. "I hate that you made me care. You kidnapped me and here I am, bawling my eyes out over you… This can't be it. This isn't how you were supposed to die…"

Sitting up and closing my eyes, I hold my hands out, trying to calm myself. There's only one thing I haven't tried… I draw power to me and my fingertips tingle as electricity flicks over them. The air crackles around us, making the hair on my arms stand on end and the buzz against my skin grows stronger. The world around me is shrouded in a veil of silence.

For the first time, I'm in complete control over my magic, my witch-based magic. It's not God-like, but it might be enough to zap him with and restart his heart.

This has to work…

Opening my eyes, I look to each of my outstretched hands, watching the capillary like tendrils of purple lightning move, circling, stretching, and growing bigger by the second. The air around me starts to pick up and my eyes flutter closed. I drag in a deep breath and move my hands slowly in front of me and turn my palms down.

"Clear," I say, mimicking the TV shows I've watched where they've shocked the patient back to life. *Here goes nothing.*

"Please don't," I hear a voice say and my eyes snap open as I look down at the man beneath me. His eyes are wide and flick back and forth between each of my hands as they hover over his chest, inches away from making contact.

The air dies down and I choke out a laugh, disbanding the electricity. The air feels staticky and frizzes my hair when I do, and I throw myself down and hug against his chest.

"I thought you died," I say, as the tears break through once more.

"So, you were going to Frankenstein me like a mad scientist?" He groans as I sit up and I climb off of him, helping him sit up.

"I was going to do what it took to restart your cold dead heart." I glare at him, but it's hard not to smile when he rubs at his chest.

"Jesus, woman, how many times did you zap me?"

"I hadn't yet," I say, leaving out the part on how I thrashed my fists at him, attempting to reboot his ticker before resorting to magic. He winces as he tries to adjust. "Your wing..."

"It'll heal. Surprisingly, this isn't the first time I've broken it, but it is the first that I almost had it gnawed off. That thing that was chasing you followed us over the cliff," he says, closing his eyes to try and ignore the pain.

"Why did you come in? You said we can't open the barrier from inside, right?"

"You and your questions..." He pinches the bridge of his nose before answering, "What was I supposed to do, Alice? Allow you to get eaten?" he snaps.

I flinch at his words. Hating the way he says my name. It's been one of my favorite words to roll off his tongue, but now, with the anger behind it, it just doesn't sit right. My eyes fall and I turn away from him, hugging my knees to my chest.

He sighs but I don't look at him.

"That's not how I meant it," he says, reaching his arm out to turn my face to look at him. "I meant that I wasn't going to make you survive here alone. Finn is going to get my dad and he'll be able to open a hole for us." His amber eyes search over my face as his thumb strokes.

His hand drops and we sit for a moment in silence.

"So, do you cry like that for all of the guys you like?"

My face falls and I jerk my head toward him to glare. "Just the assholes who kidnap me."

"We didn't kidnap you. Your parents gave you away. Huge difference," he argues as something in his wing pops, making him wince.

CHAPTER THIRTY-THREE

Kai

It takes almost an hour for my wing to heal enough for me to hide them, but finally, I'm able to pull them back inside and the pain eases a bit. It won't be long before it's completely back to normal, but dear lord, I don't want to ever take on that thing again. The kitty had claws, and they fucking hurt.

"Are we ever going to talk about what you saw in that cave?" I ask, looking around to the thick woods that surrounds us and remembering her warning. "You said no forests, but it looks like we won't have much of a choice. It's getting dark and we're going to have to find somewhere to hide out. I don't want to find out what lurks around here at night."

She sits a couple feet away, skipping some of the flat stones across the water. Her jaw flexes and she swallows hard. "I saw some man and you fighting,

He had shadows that peeled away from his body, and he hurt you…" she trails off, staring at the water like she's gathering the courage to say what happened next. "My spell binding broke, and I burnt the forest down with you in it."

I don't know how to take it. My mouth gapes and snaps shut repeatedly while I try to find the words to respond. We knew her binding would break at some point, but we didn't expect it to happen this fast.

"You sure what you saw was his shadows?" I ask, picking at one of my feathers that came out when I crash landed.

"Yeah, I'm sure. His hands became like yours almost… Sort of and he cut through your side."

Of course, he'd show up.

"That's Pan and he's definitely here. We shoved him in a long time ago."

"Like Peter Pan? You're kidding, right?" she asks, turning toward me.

"Nope. Before my dad came here, there wasn't a system like we have in Limbo, where souls are either stored, sent to Heaven or reincarnated. They just wandered and if they went into the forest and Pan found them, he would turn them into children poltergeists that would obey his every request."

"At least he doesn't have his child army then," she says, skipping another rock.

"I wouldn't be so sure. We don't collect the souls here. There's a chance that he's been and if that's the case, he's dangerous," I scrub a hand over my face as it gets darker around us. Only one moon left... We need to find a place to hide. "Come on, princess."

I stand and hold my hand out toward her. She takes it and for a moment I revel in how dainty it feels in mine.

"Where are we going?" she asks.

"We'll know when we find it, but we can't stay here."

"Wouldn't it be better to stay on the bank? We have more visibility here and when your father comes—" she counters, but I cut her off.

"This isn't wonderland, Alice. There won't be a search party. My father will open a break to let us out, but we have to get back up there," I point to the top of the waterfall, "by ourselves. There's no way up that doesn't involve the forest."

"You can fly us up."

"No, I can't. My wing will heal but not before it gets dark."

Her nostrils flare as she stomps toward me. "Fine, your *majesty*. Let's go into the woods that have your death written all over them," she says, causing my teeth to grind. *This woman… I swear.*

"You don't know that." I try to reach forward and reclaim her hand, but she snatches it away and storms past me.

"I know enough," she yells back.

"Would it kill you to not stalk away from me? You need to stay close."

Alice answers me with the middle finger as she steps into the woods. I grumble and jog to catch up with her. My wing might not hurt while it's inside, but it doesn't mean the rest of my body doesn't ache from slamming into and skidding across the shallow water like one of her stones.

We walk in silence for what feels like forever, climbing up the mountain toward the top of the waterfall. Something flutters beneath the leaves on the ground above us and I snatch Alice, holding her to my chest and my hand over her mouth as I back against one of the thicker trees.

Breathing. Between the climb and not knowing what the fuck is coming out of the ground, it seems futile. I close my eyes for a moment, gathering the nerve to look around the tree to see if I can see anything. When I do, the creature is closer than expected and I jerk back, picking up Alice and slowly, quietly, sidestep around the tree to not tip off the monster that lurks on the other side of it.

From what I saw, it had looked like a giant spider, judging by its long legs and eyes. However, instead of being fuzzy, its skin is almost metallic. I'm thankful that Alice chose to not be stubborn and went along with it. Had she fought, it would've sniffed us out. I peer around the other side of the tree and see that it's carried on, none the wiser to us being here. My hand releases Alice's mouth and I set her down.

"What was that?" she whispers, peaking around the tree before lurking back against the bark beside me. *"Holy shit."* Her chest swells as she takes a deep breath and her hand presses against her heart, as if she can settle it with a touch.

"Hence why I wanted to find a place to hide out. So that we don't bump into things like that."

Her head tips as she scowls at me. "Don't do that."

"Do what?" I ask as we start walking again.

"Say I told you so. You don't know if the water would've been safe or not."

"Alice. They're creatures, not ghosts. Things need water to survive. Where do you think they're going to find it? The watering hole, aka the waterfall. Now, come on, I think I see a cave up ahead."

She groans, ending the dramatic expression with a rattled scoff. "Can you not be an asshole right now?"

"I don't know. Can you not be so stubborn for a minute? I'm trying to get us out of here in one piece. You didn't grow up here. You have no idea what you're up against. Maybe instead of questioning my judgment on how to survive in my homeland, you could say a simple thank you."

The leaves behind me stop crunching and I turn around to see her standing with her arms crossed over her chest. "I'm sorry. Maybe I should just trust the judgment of the man who decided to meet with the most ruthless king in history. That sounds like a smart move."

I inhale until my lungs ache, shoving the need to put her in her place down deep. Instead, I keep walking, but she in turn, keeps pushing.

"And I could say thank you for catching your fiancé and not letting me fall to certain death. But it's just that I didn't exactly choose to come here to Hell, did I? I was forced to leave my world where the only thing I had to worry about was the guy in my Organic Chem class not knowing who I am. You brought me here. You told me I had to marry you. You promised to protect me in exchange for my compliance and I agreed. Yet you allowed me to get trapped in this god forsaken hell hole. So, am I thankful to not be dead? Yes. Am I going to get to my knees and show my appreciation for your oh, so chivalrous act? Fuck no, sir."

She stomps past me, and I reach out, grab her hand, yanking her backward and she spins to face me. Her face lands an inch from mine. Her eyes promise to melt me alive, but she's not the only one that can touch hell fire and survive. My jaw ticks as it flexes but she refuses to back down, pushing closer until our noses almost touch.

"Woman, you better keep your fucking voice down. You want to be mad at me? Fine, but I'm not going to let you get us killed."

"Fuck you," she whispers. At least she lowered her voice.

I turn my head, grabbing the bottom half of my face and chuckling at the balls this woman has.

"Do you think this is a game? We could die here. We're immortal to most things. We don't age and can heal, but getting eaten and digested? We can't survive that and trust me, there are plenty of things that would love a taste of you. Including this realm's King." Her eyes still glare into me. "Or maybe you want him to find you, maybe you want to be used and abused by him, is that it?"

As soon as the words leave my lips, I regret them. I said it because I wanted her to feel how infuriated she's made me, but the hurt that reflects in her eyes makes my chest squeeze tight.

"Screw. You," she says, drawing out the syllables.

I bend, clamping my hands around her waist and throwing her over my shoulder. Kicking and screaming. I wave my hand and silence her, which only makes her kick harder, but at least it won't draw every monster in earshot to us. I make my way to the cave in sight and by the time we reach it, she's given up, hanging limp as I haul her off to a cave of all things.

I summon my sword, the green flames licking off the blade and lighting the hollowed tunnel of the cave. Raising the blade to put the hilt against my mouth, I blow and a green ball of light shoots through the cave. I follow it as it lights the way and find it to be empty. It's not shallow, but there's no exit out the back. It's more of a long hallway made from red clay and crystals that opens into a small cavern.

It will work. Whispering in Enochian, I place a spell on the mouth of the cave, sealing it off to the outside world. We'll be safe here. I set Alice down and she glares at me, sitting on the cave floor, arms crossed.

"Stay here. I'm going to get wood for a fire."

"Don't hurry back," she chimes and every muscle in my body flexes and my jaw grinds so hard it hurts.

CHAPTER THIRTY-FOUR
Alice

"I'm starving," I say, leaning against the cave wall.

We've been in here for most of the night and neither of us dare to sleep. Kai did make a fire, and I'm thankful, since the temp drops to the point that goosebumps refuse to leave my arms, regardless of how close I get to the fire. My teeth chatter and my breath fogs as soon as it leaves my lips.

"We'll find food when the sun comes up. You should get some sleep," he says, leaning against the opposite side of the cave.

He can keep his ass over there. As much as snuggling could help with the cold, we still haven't fully resolved our argument. I don't want to die here… Yet, in this part of Hell, everything wants to kill me or use me. Hell, even Kai and Lucifer do, to an extent. They're using me to fight for their cause.

They need the power I'll wield after the binding breaks or else Lucifer would've never made a deal with my mother.

Michael and the angels want me dead for simply being born, and the two people who brought me into this world get to just skip around Heaven with their halos, without a care in the world. My existence puts the little bit of family I have at risk.

"Penny for your thoughts," Kai says, and I roll my eyes hard enough to crack an eye socket. "Or not. Jeesh."

"Earlier, in the woods, I was thinking that maybe I should stay here… Being here keeps everyone safe. Heaven doesn't know you're not in the void. They only know I exist, and Michael is still looking for me. Regardless of whether you stole me, or not, I would've had to leave home to keep my family safe, but if I stay in Hell Hold and Michael finds out, they're going to come for you too. They'd never dare look for me here." My eyes drop to the cave floor between my folding knees that my arms are propped on. "So, earlier I was trying to figure out how I'd survive here when you got back…"

"And you were thinking about submitting to the king…" he says, and the malice in his tone is enough to make me shiver to the bone. Kai doesn't look at me, but the twig he's picking at in his hand breaks.

"Yeah. Maybe then, I can convince him to join your war," I say.

His laugh is intoxicating and yet sends a fresh wave of chills through my body. "You're not… No. It's not an option."

"Why? Because he's your grandfather? Just out of curiosity, are there any other family members I should know about?"

"I didn't know either. If I had, I would've never put that bubble up. Had he not been projecting inside; he could've walked out of it. It's blood magic and just as I can manipulate my father's boundary —"

"He could've yours since you're his grandson," I say, finishing his sentence.

Kai nods. "I get it if you're still not sold on the idea of being with me, but I'm not going to hand you over to a monster, either. The man has children constantly, trying to produce an heir, but he only ever has girls. So, he hosts a gauntlet every time one of them comes of age and gives them away to whoever the winner is. When my father landed here, he met my mother and fell in love. He played the gauntlet and won it to save her. I just didn't realize her father and the High King were the same person."

"That's fucked up," I say, curling against the cave wall.

"Am I that bad that you'd rather be with a man like that?" His words slice through to my core, leaving me bloodied and broken.

"No, you're not, but if I stay with you, I'll never go home. Not to mention the risk of Michael finding out and killing you, too." His mouth quips up, no doubt realizing that I'm worried about him. "Oh yeah, and the fact that it seems like I distract you every time things come down to the wire."

"Is that what you want? To go home after the war?" he asks, ignoring everything else I just said, as if me going back to Earth is the worst of our worries right now.

I hesitate a moment before nodding. "I do. I want a normal life and to live in my world with my family. I'll never have that here, the closer I get to you... I'm worried I won't be able to get myself to leave."

He drags in a breath and relaxes into the cave wall, his eyes skimming over me. "Is that what changed today? You seemed off before we left the keep and it just kind of got worse from there." I nod, unable to bring myself to meet his eyes. "If that's what you want, when the war is over and it's safe, I'll escort you back to Earth myself. Regardless of what you think of me, I do want you to be happy, Alice."

My stomach grumbles and my hand settles on top of it. I look to the neon yellow mushrooms that peek out of the cracks in the cave walls and as much as they gross me out, they look really good right now.

"Do you think those are poisonous?" I ask. Honestly, it doesn't matter if they are or not. I still want them. If they're poisonous, I'll keep them just in case it looks like I'm about to die a gruesome death, and if not? Well, come to momma.

"Yes. Very. We have them in Hell Hold too," he says, throwing the twig in his hand into the fire.

"Perfect," I say sarcastically, tearing off a piece of my shirt and picking a couple, wrapping them in the fabric.

"What are you doing?" Kai asks.

"Saving them. I'd rather be poisoned than have some fucking monster eat me alive and use my bones for toothpicks. So, should shit hit the fan…"

"You are not eating poison mushrooms, Alice," he says. As if he could stop me should that moment come.

I hold the wrapped mushrooms in my hand and stop to look at his glare that makes me want to shrivel up and hide in the cracks of the cave. "So, you'd rather me die horrifically? We're not exactly at the top of the food chain here, Kai."

"But we're not at the bottom either."

"How? Your father has to open the boundary and as far as I can see, no one knows where we are or whether we're alive or not. So, how long do you think Lucifer is going to wait for us to get back to where your men are camped before he believes we're dead? A day? Two?"

He's quiet and stares at the flames of the fire. I knew he couldn't answer the question when I asked it. "Great. So, should I grab extra for you, too?"

Kai shoots me a venomous look, his eyes growing dark, but not quite demonic. His nostrils flare as his jaw clenches. "Drop the fucking mushroom, Alice," he seethes, standing to walk across the cave and yank me up from the ground to look him in the eye.

"No. I don't want to be eaten alive. I'd much rather be dead first. So, no. It's my back up plan. You should know all about those," I mock him, referring to his decision to open the bubble in the first place.

He tries to pry it out of my hands. "Let go of me," I command, but when he doesn't stop, I reel back and smack him across his cheek. His head turns to the right, and his body freezes.

Fuck... That was not a good idea. I should apologize. I should beg, but my pride boils inside of me, preventing me from doing so.

A hand shoots out and wraps around my throat, dragging me to him so he can stare through my eyes, straight into my soul. His chest rises as he inhales deeply, likely trying to talk himself out of killing me right about now.

"Drop the mushroom," he says again, his eyes so dark, they put the obsidian stone to shame. The veins around his eyes raise, wiggling beneath the surface of his skin. My eyes flick down to his lips, and he doesn't miss it, yet still doesn't move.

Slowly, I lean forward, and his grip loosens as I stare into his eyes. Our lips connect and my eyelids flutter closed. His lips stay deathly still, not giving in to the kiss, not showing any sort of emotion. When I back away, I search his face for some kind of silent invitation to continue, only to find anger brewing in his features. Instead, he looks away toward the fire.

"For what it's worth, I don't want the High King. Or anyone else for that matter," I say, resisting the urge to kiss him again and slightly hating that he didn't kiss me back. "The idea of losing you terrifies me. I distracted you in my vision. I did the same today. Had I not been at the meeting, you wouldn't have hesitated. You wouldn't have had to come after me." My hand reaches up to force his eyes to mine. "I'm falling in love with you. Everything else aside, I don't want to be the reason you die and staying away from you is the only way to avoid that."

Kai's quiet as his haunting eyes flick across my face, as if he's trying to figure out if he can trust what he's hearing. His lips are so close that I can feel his breath warming me, while at the same time sending goosebumps across the rest of my body. I swallow, wishing he'd close the gap, and that sheer need goes against everything I've said so far. But it's there. The memory of the way he tastes, the way his hands feel on my skin, is etched into my brain. It taunts me every time he smiles–with every word he speaks. If it weren't for the stare he has on me right now, my eyes would be glued to that gorgeous mouth until he fulfills my wish.

"It's hard," I say, trying to fill the awkward silence, "I don't want to feel this way and I wish I could just turn it off, but I can't. So, please. Don't make it harder. Let me stay here."

"No," he says, crushing his mouth to mine as the mushrooms drop to the ground.

THE DEMON PRINCE

CHAPTER THIRTY-FIVE

Alice

I already crave the way his touch scorches my skin, the way his taste makes me moan, and the liquid heat that dances in his amber eyes, but this is more. This is a kiss that promises to leave me boneless and my heart full. It causes the world around us to fade into background noise, taking with it the worry of being in this realm, where every creature and plant threatens our lives.

Our kiss is feverish, *hungry*, like both of us can't get enough. Both of our souls are worn on our sleeve, and we're stripped down to a state in which everything else is secondary to the need to feel skin against skin. We're two people who can't get any closer yet, have to be, and won't rest until we are. His lips part in silent invitation and I take the opportunity to capture his bottom one, nipping it between my teeth, and pulling until he moans low in his throat. My heart beats faster, until it echoes in my ears, drowning out the sound around me as I give in to the moment.

Unzipping my jacket, I shrug it off my shoulders before gripping the hem of my shirt and yanking it up and over my head. It drops to the ground as warm fingers slide across my skin, committing every surface to memory. Goosebumps raise in their wake, and he smirks against my lips before blanketing my jaw and neck in kisses. His hands grip behind my thighs, lifting me up as he sits down, locking me against him as I straddle his folded legs. The contrast between his calloused fingers and how soft and slow they travel up my side has my eyes rolling back inside my head. He circles around to my back, undoing the clasp of my bra and my arm flies up to catch the contoured cups before it can fall.

"Let it go," he demands. His voice is lust-driven and dark, yet, so fucking sexy that I want to heed every command he gives me... *or thinks*. I swallow, letting out a shaky breath and do it. It drops to the ground next to us and he tosses it away.

One of his strong arms wraps around my waist, and his other hand pushes the hair away from my neck, revealing my throat to him. I tilt my head, allowing him access as he places a kiss on my pulse, then without wasting a second, descends. His parted lips and the top of his tongue slide down my chest, up and over the mound of my breast. He captures one of the pebbled peaks between his teeth and pulls until my hands bury into his hair, holding him to me as a wave of pain and pleasure spikes through my stomach. I feel him chuckle against my skin, pleased with himself; his breath causing the trail his tongue left to go cold. He repeats the process on the other side, and I moan as my head tips back.

His mouth hovers above my skin so his bottom lip is the only thing that grazes me as he rocks his head side to side in the valley between them. "You're so responsive to me, little witch," he says, pressing a hand against my lower back as he flips to the right, laying me down against the cave floor. My body arches away from the cool stone, intently aware that his amber eyes are watching my every move. His teeth sink into the swell of my breast hard enough to leave a mark, *his mark*, but not hard enough to break the skin. I yelp but as he releases his hold and his tongue laps across the reddened skin, the noise in my throat quickly turns into a moan, followed by a purr. "And you thought I'd let the High King have this? Not a fucking chance."

I wiggle my hips beneath him, and he takes that as an invitation to slide lower. Kai sits back, watching me as he unties the laces on my boots, taking them and my socks off. Then he leans forward, propping himself up on one arm as his other palm presses and rubs down the seam of my pants between my legs. My knees close around him as my hips tilt, needing more. He kisses the hollow between my belly button and my hip bone as he unzips and unbuttons my pants. His fingers hook around the waistband and pull them, along with my panties off and tosses them to the ground.

I'm immediately aware of how naked I am and how *not* he is. His hands knock my legs apart but before his head can dip to taste me, my fingers weave into the hair at the base of his neck and pull so he has to look up at me.

"Oh no. Tit-for-tat, sweetheart," I say.

Amusement flashes in his eyes as he smirks. He sits up as my hand untangles from his hair and he pulls the hem of his thin shirt up and over his head revealing abs I want to trace with my tongue across and pecs my hands ache to dig my fingers into. He bounces them and lifts a brow like he's taunting me to come and get him. That's an offer I won't refuse. Not again.

I lift my foot and plant it against his chest, kicking him backward as I roll forward onto my hands and knees, and crawl forward until my face hovers over his. "My turn," I whisper in his ear and he audibly swallows. Lifting, I glimpse the longing that burns behind his eyes, and it tempts me to lick my lips. Instead, I dip to kiss him deeply and his body melts into a pool of liquid lust beneath me.

"Have your way with me," he says against my lips. I skim feather-light pecks down his throat and across his chest before I bite him in the same spot. He sucks in a breath when I let go. My hand slides down the front of his pants over the length of him and his head thumps back against the cave floor with a rugged groan.

"Oh, I intend to." My words don't have a threatening ring to them, they hold a promise.

"*Jesus...*"

"Excuse me. It's *princess* to you," I say as his head snaps up and his eyes connect with mine. My cheeks flush and a smirk spreads across my face as my fingers undo his pants. I'm not sure if I shocked him or turned him on, but either way works in my favor. I continue to slide his pants, along with his boxers, down just enough to free him from the confining fabric.

Straddling his thighs, the rock-hard length of him comes up past my belly button and I swallow. He's by far the biggest man I've ever been with, and I'd be lying if I said I wasn't scared... but regardless of my nerves, I've never wanted anything more.

I slide backward, raising my hips in the air as my hands circle his cock, bringing it to my lips and I enjoy the way his pupils blow as I lower my mouth. My tongue whips back and forth, wrapping around him as I take his cock as deep as my throat will allow.

"Bloody hell, woman," he curses under his breath, wrapping my ponytail around his hand.

Bobbing up and down, he guides me with my hair as I open my throat to allow more and more of him to sink inside it until his eyes flutter closed and his breaths turn into moans. There's something about having a man this powerful at my mercy that excites me more than I care to admit. Suddenly, the hand in my hair grips tighter and I swirl my tongue and increase my speed. *That's it.* Let's see how *you* come undone.

He yanks my head back, leaning forward to look at my eyes, as if he's seeking permission to take it further, but he falls silent, like he can't find the words to ask. His thumb wipes the saliva from my chin, and I capture it, sucking it between my lips before letting it go with a popping sound.

"Are you going to fuck me with your eyes or your dick?" I ask, and he groans, swiveling his neck as he pulls me backward.

"You have a filthy mouth, you know that?" he asks, running his fingers through my slit and before rubbing circles around that magical spot that stokes my fire.

"Did you expect anything less?" I ask, but he doesn't answer me. Instead, he slips a finger inside me, then two, and my hips rise to meet his thrusts. It doesn't take long before I'm clenching around them, and my legs shake. Kai retreats, cupping his hand over my sex and I gasp in air, trying to steady my racing heart, knowing I was so close to falling over the ledge that I can still feel it shuddering through me.

"You don't get to come yet. Not until you take every inch of me. Not until you admit who you belong to. Don't think I've forgotten about your wish to become a martyr. You don't get to decide what I deem is worth fighting for. I've been very forthright from the moment I met you, letting you know that I'm yours, but I think it's time for you to admit that you're mine."

He pauses, toying with me, teasing me but never giving me what I truly want.

"Come on, Alice. Who do you belong to?" he whispers in my ear, his hair tickling my cheek. I try to rock my hips forward, desperate to ease the ache, but he jerks his hand away, preventing me from grinding against it.

"I care about you, but I don't belong to anyone. I'm a *person*, not a *possession*," my voice is barely a whisper. It's weak, feeble, and unrecognizable, and it sounds like I'm trying to convince myself more than him.

The tick in his jaw hammers as he leans back to rest on his heels. "Wrong answer, little witch." He links his arms under my thighs and jerks me toward him, but before I get my bearings, his mouth skims my thighs making them tremble with anticipation.

"God, *please*," I beg, my hand finding purchase in his hair, trying to push him to the place I want him.

"Don't pray to God, love… He's not going to save you," he says between kisses.

"Don't be an asshole," I say, giving up on moving him, and trying to contort my body instead. He chuckles against my thigh as his hands curl up to press against the flat plane of my stomach, locking my hips to the ground.

"Don't be so stubborn. You can put both of us out of our misery with one word. Say it, Alice, and I'll eat your sweet pussy until you forget your name." He swipes his tongue over my clit once, causing my body to jerk. "No? Maybe you need more convincing."

One of his hands leave my stomach and he nips the fleshy part of my thigh as two fingers shove inside me, curling and scissoring as he laps me up, devouring me whole. I climb again, grinding into his face as I chase my release. I'm so goddamn close that I can taste it. His tongue flicks and his eyes watch me and just as I'm about to fall again, he bites my clit, shattering my chances.

I groan, closing my legs around him and throwing my arm over my eyes.

"Who do you belong to?" he asks again, and I debate denying him an answer, but he flicks my clit, making me buckle.

"You, asshole!" I yell, not needing to see his face to know he's smirking triumphantly.

His hand reaches up to cover my mouth and he bends forward to whisper in my ear, "Shhh, princess. Trust me, I love all the noises that come out of your pretty mouth, even your insults, but I don't want to fight every monster in this realm to keep you to myself."

His hand settles between my thighs again, but this time, he doesn't hold back. His fingers pump in and out of me, twisting and curling. I cry out against his palm that is still clamped over my mouth and my eyes flutter, rolling toward the back of my head as I come so hard my legs shake. My body trembles as he nips at my ear.

"There we go... See? Now, was that so hard?"

Kai plants a kiss against the pulse that hammers in my throat before releasing my mouth and moving his body between my legs. My muscles feel like jelly; weak, but oh, so satisfied. I feel the head of his cock rub against my clit, circling until I squirm beneath him. Only then does he slide it down to rest at my entrance. His hips roll forward, slowly inching himself inside while I stretch to accommodate him and his obnoxious size.

"Breathe, Alice," he says, and I blow the air out, and as if on cue, he shoves all the way inside, burying himself to the hilt. My eyes flick open wide as I try like hell to catch my breath. Luckily, Kai stays still, allowing me a moment to gather my shattering resolve.

"There you go, sweetheart. I knew you could take it…" He gyrates his hips, circling while buried inside me, forcing my walls to loosen.

Slowly, he pulls back as he collects saliva on his tongue, letting it drip from his lips and slide down before he shoves back in, and I cry out.

Kai's body stills as he leans forward, inadvertently, pushing himself deeper. "You can't scream, love. I want you to, but you can't. We don't know what will hear it," he whispers against my lips before claiming them. His hand slides under my back as he rolls on to his, taking me with him. "Here. You take control. Use me."

I stare down at him for a moment, as his fingers pull the elastic out of my hair, and my red curls fall free, hanging down to my hips. He smirks, rolling a curl around his finger. "You drive me fucking mad,

Alice, but you're by far the sexiest woman I've ever seen in my life. So, show me what you're made of. Show me how hard you can come for me."

My mouth gapes but his hands grip my waist, rocking my hips as my head slips back and a moan escapes my lips. No one has ever been that deep. Its uncharted territory, but it feels *so fucking good*. I catch the rhythm, grinding against him, and his hands roam, leaving heated trails in their wake.

He palms my breast, dragging the other into his mouth for his teeth to toy with. I roll my hips, over and over, as he switches sides, feeling myself clench around him as ecstasy builds, igniting nerves I didn't know existed. He growls as his eyes roll back into his head and just when I think I can't take it anymore, I come, biting my lip to keep from making noise as it pulses through my body, wave after glorious wave. My back arches and my toes curl. I feel everything and nothing at the same time.

I'm still rocking my hips, riding out every last second of the euphoria when Kai's body tightens, and his abs flex beneath my fingers. His head tips back, bumping into the ground of the cave as his hands lock my body to his. After a second, he relaxes, exhaling the air that was trapped in his lungs.

"God, you're fucking perfect," he says, brushing the hair out of my face.

I open my mouth to speak, but someone clearing their throat makes my head jerk toward the noise. Lucifer stands with his back to us, facing the mouth of the cave. Gasping, I roll off Kai, trying to throw my clothes on. *Kill me now.* Of course, Kai just lazily rolls to his side, draping his shirt over his crotch while watching me get dressed. The man has no shame.

"Well. I'm glad you're not dead," Lucifer says, "I'll be opening a bubble at high noon tomorrow at the same place you came through. Don't miss it." Then he disappears without another word.

CHAPTER THIRTY-SIX

Kai

My father astral projecting into the cave was… definitely not planned. On the bright side, he didn't stick around to scold me, like I expected him to, which could've been due to our nakedness or just him deciding to wait until we're not at risk of dying to do so. Either could be it.

Alice shoves her shirt over her head and shoots me a death glare that makes my heart throb. Like hell is she going to wear something dirty and covered in lake water. I can't conjure things into existence, but if I know where something is, I can summon it to me. Closing my eyes, I picture her side of the closet, and snap my figures as one of her band shirts and a pair of fluffy pants land in my hand, along with a pair of sweatpants for me.

Opening my eyes, I see her look at the pile of clothes.

"You could've done that the entire time?" she asks, pressing her lips together.

"I guess. I didn't think it would work across the boundary, but..." I snap my fingers again and the couch from our room, along with pillows, a blanket, and chips appear next to us.

She sighs as her head tilts back. "If I didn't love you before, I do now," she says, then her eyes bug wide as if she didn't plan to say that out loud. My heart sings in my chest and my tongue runs along my lip. Do I say it back? I mean, I know I'm falling for her, hard, but I don't think she wants me to acknowledge the weight behind what just slipped off her tongue. Maybe it was innocent... Maybe I took it in the wrong context.

After she's had enough time to eat something and change clothes, I scoop her up and hug her to me on her side, trapping her between me and the back of the couch. I pull the blanket around us, and she strokes her fingertips across the arm I have wrapped around her.

"For the son of the Devil, you like to snuggle a lot," she says.

"Is that a bad thing?" I ask, not wanting to smother her.

"No. Just unexpected."

I smooth her hair down, so I can kiss her cheek. "I've never wanted to snuggle with someone before, so it's new for both of us. But now, I don't know if I'll ever get enough of having you wrapped up against me, feeling your heartbeat on my skin. It's peaceful."

"You're annoyingly perfect," she says.

A laugh escapes from my throat. "Why is that?"

"Because you're so smooth…"

I chuckle and kiss her throat, sliding my hand up under her shirt to cup her breast. "I don't know. Your skin feels pretty smooth… I think you got me beat."

Her hand wraps around mine through her shirt. "Go to sleep," she says, and I grumble, but agree. We have a hard hike tomorrow and I'm not looking forward to what comes after we cross that boundary.

My father might be a stand-up man, all business and calm, but when he's pissed, it's not pretty.

***

"Remind me... to never... go hiking... *again!*" Alice complains from behind me.

"Come on, princess. I don't want to be in these woods any longer than we have to." She groans quietly. I guess that's not what she wanted to hear, but we can't stop and take another break again. Not if we're going to get to the boundary in time. I don't want to risk cutting it close, not when she had a vision of Pan. It's coming, I just don't know when or how much that will slow us down.

As soon as I reach the top of the plateau, the forest levels and the brush grows thicker but the trees are more sparse. I try to catch my breath and wait for the woman behind me to clear the top before going any farther. Minutes pass and she still hasn't crested the plateau.

Something's wrong. I look down the hill, searching for Alice, but she's not there. She was right behind me... where the hell could she have gone?

"Alice?" No answer. The panic sets in as my body runs cold. *No, please no.*

"Alice!" I yell again, not caring who or what hears. Still, no answer.

I slide down against the side of the hill to where I saw her last while my heart thumps in my chest, drowning out everything except for the need to find her.

"Up here!" I hear her voice yell and my body stills. There's no way she made it past me. There's no way she could be at the plateau already. I crane my body around to face the crest that I just slid from.

"Look over the edge. I need to see your face," I say, but she doesn't answer.

Fuck me. I shrug my wings out of hiding. They still ache from my crash but I'm hoping I'll be able to push through it to at least get to the plateau. They reach up and flap down, sending a gust of wind beneath me while I cringe. My teeth grind, as I do it again and again, feeling the tears that prick my eyes but don't fall. The moment I reach the top, I shove them back inside as my face contorts as a sharp pain shoots through my shoulder blades. A groan leaves my lips as I breathe out and look around the plateau. There's no sign of Alice… because it wasn't her. It was one of Pan's children.

They mimic voices, leading people away from one another while Pan picks them off one by one. He steals their shadow and uses them as a power source against his enemies, then eats them until all that's left is a pile of bones. I have to find Alice before he does. I look both ways, trying to decide which to search first, then take off looking down the tree line for her red hair.

Cursing at myself once I reach the end of the plateau, I go back the other way. I stop at the end, my lungs starving for air. Bending over to rest my hands on my knees, I try to slow my heart and catch my breath.

Where the fuck is she?

Someone slow claps behind me and I straighten, turning to find Pan standing a few feet away.

"Look at you. All grown up. I think I liked you as a child better, sweet prince." My heart skips and I hold my breath, remembering how I almost became one of his victims.

I had tried to run away from the keep, pissed that my parents kept me in a bubble, hidden from everyone and everything. I didn't like being alone…

Outside my bedroom window, I would watch kids my age playing games in the courtyard, and I hated it, wanting to be down there, too.

Six-year-old me thought it would be a great idea to pack a bag and sneak out, to run away and take control of my own life, but I didn't make it far into the woods before the man in front of me came. He promised that I'd have kids to play with, that there would be no rules. I was dumb enough to listen to him.

It just happened to be the day that Michael was visiting to go over the numbers with my father in Limbo. When the monster before me tried to take my shadow, I screamed so loud that it shook the seven realms, and my father came running with Michael in tow. Together the two threw Pan into the prison world, but after, Michael made my father throw me into The Void.

Lucifer fought it so hard, even after I told him I understood and did all but ask him to do it. No one stood up to fight with him, but Michael and his guards held nothing back. Together, they overpowered my father and beat him until he no longer resembled a man, but rather a walking, swollen heap of torn flesh and broken bone. It was then, that I opened the door and stood in front of the portal. I remember the way my father's hand trailed over my cheek before I stepped back.

Only Michael didn't stop there. After I was gone, my father threatened to kill him, even if it was the last thing he did. Still, the archangel left him, finding his threat weightless. That night, my mother tried to scry the future in the temple beneath the keep, hoping that maybe, there would be a loophole and they would get their son back. Michael came back and while she was in the trance, and while my father was healing, he ripped her soul from her body, putting it in a jar and taking it with him to Heaven.

This monster, beyond my own fault and Michael's deadly vendetta against what I am, he's partly responsible for my mother's death. He won't take Alice from me too... I summon my sword, igniting it with hellfire as I spin and slash it toward him. He deflects it, slamming his magic into me, but

I cut it with my own, directing it toward each side of my body.

"You've grown stronger," the wicked god says, circling me.

"Is that supposed to flatter me?" He shakes his head no, right as a scream tears through the forest, sending birds rushing from the treetops. *Alice...*

"You could still save her, you know. I'll even let the girl keep her shadow, but only if you give me yours," he bargains, but I take off toward the noise, hoping that it's not one of his children's mimics I'm following.

I break through a small clearing in the woods, searching around. The sound couldn't have come from that far. Closing my eyes and dropping to my knees, I let my power search through the woods, looking for anything resembling a red-haired princess but coming up empty handed. My fist slams into the ground, hard enough for the ground to shake. I grab my sword and get to my feet, ready to go after Pan, but when I turn around, he's already behind me, grinning with sharp-ass teeth.

"Where is she?" I demand, storming up to him, sword drawn and pointing at his throat. "Tell me, or you might want to start praying for both of our souls because I will rip you limb from limb until you talk."

"So angry, these days. Calm down. She breathes. Her shadow is still intact, as I promised, but it won't be for long unless you pay up."

"How about option three," I spin and slice my sword through the air. The god jumps back, but not fast enough. My blade cuts the fleshy part of his shoulder, drawing blood. He yelps and reaches his hand up to heal it. "The wound might close, but you know those made by hell fire never heal."

The god grinds his teeth as I prowl around him, letting the predator become prey. Pan smiles at me, like he could care less about my need to strike him down, instead, he looks down at me like I'm a small child, beating my fists against his leg in a futile attempt to fuck him up. He lifts his hand and the sword rips from mine, clattering against the rocky ground to my right.

Power slams into my gut, sending me sliding backward until my feet catch on a raised root and I push off, holding my hand out to recall my sword and it materializes in my grip again as Pan rushes toward me. Rage ignites my bloodstream as I charge, feeling his dark magic slither over my body, the sheer smell of it burning my nose as my nostrils flare.

Shadows swarm around the man, peeling off his body as they whip around us at our feet. I slice at the god again, determined to end this, but he dodges and shoots me a smile so sinister, it makes my soul quiver. His fist collides with my ribs, breaking them like twigs under a foot and I gasp, taking a step back to bite down the pain.

Someone gasps, someone feminine. I turn my head to see Alice standing on the edge of the clearing and as I turn back around, I watch in horror as Pan's talons extend, slicing into my chest and tearing out my side as I fall to the ground. The world around me slows and an eerie feeling settles in before I even attempt to breathe. My lungs ache, my heart spasms inside of my chest. Then Alice's scream cuts through the euphoric haze and the clearing ignites in hell flame.

THE DEMON PRINCE

CHAPTER THIRTY-SEVEN

Alice

My vision unfolds before my eyes, as the scream tears through me, and the goosebumps rise across my body. My lungs burn, my throat bleeds, my ears ring… The smell of burnt flesh fills my nose, scalding me and forcing bile up my throat.

All forms of sound disappear until the only thing left is a ringing that rattles my ear drums while the clearing in front of me burns to ash, taking the men with it. Taking *my man*, with it.

Pan screams, flailing on the ground until he simply stops, and my fingers slide beneath the blacked dirt as the spellbinding shatters to pieces. Knots untie as power floods my every pore, every cell, blinding me with white hot pain. My mouth gapes as the need to scream again pulls at my chest and a drunken feeling takes hold. The world spins and I fight for my balance, but just as quickly as the feeling washes over me, it dissipates.

I climb to my feet, numb to everything except the need to have the god's fucking spine in my hands... to make him pay for what he's done. Walking through the green flames that lick at my feet, I feel my eyes go black with rage as I rip the god from the ground. He's still alive, silent, but alive, and the only thing that moves are what's left of his burnt, swollen eyes.

"Good. I want you to feel this," I say, no longer recognizing my voice.

Remembering a spell to turn things to stone, I mutter it as his eyes flick over my face. Slowly, charred skin turns hard and a sound like someone squishing bubble wrap hits my ears, pulling my lips into a smirk. I drop his feeble body as the spell finishes but then continues to deteriorate further until the statue he's crumbles into dust.

"Alice..." I whip around to find Kai, on the ground, coughing up blood and every thought, every part of the world around me disappears as I drop to the ground and search over his body. It's been untouched by the hellfire.

My hands press against the wound on his chest as I close my eyes, but his hands cuff my wrist, bringing me back to meet his gaze.

"You can't. You've already used too much."

"I have to. I know you'll heal but we don't have the time. If we don't show up, your father might not hold the bubble. He'll think we're dead. You can't walk the rest of the way like this and I can't carry you."

"Go," he says. It's only one word, but it's enough to set me off.

"No! I'm not leaving you." I start to put my hands on his chest again, already halfway through muttering the spell Elise taught me, but he holds my wrists away.

Then a growl comes from behind me and my heart stops. Slowly, I crane my head around, seeing the creature I ran from when I first got trapped inside the barrier, walk through the tree line.

"We have to go," I say quietly. "Can we teleport?"

"I tried already. I don't have a clear enough image of where we need to go in my head. I didn't exactly take a second to look around while running in here."

Fuck. "Okay, teach me. Fast."

"I can't. If you mess up, if you land us on the other side of the barrier, we're dead. You have to go. I'll slow you down, but if you run, it will probably chase you instead of eating me."

Not the best of plans… but it might be the best one we got.

I stand, summoning the red ball of lightning with ease and toying it in my hand as it stalks closer.

"Here kitty, kitty, come play with me," I tease, waiting for it to get close enough before I run, ensuring it follows me instead of stopping for a snack. And if Kai is anything, he's most certainly that.

The creature prowls up to me but doesn't hold the same curiosity in its eyes. The playful, 'I'm going to pounce on you while I rip you to shreds' look. Cocking my head, I watch as it stops a few feet away and simply lays down and bows its head and purrs.

"Oh my god…" Kai says, quietly. "It's your familiar."

"Come again?"

"It's your familiar—"

"I heard you the first fucking time, Kai. How?" I snap.

"You won. It can sense your power and it's bowing to show its respect. It won't hurt you, Alice. Once an animal decides to become a witch's familiar, its loyalty lasts until death."

I gulp down air and slowly walk forward, holding my hand out until it connects with the creature's soft white fur, which holds more of a pink hue when blood has stained it. It purrs louder, nuzzling into my touch as its yellow eyes slowly open and meet mine.

Holy shit.

"I have an idea," I say, leaving the creature and trying to hoist Kai up from the ground. His wound is starting to close, but he still sucks in air through his teeth and winces as he stands up right. "Come on, up you go."

"Um… I'm not riding that thing."

"Um. Unless you want to die, yes, you are. Now up," I demand.

Kai's eyes skim over the creature as he groans, drawing the creature's attention. It opens its mouth, almost like a smile, and its pupils grow.

"Bad kitty," I say, and it darts a glare at me, but complies and lets me and Kai climb onto it's back. The creature itself is easily three times as tall as the horse I rode here on, but it helps us by hunkering down.

Once we're seated, it's butt wiggles as its weight settles back and without warning, it darts forward, weaving through trees but not taking much consideration for the fact that we have to dodge branches. Me and Kai duck and weave as it flies through the forest, skidding to a stop in front of the barrier where the canopy still stands, along with the rest of Kai's men. Lucifer looks up and his eyes shoot wide when he sees us, and Finn mouths, "What. The. Fuck," as he walks up to stand beside him. Their eyes skim over the creature as it drops down to the ground and allows us to climb off.

"Interesting," I say, scratching behind its ears. "It's like it knew exactly where I wanted to go."

"Because it did. You're connected now, but like hell is it sleeping in our room. Just so we're clear," Kai says, sliding down to the ground with a cringey groan. "It might be loyal to you, but it does *not* mean it won't eat me." A laugh jerks out of me as he walks through the barrier.

I walk toward the blue wall, ready to do the same, but the creature doesn't follow, it stays, watching me, as if it's seeking my permission beforehand.

"You coming?" I ask, waving it forward and it bounds after me and slips through the veil beside me.

"What the hell is that thing?" Finn takes off his hat and scratches his head.

"Alice's familiar," Kai says, as Lucifer brings his hand to his chest and heals the wound.

"And what the fuck happened to you?" Finn asks.

"Pan." All of the men fall silent, looking between Lucifer and Kai. Did I miss something?

THE DEMON PRINCE

"We will be having a discussion as soon as we get home, just so you know," his father says, something menacing behind his tone. Then, he simply drops the bubble and vanishes.

CHAPTER THIRTY-EIGHT
Alice

When we get back, Kai heads off with his father and I make my way up the Rapunzel-worthy staircase, pissed that I can't simply poof myself up to our room. Finn follows me on orders to not leave me alone. I thought we'd be past that by now, but the order didn't come from Kai, it came from Lucifer. After having to retrieve me from The Realm of Monsters, I guess I can slightly understand his need to helicopter parent.

My creature, who I have yet to name, stayed in the forest around the keep, which I'm still reeling with the idea that it's my familiar, and how the hell I managed to manifest characteristics of it before even meeting it, but I'm sure I'll learn in time. For now, it's just nice to feel whole, like all the parts of my soul are there and not locked away in a box.

"So, how was your pre-wedding vacation?" Finn asks, as we take a seat in what's left of our living room furniture. We're going to have to get a new couch, but it was better than sleeping on the ground.

"Pre-wedding?" I ask, realizing that no one actually told me when the ceremony would be.

"I'm joking. It was supposed to be tonight, but Lucifer asked me to postpone it until you and Kai say otherwise. So, I spent my morning calling florists, the seamstress, the honorary guests. It was a blast."

My cheeks flush and I press my lips together to keep from laughing. Imagining Finn in his armor, twirling an old-fashioned phone cord, calling to chit-chat those people is just too good of a mental image to pass up.

"I'm sorry," I say, and his lips tip up.

"No big deal, princess. I'm just glad you guys got out. No one ever has before. Had it been anyone else, Lucifer wouldn't have poked a hole."

My eyes drop as my brows furrow together. "I'm sure he's not exactly happy about that, is he?"

"Not by a long shot. I'm sure he's ripping Kai a new asshole as we speak. I told him it was a dumb idea to meet with the king without Lucifer's permission, but he's also supposed to be taking over for him after the war, and I think that's gone to his head a bit. It's not your fault that you got trapped. The meeting should never have happened," Finn says, his armor screeches as plates slide together so he can readjust in his seat.

"That's not true. I supported it. I didn't agree, but I still told him I would go in with him and I could've talked him out of it," I say, rubbing a hand down my face. "Where are they?"

"Why do you want to know?"

"Because he doesn't deserve to get his ass beat alone…"

Finn's eyes meet mine and he doesn't answer, just stands up and holds a hand out to me. I get to my feet, and he leads me through the keep, down to the main floor and then down farther until I lose count of how many floors we've descended. Then, he points to a large wooden door at the end of a dark hall.

"They're in there. It's Lucifer's room… and his wife's crypt."

I can hear them arguing, their voices raising, and traveling down the tunnel, even though I can't make out the words. Nodding a thank you to Finn, I walk toward it, and turn the latch. The wooden door creaks open on old, worn hinges and Lucifer turns to face me, clasping a hand over his mouth as if it would be unfortunate for me to hear the anger that spewed from it.

"What are you doing here, Alice? Go back to the room," Kai says without taking his gaze off of his father.

"No. She needs to hear this just as much as you," Lucifer says, snapping his fingers and I'm dragged inside as me and Kai are both sent hurling into seats as he paces back and forth in front of us. "You are supposed to be taking over my throne. How can that happen when you do things as idiotic as breaking down the boundary that contains a realm full of monsters that would rip everything I've built to ruins?"

His question wasn't meant to have an answer. It was to prove a point.

"I could understand a six-year-old, defying me and making a mistake that cost people their lives, but you're much older, you knew exactly what the stakes were and didn't care about the consequences. I know you're scared. We all are, but it doesn't give you the right to put innocent lives at stake," he says, staring at Kai. He looks off to the right and I follow his eyes, finding a glass coffin with a perfectly preserved woman inside. "What would your mother think?"

Kai snorts. "My mother would've been proud of me for trying to protect the woman I love. Not scold me for it going wrong. She'd tell me to pick up my sword and try again, to find another way."

His mention of the L-word stops my heart and I slowly turn to face him, mouth gaping, before looking to Lucifer's expressionless face.

"She would've, but she would never have encouraged you to open that realm. She would've made damn sure her plan would've worked first. I wasn't against talking to the king, but we didn't have the ability to scry and make sure it wouldn't end in chaos."

"I don't have her ability to see the future. I can only see the past," Kai retorts.

"You're right. Which is why I needed Alice's spellbinding to break first, because she can. You didn't even give me the chance to explain that before you just planned to do it anyway." Kai settles back into the seat, his eyes dropping to the floor in defeat. I watch his father drag his hand through his hair before letting it fall to his side.

"I postponed the wedding until further notice," Lucifer says to us, letting his eyes look to me for the first time since I sat here. "When you're ready, we'll plan it. Now that your spellbinding has broken, there's no reason to rush. You're clearly more capable at handling yourself than I gave you credit for."

The room falls silent for a beat, and I slowly take it in, twisting my engagement ring around my finger with my thumb. It's windowless, but the walls are made from the same obsidian stone. A large painting of Lucifer, his wife, and a young Kai hangs on the far wall. It's huge and is easily as tall as a single-story house. There are more earthy wood tones than our room and bookshelves that line every open wall, but everything here seems to frame the glass coffin like a shrine.

"Lock the door on your way out, I have to go finish cleaning up your mess," he says to Kai before turning on his heels and leaving the room.

The man next to me slumps backward, running his hands down his face as he grumbles, and I ignore it. Lucifer was right, he went balls to the wall, and I knew it was a bad idea, but I didn't exactly try and stop it either. It was reckless, dangerous, but there were some moments of the journey that I don't regret experiencing either.

"Is that your mother?" I say, getting up to walk over and peer through the glass. She's beautiful. White hair, silk-like skin... Her hands are crossed over her chest with a single golden rose beneath them.

"Yes," he says, breathing out heavily as he walks up behind me.

"Why is she in here?"

"My father still has hope..." he says, and it instantly makes my heart ache. I might not have known Kai for long, but almost losing him, knowing what it feels like to be helpless and to help someone you care for... I'd hold out hope too.

Kai inhales, settling his hands on my hips. "When I was six, I ran into Pan in the forest. I was supposed to stay in the keep, to stay hidden. I left anyway and my father had to leave his meeting with Michael to save me. It's how he found out that I existed. After I was thrown into the void, my mother tried to scry the future to see if I'd ever return to her and Michael was pissed that my father threatened him. So, he took advantage of her vulnerability and stole her soul, shoved it into one of the jars we use in Limbo, and took it with him to Heaven as a punishment. My father found her and put her body under a spell, freezing it in time. He's still holding out hope that when the war is won, he'll be able to restore her soul and get her back."

"And what do you think?" I ask, hating the guilt I hear in his voice. He was a child... he couldn't have known. Yet the sheer weight it holds over him... I'm surprised he hasn't crumbled from the pressure.

"I think my mother was gone a long time ago," he says. I turn to look at him, seeing his jaw clenching as it ticks and his eyes gloss over. "If he hasn't shredded her soul already, he'll do it the moment we march against Heaven."

I cup his jaw, tilting his head up so he has to meet my eyes. "Let's hope that doesn't happen, but it's strong of you to prepare yourself for it if it does...Can I ask a question?"

He smiles, sniffing and trying to pretend that he wasn't on the verge of crying. "What do you mean by jar? Are we talking about putting souls in mason jars? Or is that just a term that doesn't translate?"

Kai smiles, tucking a chunk of hair behind my ear. "Yeah, it's exactly as it sounds. I'll take you there one day. But when a soul crosses over after someone dies, it gets judged. If it's bad, they suck them into a jar that they can put on a shelf in Purgatory, so their soul doesn't get reincarnated. If it's good, they get to go to Heaven until such time that they want to be reborn."

I'm quiet for a moment, trying to image the logistics.

"Have you seen the movie *Ghost busters?*" he asks, and I nod. Who hasn't? "Well, we have backpacks that are similar, and it just sucks their being inside the jar."

Huh...I resist the urge to laugh, imagining the man who brought me here, Allister, sucking off some guy into a jar. "So, do they just accumulate in Purgatory? Or could you break them down and create a new soul with what's left?"

"So, you giggle at us for having backpacks, but putting souls through a meat grinder is completely realistic?"

I shrug my shoulders and he chuckles. "We could, but instead, we just leave them to rot. Eventually the jar will glow green, and we can send them to the pool to be reincarnated, but I've never thought of the meat grinder idea."

We're both quiet for a moment while I look in the glass box. She looks so peaceful...

"She'd like you, you know," Kai says, making my cheeks flush. He's quiet for a moment, searching my eyes. "Do you still want to marry me?"

I suck in a breath, unsure of how to word how I feel. "Yes. Not right this second, but yes."

He leans forward, brushing his lips against mine. "I understand. Let's go, princess. I think we could both use a nap."

THE DEMON PRINCE

CHAPTER THIRTY-NINE

Alice

He teleports us up to our room, which I'm incredibly grateful for. My thighs are burning from stairs, running through the woods, *coming*... They've been through hell. I wouldn't have made it if I had to climb all the way up here.

It's ridiculously awkward. I'm not even sure where to put my hands, or whether to keep them to myself. To avoid the weird conversation that I know is coming, post-pound town, and now that things have calmed, I head straight to the bathroom to take a bath and wash the monster realm ick off me.

Stripping from my clothes, I dip my toe in the pool, testing the water... like it would be anything other than hot? I'm not sure what I expected, but I can guarantee that I didn't foresee the hand wrapping around my throat right as I'm about to step in. Kai gently tugs back until I feel his naked chest behind me and his cock pressing against the curve of my bare backside. His other hand flips my hair over my shoulder, exposing my neck to him. Lips press against my shoulder as his hands roam, blindly. One reaches around to pinch my nipple, rolling it between his fingers while the other, dips between my legs to do the same to my clit.

He kisses my shoulder again and whispers, "You like it when I touch you like this... don't you?"
Is that a real question?

"Yes," I say, my reply coming out as a moan more than an answer.

My hand reaches up to lace into his hair, drawing his face back to my neck. His kisses feel phenomenal and there's not a single cell in my body that wants him to stop or even wants to fight it.

He wasn't kidding... This feels different. Now that my spell binding is broken, my body craves him like I never thought possible, and him being this close, our power mixing in the air around us, is intoxicating.

Is this how he's felt this entire time?

"Are you sore?" he asks, taking his fingers away and I audibly pout.

"Are you looking for an ego boost or permission?" I wiggle my hips, hoping he'll put them back.

He snorts. "Both?"

"Not enough to say no."

I barely get my response out before he wraps his arms around my waist and picks me up. Carrying me over to the counter, he sets my ass on top of the cool marble and my back straightens but relaxes the moment his body presses between my legs. I rock my hips forward, grinding against the length of him and his pupils blow.

His hand brushes his hair back as he watches where we connect with a hunger I've yet to see on him. "Tell me, princess. Do you crave me right now? Does all that power in your veins make you greedy enough to want my dick buried inside of you?"

I don't answer, not even when his hand slides up my throat and his thumb forces my jaw up. I stare at him as he leans forward, hovering his lips an inch away from mine. I don't need to say it. My tattletale heartbeat already has answered his question, and I know he can feel my pulse thumping against his fingers.

"That's what I thought," he growls before kissing me as if I was the oxygen his lungs starved for. My blood spikes in my veins as I let my fingers roam, tracing down the hard indentations of his abs and then around his back so I pull him closer. My nails nip against his skin in silent warning. He pulls away to suck in a breath, searching my eyes.

His dick throbs against my center as his thumb slides across my swollen lips and I chase it with my tongue. "Please," I release a heady whisper and the air leaves his lungs as he reaches down to line up with my entrance and pushes inside. My back arches as his cock spreads me apart, stretching me from the inside out. "Fuck me," I groan, letting my head fall back.

"Oh, I intend to," he says, repeating my own words back to me from the night before.

A smile touches my lips as he plants kisses down my neck, sparking the inferno that ignites inside of my body. I feel his finger trail down my spine, so lightly that it causes a shiver to rush through me and my back to bow allowing him to capture one of my pebbled peaks in his mouth.

His tongue swirls as I wiggle my hips. Heat soaks my core, pooling around his dick as my pussy clenches, begging him to move, to push in deeper than just the tip. Warmth slides over me as he smiles with my nipple pinched between his teeth. I cry out as pain and pleasure ripple through me, and he shoves all the way inside, bottoming me out, making me gasp as tingles erupt through my stomach. He repeats the process with the other nipple before rocking his hips slowly, coming almost entirely out before filling me up again.

I moan as my head falls against his shoulder, trying to muffle the sound, but his hand wraps inside of my hair without missing a beat, pulling my head back.

"Oh no you don't. You don't need to be quiet here and I want to hear you when you come," he hisses, and butterflies storm my stomach from his words.

He lets go, before pressing my knees wide and slamming inside of me, over and over until my legs shake. Kai traps one leg between his elbow and his torso as he reaches up to swirl his thumb over my clit. It takes me up and over until I cry out and shatter into pieces, but he doesn't stop. He continues stoking my fire and grinding his hips against my center, rocking in a circular motion.

It feels too good, and him rubbing against all my walls that deep, ignites already sensitive nerves... I can't take it anymore. *I can't breathe.* My hand flies down to stop him from circling my clit, as I come again, squeezing my legs together as my entire body falls apart, and my walls clench, holding him inside of me.

"Fucking hell, woman," he growls before claiming my lips as I pulse around him.

Kai's fingers slide beneath me, squeezing the flesh of my ass hard before driving back inside, forcing me to take more until I see stars. His breath dances across my skin as my fingers thread through his hair holding him against me.

"I love watching you writhe for me. The way your eyes flutter shut. The way those full lips part… You make the sexiest noises when I'm buried in you. It makes me never want to come out," he says before biting my lip, pulling at it seductively.

His hands hold my hips steady as he sinks inside of me, and I feel the sensation build again. My hands grip on to the counter top his thrusts become carnal, visceral, as he chases his own pleasure. His eyes stare down to where we meet as he watches me break apart into a million pieces again.

This man has destroyed my deception of normal, and nothing and no one besides him would ever be able to make me come undone so sweetly, yet so savagely, that my mouth will water every time I think of how he will ravish me.

His body jerks, as I clench around him, coming down from the high as he groans his release. Dropping his forehead against my shoulder. A purr rolls through my throat as I hug him closer, my heart hammering against his.

"Fuck, princess, you absolutely destroy me," he says, kissing my pulse.

"You like it though." I press my lips to his cheek before sliding off the counter, pulling his hand along with me so we can both get into the pool.

The warm water soothes my muscles as Kai snuggles into my back as we float along the surface.

"So, what now?" I ask, playing with his fingers, entangling them with mine.

"For us? Or for everything?" he asks, his lips grazing my ear as they move.

"Both."

"We teach you how to use your magic." I sink into him, enjoying the way his body fits perfectly against mine.

"Hmmm. That could be fun." He chuckles into my hair.

His thumb strokes over my fingers. "Then we fight a war."

"That could be fun too. After hearing what Michael did to your family, my anger toward him goes a hell of a lot deeper than him just taking away mine. I'm going to enjoy kicking him off his throne," I say, bringing his hand to my lips. I kiss it as he smirks against the side of my face, kissing my cheek.

"And after?" he asks, quietly.

"Are you asking if I'll go back to Earth?"

He hesitates before saying, "I'm asking if you still want a normal life."

"I lived a normal life once upon a time. Then, some asshole with tattoos kidnapped me and brought me to Hell… where I met you. I know it sounds cheesy, but even then, I knew a normal life wasn't in the cards for me, because a normal life doesn't involve you."

I turn around in his arms, linking mine behind his neck.

"I love you. I tried so hard not to, but I do and the thought of leaving here without you… it makes my heart ache. Even a week ago, if you had given me the opportunity to leave, had Michael's wrath not been in the picture, I wouldn't have been able to. From the moment you kissed me in that crappy frat house, everything normal about my life ended and I don't regret it one bit."

His hand cups my cheek as he leans forward, kissing me so tenderly that my heart feels whole.

"I love you too, princess. Always have, even when I didn't know it."

To be continued….

BOOK TWO COMING SUMMER OF 2022!

Enjoy the book? I would love it if you could leave an honest review on [Amazon](#) or [Goodreads](#)!

AMANDA AGGIE

FOLLOW ME WHEREVER YOU HANG OUT TO BE THE FIRST TO KNOW WHEN BOOK TWO DROPS!

THE DEMON PRINCE

COMPANION GUIDE

(This will be updated with new content from each book)

THE SEVEN REALMS OF HELL

LIMBO
The processing center of the afterlife. Souls cross over through a door where they are weighed in Limbo on a vegetable scale. Once they're determined as 'good' they are given a halo and escorted to Heaven. If they're 'bad' they ghostbustered into a glass jar and then shelves in Purgatory.

PURGATORY
This is the warehouse of Hell. All of the bad souls that they don't want to be reincarnated are stored here in glass jars. After time has passed, and the soul has been 'rehabilitated' (accepted what they did wrong and served their time out) the jar will glow green and will be reincarnated.

THE SOUL WELL (THE POOL)
Souls that are ready to leave Heaven and be reincarnated cross over here and are put into the pool, via transport tubes (think what you see in the drive through of a bank). This is also where the rehabilitated jars from Purgatory are sent and reincarnated. From the outside, it resembles a lake that shimmers and has a beam of light that shoots up through the 'ceiling' of Hell. The souls are sucked up and put into the next available baby.

HELL HOLD
This is where the keep is (the main castle) as well as the marketplace. All of the creatures and demons in Hell live here either in the keep or in the surrounding village.

THE REALM OF MONSTERS
When Lucifer fell, any of the living creatures that wouldn't submit to his rule were imprisoned here, inside a force field boundary. This is also where creatures that the jars in Limbo and The Void can't hold are banished to.

DEVIL'S VALLEY
This is where Lucifer and the other fallen angels touched down. Directly above it is a hole that goes all the way to the Bermuda Triangle in the North Atlantic Ocean. Things tend to fall through on occasion.

THE VOID
This is where angels go to die. It's basically a realm of complete darkness and no one that goes in can get out. The only creatures that are the expectation to the rule are nephilim.

LANDMARKS & PLACES

TREE OF LIFE
This is actually nine trees (one of each of the sacred woods) that are twisted together and over time have become one tree. Inside it, is a hollowed cavern between the trunks that is filled with crystals. It's used for rituals and spells.

THE FALLS OF BONES & TEETH
Also known as 'The Falls of Jupiter. This is the waterfall in The Realm of Monsters. Beneath the surface toward the bottom of the lake are skeletons of all the different creatures.

TITAN'S TOMB
A field of gigantic statues that used to be the titans until Zeus killed them and rendered them stone.

THE FOREST OF LOST SOULS
A massive forest that used to be controlled by the lesser god, Pan. He would collect souls (before there was a system in place like Limbo) that wandered about Hell after it was abandoned by God. He turned them into children so that they could lure people to him and steal their shadows. Pan was sent to The Realm of Monsters, but a majority of the souls remain and haunt the woods.

THE RIVER OF STYX
A river that runs through Hell and patrolled by the ferryman. It branches into four different directions and the branches are known as Acheron, Lethe, Phlegethon, and Cocytus.

APHRODITE'S TEMPLE
It's in The Realm of Monsters but it's where the main fertility crystal is (a shard of it was bound to the cave in the Tree of Life).

HELL FLAME
A ball of fire that acts as Hell's sun.

THREE MOONS
Three large island like masses that float in Hell. When the three of them cross in front of the Hell Flame, it becomes night. It's also where a lot of winged creatures such as the dragons live.

SNAPSHOT OF HELL'S HISTORY

(As per the book so far and in relation to this world. It's not 100% true to Greek Mythology)

FIRST, GOD CREATED THE WORLD.

- **Gaea**: The earth
- **Tartarus:** Hell
- **Eros:** Love & Soul Mate Attraction
- **Erebus:** Night
- **Uranus:** Heaven
- **Mountains:** Land
- **Pointus:** Water

SECOND, GOD CREATED...THE LESSER GODS / THE OLYMPIANS (FIRST ATTEMPT AT CREATING A CIVILIZATION).

- **Zeus:** The god of Lightning
- **Hera:** The goddess of childbirth, marriage, & women
- **Hades:** Also known as Lucifer & the god of the underworld
- **Poseidon:** The god of the sea
- **Demeter:** The goddess of growth & wheat
- **Hestia:** The goddess of hearth
- **Leto:** Mother of Artemis and Apollo

THIRD, GOD CREATED...THE TITANS TO CONTROL THE LESSER GODS
(The statues they see in the fields)

- Cyclope
- Hecatonchire
- Cronus
- Rhea
- Coeus
- Phoebe
- Oceanus
- Tethys

WHEN THE TITANS FELL TO THE LESSER GODS, GOD MADE THEM MORTAL AND TRAPPED THEM BY BUILDING EARTH AROUND HELL. IT'S NOT UNTIL LUCIFER FALLS FROM HEAVEN THAT HELL GETS UNDER CONTROL AGAIN.

CHARACTERS

WITCHES

Alice Whittaker: The main character who is part witch and Angel/Demon. The daughter of Celeste and Azazel who was 'kidnapped' from Earth and promised to Prince Kai. She's prophesied to help win the war with Heaven.

Celeste Whittaker: Alice's mother who is also a quarter demon. She was the headmistress of the Faction Council before her demise. She's Azazel's soulmate.

Elise Flynn: Alice's aunt. She became more of an adoptive mother who raised her after her parents passed. A time spinner.

Bessie Whittaker: Belphegor's soulmate and was killed by Michael and the other archangels for having a nephilim child. Later, she's reincarnated and reunited with Belphegor and has a second son, thus becoming Alice's great grandmother. Also was Headmistress of the Faction Council.

Agnes Whittaker: Belphegor and Bessie's first child. Killed by Michael and the other archangels.

ANGELS

Michael: The archangel in charge of Heaven. The first born of God's second attempt to make angels. Wants nephilim dead and is Lucifer's nemesis.

DEMONS

Azazel: Used to be an archangel and was the head of the Watcher Brotherhood (a group of angels who were tasked to watch over Earth and protect the humans from paranormal kind). He fell for Celeste during his last tour on Earth before dying.

Finn: Kai's best friend and right hand.

Belphegor: Alice's great grandfather. The founder of the Belphegor Academy and the Faction council. He used to be one of the original watcher angels before he fell in love with a human and married. He was sent to The Void but later retrieved by Kai. After returning to Earth as a demon in search of his soulmate, he conceived Alice's grandfather.

Ivar: The demon guard tasked with keeping Alice safe and showing her around Hell Hold.

LESSER GODS

Prince Malikai (Kai): The son of the Devil and Persephone. He's full Nephilim (well, the lesser god kind). He's supposed to take over Hell after the war with Heaven and is engaged to Alice Whittaker.

Lucifer (Hades): Ruler of Hell and God's first-born child. Ascended to Heaven when God locked away his brothers and sisters in Hell. He fell from 'grace' after confronting God, saying that his judgment system was flawed and then started a rebellion and was sent to Hell as punishment, tasked with redoing the judgment system in the afterlife and controlling the children of his siblings that were left in Hell.

Persephone: The daughter of Demeter and The High King. The wife of Lucifer and the mother of Kai. Currently preserved in a glass box in Lucifer's quarters since her soul is with Michael in Heaven.

The High King: Zeus' son and the ruler of The Realm of Monsters. Persephone's father and Kai's grandfather. Can mimic other's power just by touching them. He's immortal because he touched Lucifer.

Pan: A lesser god who used to run The Forest of Lost Souls. He's notorious for collecting souls and turning them into children so they can do his bidding and steal shadows. Tried to take Kai's shadow but now is in The Realm of Monsters until Alice killed him.

EMPATHS

Clamara: The keep's head maid who can make you feel emotions.

WOLF SHIFTERS

Noah Flynn: Alice's uncle, husband of Elise Flynn. He's a wolf shifter and part of a cursed bloodline, Alice cured him of it as a toddler and he helped raise her after her parents died.

HUMANS

Charlie: Alice's college roommate.

Cameron Till: Alice's college crush.

OGRES

Thorben: The leader of the ogres.

FAMILY TREE

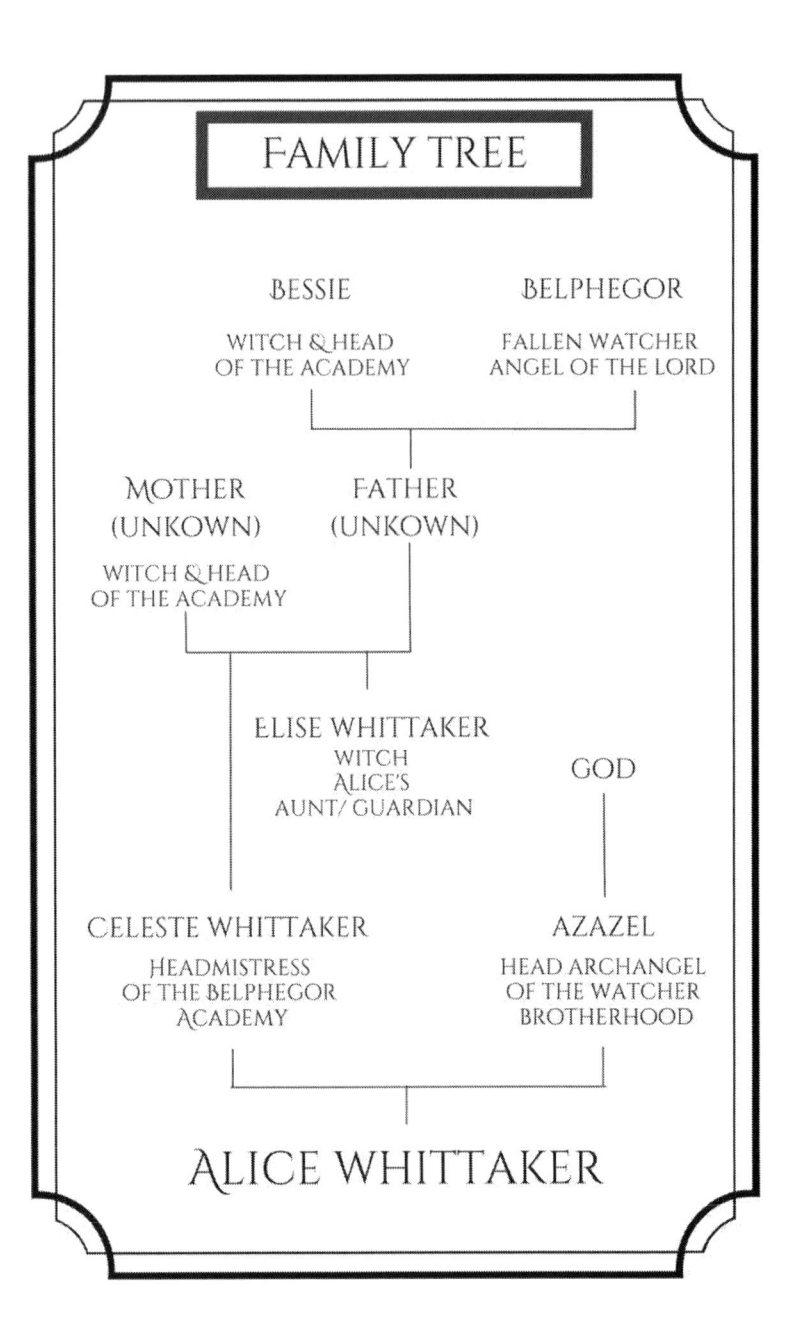

BESSIE
WITCH & HEAD
OF THE ACADEMY

BELPHEGOR
FALLEN WATCHER
ANGEL OF THE LORD

**MOTHER
(UNKOWN)**
WITCH & HEAD
OF THE ACADEMY

**FATHER
(UNKOWN)**

ELISE WHITTAKER
WITCH
ALICE'S
AUNT/GUARDIAN

GOD

CELESTE WHITTAKER
HEADMISTRESS
OF THE BELPHEGOR
ACADEMY

AZAZEL
HEAD ARCHANGEL
OF THE WATCHER
BROTHERHOOD

ALICE WHITTAKER

FAMILY TREE

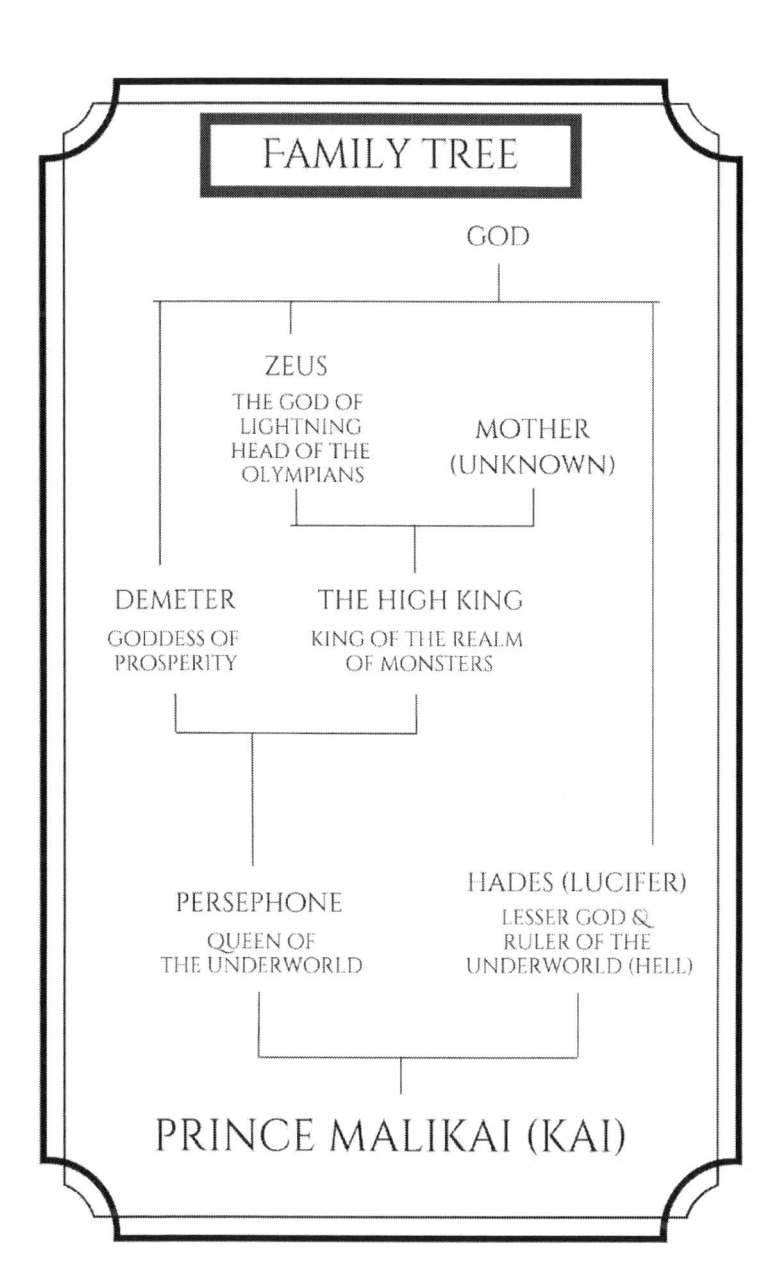

GOD

ZEUS
THE GOD OF LIGHTNING
HEAD OF THE OLYMPIANS

MOTHER
(UNKNOWN)

DEMETER
GODDESS OF PROSPERITY

THE HIGH KING
KING OF THE REALM OF MONSTERS

PERSEPHONE
QUEEN OF THE UNDERWORLD

HADES (LUCIFER)
LESSER GOD & RULER OF THE UNDERWORLD (HELL)

PRINCE MALIKAI (KAI)

SOME EYE CANDY?

MAP OF THE SEVEN REALMS OF HELL

SEE THIS IN COLOR ON MY WEBSITE
(WWW.AMANDAAGGIE.COM).

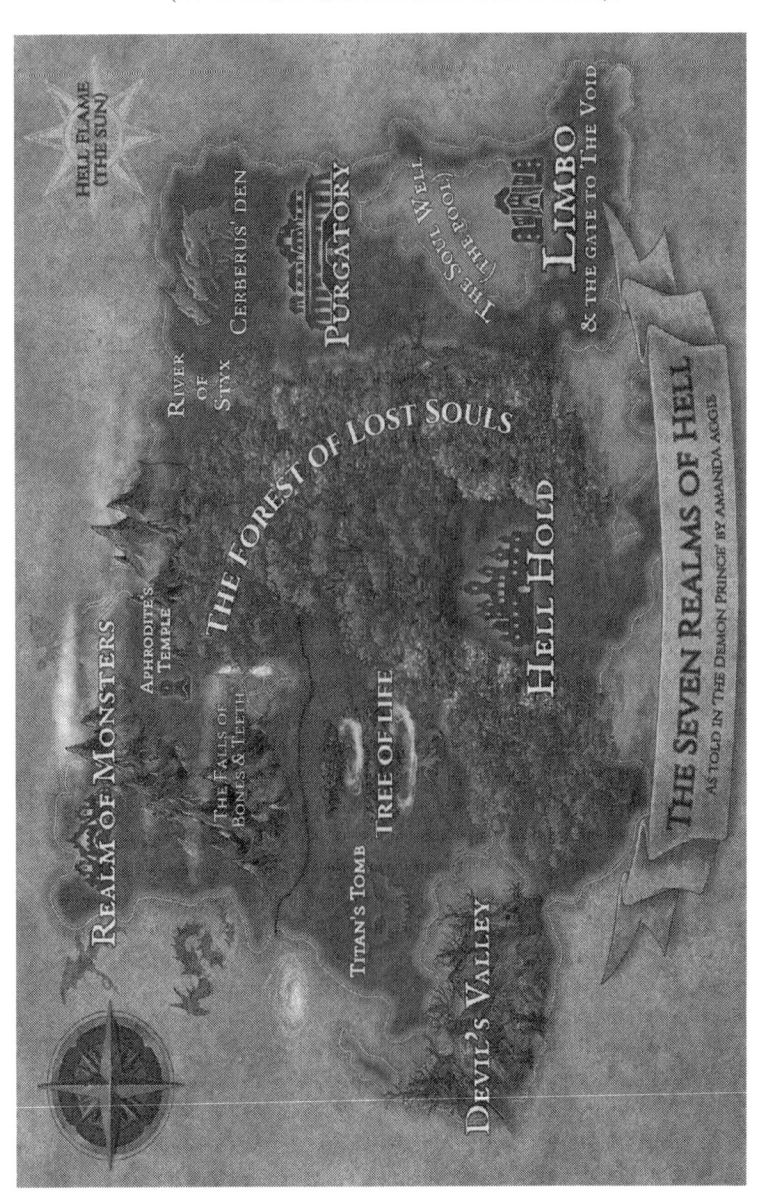

ABOUT THE AUTHOR

Normally these things are told in third person, but that's not my style. I'm a real girl, not some bland biography you found on wiki. So, rather than tell you about my birthplace, I'll tell you about myself and my love for books.

I'm a mom to two beautiful tiny humans and my Border Collie-Aussie rescue. My favorite holiday is Taco Tuesday, and season is…well, whenever I can get away with wearing oversized sweaters. I'm happily married to my best friend and laugh a bit too hard at corny puns, but I wouldn't be me if I didn't.

Growing up, I'd read books that took me to magical worlds and idolized the people who created them — authors. Back then, I was oblivious to the fact that they were real, dangerously over-caffeinated people who just enjoyed stories as much as I did. Really, not much has changed since then. I still read books and become overly obsessive over the ones I love, just the romances became steamier, and the fairy tales fractured and grew darker.

As for my written works, if you enjoy choking hazard paranormal or fantasy romances that are unsafe to eat or drink while reading, I'm your gal! If you like dark, morally grey anti-heroes that you hate to love, I've got you, boo. Go get some pearls to clutch, or maybe a rosary — just in case it gets too hot — and check out my stories here: www.linktr.ee/amandaaggie

Thank you for making it this far and for being you! I wouldn't be able to do the job I love if it wasn't for ravenous readers like yourself. <3 Read on, fellow humans!

Printed in Great Britain
by Amazon